Ruth Dudley Edwards

Ruth Dudley Edwards was born and brought up in Dublin. Since she graduated she has lived in England, where she has been a teacher, a Cambridge postgraduate student, a marketing executive, a civil servant and finally, a freelance writer and journalist.

A historian and prize-winning biographer, her most recent non-fiction includes the authorized history of *The Economist* and a portrait of the British Foreign Office, written with its co-operation.

She feels intellectually English and temperamentally Irish. *Murder in a Cathedral* is her seventh crime novel. The sixth, *Ten Lords A-Leaping*, was shortlisted for the Crime Writers' Association's Last Laugh Award for Funniest Crime Novel of the Year.

By the same author

Fiction

PUBLISH AND BE MURDERED
TEN LORDS A-LEAPING
MATRICIDE AT ST MARTHA'S
CLUBBED TO DEATH
THE SCHOOL OF ENGLISH MURDER
THE ST VALENTINE'S DAY MURDERS
CORRIDORS OF DEATH

Non-fiction

TRUE BRITS: INSIDE THE FOREIGN OFFICE
THE BEST OF BAGEHOT
THE PURSUIT OF REASON: THE ECONOMIST 1843–1993
VICTOR GOLLANCZ: A BIOGRAPHY
HAROLD MACMILLAN: A LIFE IN PICTURES
JAMES CONNOLLY
PATRICK PEARSE: THE TRIUMPH OF FAILURE
AN ATLAS OF IRISH HISTORY

RUTH DUDLEY EDWARDS

MURDER IN A CATHEDRAL

HarperCollins*Publishers*

This novel is entirely a work of fiction. The names, characters and incidents portrayed in it are the work of the author's imagination. Any resemblance to actual persons, living or dead, events or localities is entirely coincidental.

HarperCollins*Publishers*
77–85 Fulham Palace Road,
Hammersmith, London W6 8JB

This paperback edition 1998

3 5 7 9 8 6 4 2

First published in Great Britain by
HarperCollins*Publishers* 1996

ISBN 0 00 649864 7

Set in Meridien

Printed and bound in Great Britain by
Caledonian International Book Manufacturing Ltd, Glasgow

To Una, Chief Accomplice, and, of course,
as usual, to John

As always, I had advice and help from countless friends, but special thanks are due to Andrew Boyd, Nina Clarke, Paul Le Druillenec, Gordon and Ken Lee, James McGuire, Neasa McErlean, Jill Neville (versifier laureate), Carol Scott, Julia Wisdom, my tough and tiny publisher, and my favourite dean (who had better remain anonymous).

In the interests of the plot I have taken some small liberties with details of customs and procedures in the Church of England – and particularly in the running of cathedrals.

Both read the Bible day and night,
But thou read'st black where I read white.

From 'The Everlasting Gospel'
WILLIAM BLAKE

PROLOGUE

'Of course you will.'

'No, Jack, I bloody well won't.'

'Give me one good reason why not.'

'Because I don't believe in God and I don't much care for pomp and circumstance.'

'What's God got to do with it?' Baroness Troutbeck sounded baffled. 'We're talking about the Church of England here, not some crowd of born-again fruitcakes. Nobody will be indelicate enough at this shindig to enquire as to whether or not you believe in God. Good grief, these days, in the good old C of E, that's almost a disqualification for office.'

'I'm not looking for office.'

'Stop arguing. For Christ's sake, Robert, all I'm doing is asking you to come to an amusing occasion and do me a good turn into the bargain.'

Amiss looked at her suspiciously. 'What kind of a good turn, Jack?'

'I won't enjoy this without someone to snigger with and I've suddenly been left partnerless. I need a walker. That's what they call blokes who act as escorts for women who don't shag them, isn't it?'

'Do I gather you're short of those who do? Have you and Myles had a lovers' tiff?'

'He's got to go to the funeral of some old mate from the dirty-tricks brigade.'

'Mary Lou?'

The baroness grinned. 'If I took Mary Lou, every red-blooded cleric – every heterosexual red-blooded cleric, that is, if there are any left in Westonbury, which I doubt – would be sniffing and slavering round her. I'd rather have someone unobtrusive.'

'Thanks. You really know how to make a chap feel good. Makes me sound like a valet.'

'Stop being temperamental. We've got quite enough of that ahead of us. And stop playing hard to get. It's not every day you get invited to a ringside seat at a great British occasion. You've seen me ennobled; now you can watch David being episcopated, or whatever it is they call being bishoped. Besides, it'll do you good to get away from this dump for a while.'

'It's not a dump,' began Amiss indignantly, recognizing as he did so that he was letting himself get sidetracked. The baroness threw a disparaging glance around his living room; he followed her eye, as if he were a stranger, and took in the undistinguished furniture, the posters from undergraduate days that he'd never got round to replacing, the makeshift bookcase of planks and bricks, the Chinese paper lampshades and the sad, threadbare carpet.

'If it wasn't for the odds and ends you picked up in India,' she said, waving at a few rugs and pictures, 'this would be the appropriate background for a dreary 1970s sitcom about shiftless students.'

'I took over the furniture from my predecessors,' Amiss said defensively. 'And as you well know, since then I've never simultaneously had the time and the money to get around to turning the place into a home. Anyway, what's the point? I'll be moving out when Rachel gets back.'

'Which is when?'

'In three months. Beginning of June. It's a bugger that it's another postponement, but at least this time it's definite.'

'She'll be staying in London?'

'For the next few years at least. So she's given notice to her tenants and I'll move in with her.'

'Oh, good, good.' She sounded vague. She looked at her watch and vigorously knocked out her pipe. Plutarch, who had been slumbering peacefully on the baroness's stomach, started, yowled and propelled her vast marmalade body to the floor.

The baroness looked unsympathetic. 'Stop being neurotic, Plutarch. As for you, Robert, you'd better get moving. I'll have to put my foot down hard if we're going to make Cambridge in time for dinner.'

'Jack! I said no.'

'Rubbish. By your own admission you've nothing to do until some job applications bear fruit. If they ever do, that is. Now stop being coy. You'll have an enjoyable few days in Cambridge and we'll take off on Sunday at sparrow-fart for Westonbury. Besides, you can have a loving reunion with Mary Lou.'

Amiss looked at her sternly. 'These days my feelings towards Mary Lou are entirely platonic. Just because you put it about at every opportunity doesn't mean that the rest of us behave similarly.'

'Good God, Robert, I'm not going to throw you back into bed with her.' She leered. 'I prefer her to be in mine. But you'll enjoy seeing her. Now come on, go and pack your Sunday suit and some clean knickers, stop being such a prig and say yes to life.'

'When you drag me into anything it usually means death.'

'For heaven's sake, man, this is the Church of England we're talking about. They may be having their differences in Westonbury, but they haven't taken to rubbing each other out. Yet, anyway.'

'You should bully for Britain,' he snarled, as he headed for the door.

She smirked. 'I do. Now, where's Plutarch's basket?'

'I don't need to take her. I can get a neighbour to do the necessary for a couple of days.'

'Better to take her. It'll be nice for her to see old haunts.'

'I thought she was a *feles non grata* at St Martha's.'

'They'll put up with her for a short time. And Mary Lou actually likes her, so she'll be looked after while we're in Westonbury.'

'Oh, all right then. You feed and water her and get her equipped for the voyage while I change.'

Plutarch, who had just jumped back onto the baroness and was draping herself around a particularly comforting curve, found herself unceremoniously dumped on the floor. 'Right, old girl. Let's get cracking.'

Amiss, who had frequently suffered the rough edge of Plutarch's tongue and claws for much lesser acts of *lèse majesté*, looked on resentfully as the animal stretched, yawned and then followed the baroness obediently into the kitchen.

1

As their speed was reduced to a slow crawl in the queue for the M11, the baroness reached down to her left and picked up a receiver.

'You've got a car phone,' said Amiss disdainfully. 'How vulgar!'

'Vulgarity doesn't frighten me.' She punched in some numbers. 'It's me. Get me Mary Lou.'

'Do you ever say hello or goodbye?'

'What's the point?'

'It's called manners. But then, I forgot. You don't have any.'

'Has he arrived? Good. Take him for a run or something to give him an appetite for dinner . . . Yes, got him . . . Within the hour.'

'You seem to regard the place as your own personal fiefdom.'

'Isn't it?' She sounded surprised. 'I'm its boss, amn't I? And a baroness to boot. Who needs democracy? I was cut out to be a benevolent dictator. I find it saves a lot of time.'

As they reached the motorway, she put her foot down and within sixty seconds had manoeuvred the car into the fast lane and was flashing her lights energetically at the Porsche in front. 'Out of my way!'

'He's already well over the speed limit,' said Amiss faintly.

'Slowcoaches like that shouldn't be in the fast lane.' The Porsche obediently moved over and she put her foot down harder on the accelerator. As they overtook, Amiss observed the look of incredulity on the face of the spivish driver when he grasped that he had been cut up by a woman twice his age and size, who was confounding her impertinence by waving at him cheerily.

'Taught him a lesson,' she cried happily.

Getting no response, she turned to view Amiss. 'You're very quiet all of a sudden. Not nervous, are you?'

'Me? Nervous? Certainly not. There's nothing I like better than being driven at forty miles over the speed limit by a madwoman keeping only one eye on the road.'

'Just as well.' She began to gain on a BMW and recommenced the light-flashing. This time the driver pulled over immediately, but sounded his horn as she flew past. Amiss looked apprehensively towards the back seat. 'Plutarch's strangely quiet. Normally she creates like hell when confined to basket. Especially when people sound horns. How did you work this magic? Hypnotism?'

'Nothing magic about a Mickey Finn.'

'You doped her?'

'Certainly I doped her. We don't want her arriving at St Martha's a nervous wreck, do we? She's much better off having a pleasant kip.'

'Where did you acquire a Mickey Finn?'

'Good grief, stop asking boring domestic questions. At a Mickey Finn emporium, of course. I always keep a supply. Cretin!' she shouted, flashing her lights furiously at a Rover that doggedly stayed in front. 'Doesn't he realize I'm in a hurry?'

'Tell me about this about-to-be-bishop. It might take my mind off your driving.'

'David? What do you want to know?'

'Why are you two so pally?'

'Usual reasons.' She chuckled.

'You're not having an affair with a bishop-elect?'

'No, no. I've rarely seen a bishop – or even a bishop-elect – that I fancied. Our fling was a long time ago. And he was no bishop at the time, I can tell you.'

'A goer?'

'Wouldn't say that. Keen when he got going, but initially young, bashful and awash with scruples. Took me quite a lot of hard work to make him yield to my girlish charms:

ordinands led pretty sheltered lives forty years ago, you know.'

'Are you telling me that you seduced bishop-to-be David when he was embarking on his clerical career? Are there no bounds to your depravity?'

She paused for a moment to launch another vigorous assault on the recalcitrant driver ahead. 'Reluctantly, I admit that he was just an ordinary undergraduate at the time. I was in my last year and he was in his first, but he was wrestling with his vocation. Meeting me did him the world of good. Mind you I think he's stayed on the straight and narrow ever since, though our dalliance has always been a matter of sweet – if unspoken – nostalgia for us both.'

'And you didn't think of marrying him?'

She smiled triumphantly. 'Ah, that got him.' The obdurate Rover had finally admitted defeat and pulled into the middle lane. 'They always yield to coaxing in the end.'

'Coaxing! I'd call it mugging. Anyway you didn't want to marry this blushing bishop-to-be?'

'If I had ever wanted to get married, it would have been to someone a bit livelier than David Elworthy, I can tell you. Anyway I don't think I was cut out to be a clergyman's wife.'

'The only suitable marital partner I can think of for you would be a pirate. Captain Morgan in his heyday, perhaps.'

'It's more fun being a pirate oneself than a pirate's moll. I rather fancy swinging around the rigging with a knife in my teeth and making my enemies walk the plank.'

'Anyway, what's he like?'

'David? Sweet. Innocent. Honourable. Reduced to total helplessness by the loss of his wife. She was the one with the balls.'

'A battleaxe?'

'Nope. Good egg, old Cornelia. Yes, she'd have been a bit of a dictator at Westonbury, but behind the scenes, and she would have sorted things out kindly and sensibly and left the place happier. David doesn't have a clue what to do now he's on his own. He'd never have been given the job if he hadn't been married to her. The gossip is the appointments unit thought the smart move was to appoint a pussycat with a tiger as minder. But Cornelia died shortly after they arrived in Westonbury and he's been floundering ever since.'

'In what?'

'Distress and dither.'

'About what?' asked Amiss impatiently, fed up with the routine difficulty of abstracting information from the baroness.

'Oh God, all the usual C of E stuff. Queers in the cloister, new happy-clappy dean, defections over women priests, fund-raising crises. No kind of environment for a poor bugger of a theologian.'

'He wasn't a vicar?'

'Never been as much as a curate. Spent the last thirty years or so in various academic jobs and ended up running . . . correction, presiding over – Cornelia ran it – one of the better theological colleges. Now that's quite enough spoon-feeding. You'll see for yourself tonight.'

'What?'

'What he's like. He's staying with us until tomorrow.'

'You didn't mention that.'

'Who did you think I was giving Mary Lou instructions about?'

'A dog, I thought.'

'Dogs. Cats. Bishops. They're all the same. Just need care, love and a firm hand.'

'Jack! I don't trust you an inch. Why am I being brought to meet this bishop? What's going on in that fat devious head of yours? You've more in mind than simply having me squire you to see Bishop Elworthy get his mitre.'

'How suspicious you are.'

'And rightly so. Come on. Give.'

'Well, I will admit I want to avoid David getting any ideas about me.'

'Come again?'

'Since Cornelia died he's been very lonely. He's the sort of man who needs to be married.'

'Jack, you're not going to tell me that any bishop would be mad enough to think of you as a potential wife.'

'I should think I'd be excellent,' she said stiffly. 'A kind of up-market, benign Mrs Proudie. However I don't think I can add such a job to my present range of duties. Perhaps I'm slowing up, but I find that between running St Martha's, throwing my weight around in the House of Lords and living a bit, I seem to have enough to do. I think being a bishop's lady in Westonbury into the bargain might be just a bit too taxing.'

'Not to speak of constraining on your love life.'

'You could say that. I'm a bit old to be smuggling lovers up the back staircase.'

'Do I understand that I'm to pass myself off as your current inamorato despite our thirty-year age gap?'

'It's all the rage these days I hear – older women and younger men. Just look attentive, that's all. A bit of doglike devotion wouldn't go amiss. David is very polite and he'll be too embarrassed to ask . . . Blimey, nearly missed it.'

She accelerated into the middle lane, braked hard and shot into the slow lane just in time to get onto the slip road. 'That was your fault. You were talking too much. You're supposed to keep your eye on the road signs. Why else do you think I take you with me?'

'You deserve to be put away indefinitely for reckless driving.'

'Rubbish. There's nothing reckless about my driving. It's sound as a bell. Never had an accident yet.'

'That's only because everybody else behaves responsibly and gives into your tyranny.'

'Story of my life,' she said. 'Lie back and enjoy it.'

2

Amiss had been expecting Bishop-elect Elworthy to be on the weedy and frail side. Instead he seemed the epitome of muscular Christianity – hair still dark except at the temples, stomach still flat, handshake vigorous and voice strong. It came as no surprise to learn that he had just triumphed at tennis over the lithe Mary Lou Denslow.

The baroness smote Elworthy on the back: unlike most people in receipt of such a mark of her affection, he did not totter under the force of the blow. 'Attaboy, David. Glad you can still show up the young. Robert, put Mary Lou down, give them champagne and we'll toast the victor.'

As they clinked their glasses, the baroness pronounced, 'That's the secret of a good old age; trample youth into the mud at every opportunity. Mind you, you don't deserve that much credit. The blighters have no stamina these days. Not like us. They're not eating enough red meat.' She plumped herself back into her armchair.

'I haven't seen you doing much prancing around the court, Jack,' observed Mary Lou amiably.

'Tennis never was my sport. Too genteel. But I fancy myself against you in the hundred yard dash. Shall we try it now?' She nodded in the direction of the garden.

Elworthy looked alarmed. 'My dear Ida . . .' She raised an index finger reprovingly. 'Oh, sorry. I'll try to remember to call you Jack, but it's not easy for me. In any case, don't you think it might be a little unseemly to have the mistress and bursar of this establishment racing each other across the lawn at twilight?'

Amiss sniggered. 'Seemly isn't the first word I would use

to describe the conduct of affairs in St Martha's. But don't worry. She's only bluffing.'

The baroness jumped up, lifted her skirts and began to tuck them into her eau-de-nil directoire knickers. Mary Lou spoke firmly. 'Just stop it, Jack. I have absolutely no intention of racing you. It would either kill you or humiliate me. And in any case, it's time we joined our colleagues: they'll be wanting to get a look at David. Francis is very excited. He'll be dying to hear all about what you'll be wearing on Monday, David.'

Elworthy assumed a hunted expression. 'I don't want to be pawed over by any Francises,' he said querulously. 'There's quite enough of that in Westonbury.'

'Don't worry,' said the baroness. 'If you evince distress, I will interpose my body between yours and his. Now come on, you lot. Duty calls.'

St Martha's hospitality was considerably less austere than during Amiss's brief tenure as a fellow. Conversation was better too. While much of the talk at high table had the parochialism to be expected of academics, the baroness on several occasions succeeded in livening things up by introducing remarks that caused consternation among some of her colleagues' guests and led to spirited arguments. Francis Pusey's interior decorator friend was outraged by her claim that there had been no worthwhile art or music in England since Turner and Elgar respectively, while her contention that far from considering sharing a single currency with Europe, the British government should forthwith abandon Johnny Foreigner to make a mess of things in his own way, and while they were at it abolish the metric system and return to pounds, shillings and pence, caused Elworthy some alarm.

'My dear Id . . . Jack! Surely it is out of the question to turn the clock back in such a manner. One must move with the times.'

'Bollocks.' She smiled genially around the table. 'This has all been very pleasant, but I fear I must now ask you to excuse me and my guests: we have business to discuss. But the bursar will do the honours in the senior combination room. I hope you enjoy the '66 port.'

'Cigar?'

Elworthy waved away the mahogany box. 'No, no,' he said. 'Bad for the chest.'

'What an old fusspot you are. Robert?'

'Love to. Can't.'

'Why on earth not?'

'Because – as I've explained to you on numerous occasions but you refuse to take in – even one puff is liable to send me straight back to the fags.'

'Ah yes,' she said. 'The fags. Exactly what we're here to discuss.' She threw herself into her armchair, lit her cigar, drew in smoke, exhaled expansively and smiled seraphically. Plutarch, who had been sleeping off the Mickey Finn and a good supper, leaped onto her lap and put up unprotestingly with some robust stroking. 'OK, David. Shoot.'

Elworthy took a cautious sip of his brandy. 'All this is a bit delicate, Ida. Sorry, Jack.' He looked nervously at Amiss.

'Stop shillyshallying. I've told you before that Robert is my faithful lieutenant.' A memory struck her. She smiled coyly. 'And more. I have no secrets from him.'

Amiss was too full of good food and drink to care how she was portraying their relationship. He settled back cosily in his armchair, his feet on the table in front, sipped his brandy and gazed contentedly into the log fire, hoping Elworthy's story would be gripping enough to keep him awake.

Elworthy turned to him. 'How much do you know about the modern Church of England?'

'Not in good shape, I gather. Short of money and members. Splits over the ordination of women.'

'Do you see any theological tensions?'

'You mean the frolicking queers at loggerheads with the happy-clappies,' interjected the baroness. 'Just like in Trollope.'

'There weren't queers . . . I mean gays –'

'I won't have that excellent word misused in my college.'

'Oh, sod off,' said Amiss. 'There weren't homosexuals in

Trollope. The war was simply between the respective enthusiasts for High- and Low-Church practices.'

She snorted. 'Same thing.'

'Is it your view that all those clergy leaning towards the High are of the homosexual persuasion, while no homosexuals lean towards the Low?'

'Oh, stop nit-picking, David. You know very well what I mean.'

'Do I? Have you not – ?'

'Listen, David, will you for Christ's sake stop trying to turn this conversation into a bloody Socratic dialogue. You're not supposed to be conducting a seminar in which you will tease out the truth; you're telling us about what is making your life a misery at Westonbury.'

He looked embarrassed. 'Oh dear. You're quite right. Indeed that's just what poor Cornelia used to say to me: "Stop pussyfooting and spit it out."'

'She was a good girl,' said the baroness gruffly.

'She was. I am utterly bereft. For I fear that apart from being a wonderful wife, she protected me so much that in addition to being a widower, I feel like a constitutional monarch, suddenly deprived of his wisest counsellor – his prime minister – just at a moment when the country faces revolution.'

The baroness spoke gently. 'David, just tell us the story of what's been going on at Westonbury.'

'I don't know where to begin.'

'Begin with your appointment.'

'I was asked last September to take the job.'

'Right.'

'I didn't really want to but Cornelia said I should. She pointed out that although our theological college had been spared the axe there was no guarantee it would survive the next round of cuts. Life is very insecure since the church commissioners lost all those hundreds of millions in property speculation. Why, there is a possibility that they may decide to sell my palace and dispatch me to a villa.'

'Surely you fancied being a bishop just a little bit? However high-minded you are, it must be a slightly thrilling prospect.

At the very least all that flummery must be great fun – swanking around in public in cloaks and purple waistcoats and silly hats. In the Lords we only get to put on fancy dress once a year. You'll be doing it at least once a week. I feel quite envious.'

'You would.' Elworthy smiled gently. 'But then you always liked showing off. I don't. Except sometimes when I win a game of tennis or score in some scholarly debate. But of course I would be deluding myself if I didn't admit I was pleased with the honour conferred on me by Her Majesty. And Westonbury wasn't a frightening cathedral. It's small, off the tourist track and it seemed quite tranquil. "Mouldering", Cornelia called it approvingly. After all it seemed to have run smoothly for twenty-five years under the same bishop and dean.'

Amiss sat up. 'Twenty-five years! What age were they when they were appointed?'

'When they died they were respectively eighty-four and eighty-two.'

The baroness snorted. 'Good for them. Though I thought they booted you out at some absurdly young age these days.'

'Yes, indeed they do. No one appointed these days can stay beyond seventy. But anyone *in situ* before that can hang on as long as they can get away with it. Hubert was lucky enough to die with his mitre on. Literally. He had a heart attack when disrobing in the sacristy. And Reggie Roper, the dean, died in his bed a few weeks later.'

The baroness scratched her head. 'Clean sweep, eh? Who's the new dean?'

'Ah, my dear Jack. You have put your finger on the nub of the matter. Though before I tell you what I know of Norman Cooper, I had better explain a little about the current state of Westonbury.'

'We know, don't we? Run by a coven – or whatever is the male equivalent – of raving Romish poofters.'

Elworthy looked uncomfortable. 'Romish is putting it a little strongly, but I must admit the force of your description.

Really the only matter on which most of the canons differ from the present pope is in their attitude to gays –'

'I told you to reserve that word for its proper place.' Her voice rose in song:

> *'Stately as a galleon, I sail across the floor,*
> *Doing the Military Two-step, as in the days of yore . . .*
> *So gay the band,*
> *So giddy the sight . . .*

'Bugger. Can't remember the rest.' She shot Elworthy a reproving look. 'Do you realize good stuff like that is unperformable these days because it makes idiots titter? We've got to fight to recapture our language.'

Seeing Elworthy's confused expression, Amiss intervened. 'Jack, will you please desist from refighting a battle that was lost about ten years ago and let David get on with his story.' He turned to Elworthy. 'You were saying – when you were so rudely interrupted – that your new colleagues are as High as kites.'

'That's right. Well, that is, some of them are. And I don't mind that really – except for the misogyny evinced by a few of them. But while I love tradition and quite enjoy Anglo-Catholic trappings like candles and incense, they've gone too far in some respects – as you'll see when you come to Westonbury. And there's worse to come!'

'What sort of worse?' asked the baroness.

'I'd rather not talk about it here. I'll have to show you the plans.'

'So your problem has to do with making these guys see reason and play down the gaiety, is it?'

'If only that were all, Robert.' Elworthy rested his forehead in his left hand for a moment. 'Let me put this plainly. What I'm facing in Westonbury is a horrifying confrontation between the spiritual legatees of a pig-headed old queen – Cornelia's term not mine – and someone equally pig-headed who despises Anglo-Catholicism and wants to try to turn our cathedral into what has been described to me as a "happy-clappy, devil-stomping, bible-thumping rave".'

'Norman Cooper?'

Elworthy nodded and shuddered. 'Or Norm, as his wife calls him. It was her description.'

'How did the appointments unit come to perpetrate such lunacy?' asked the baroness.

'He kept a rein on his excesses until he got the appointment. After that he started to let rip in his own church: I've heard some frightening stories of what goes on there.'

'Exaggerated perhaps?'

'Maybe, Robert. And I admit he's kept quiet since he was installed at Westonbury a couple of weeks ago, but his colleagues are fearful of what he might have in mind and so too am I.'

'Won't you be able to keep him under control?' asked Amiss. 'Dammit, you're the bishop.'

'I can see you have a lot to learn about the Church of England,' said Elworthy wearily. 'I have a certain amount of power over the incumbents of the parishes in my diocese, but the best I can hope for within the cathedral is influence. Those with control are the dean and five canons who are in charge of the building itself and the houses and offices within the close, the music and the services. I can't even preach there without a formal invitation.'

'Didn't you follow what went on in Lincoln?' demanded the baroness of Amiss.

'Wasn't it something to do with sex?'

'At core it was a dispute between bishop and dean,' said Elworthy. 'The dean was a tactless reformer who had upset many of his colleagues and things got so poisonous that the bishop backed the application by a female verger to take the dean to a church court, charged with sexual misbehaviour. It took eighteen months, cost a fortune, he was found not guilty and the whole thing brought shame on the church and resolved absolutely nothing. In fact the net result is that the pressure is on to keep the lid on domestic rows and sweep anything troublesome under the carpet.'

'How unlike the British Establishment,' said the baroness.

Elworthy looked at his watch. 'My goodness. Is that the time? It's late.'

'I would hardly call ten-thirty late,' said the baroness.
'I expect you don't rise at six to run.'
'You expect right.'
Elworthy drained his glass. 'My terror is that Lincoln's problems will pale into insignificance compared to what is brewing in Westonbury. If Dean Cooper is remotely as extreme as I fear him to be, much exposure to his new colleagues will cause him to run amok. The only bright spot is that there's a stay of execution: he's off to America for a month on Tuesday.' He stood up.
'When your wife died,' asked Amiss, 'were you tempted to duck out of the appointment?'
'Tempted! I've never been so tempted by anything in my life. But when she realized she was dying, Cornelia told me it was my duty to soldier on. "Pray!" she said. "And get yourself some allies to do the dirty work."'
The baroness's eyes filled with tears. 'A great woman, Cornelia.'
Turfing Plutarch off her lap, she jumped up and gave Elworthy a clumsy hug. 'Off you go now, up the wooden stairs to bedfordshire. Robert and I will take the cat for a stroll in the starlight. Sleep peacefully in the knowledge that you've got yourself two doughty allies.'
With a 'Goodnight and God bless' Elworthy departed, unaware that Amiss's pleasant features were contorted with alarm and apprehension.

3

As they emerged from the cathedral in the midst of the throng, Amiss shook his head vigorously. 'Do you think we could get some fresh air before we proceed to lunch? All that incense made me feel quite sick.'

'Really? It always gives me an appetite. But yes, certainly. Fresh air by all means. Can't have you throwing up all over the festive board. Come on, then. Turn sharp left and we'll take a canter along the river.'

By the time they had crossed the bridge to the towpath Amiss was feeling better. 'Blimey,' he said. 'Talk about smells and bells!'

'Yes, excellent, wasn't it? There were moments when I could hardly see the congregation through the smoke.'

'You're pretty High Church as atheists go, aren't you?'

'Of course. Tell the truth but don't stint on the glory, that's my motto. What's the point of religion if it isn't full of spectacle? That was terrific stuff. All those self-important bishops in embroidered copes and boy sopranos in starched surplices and poncy canons in fancy cassocks and stately processions and the right hymns and the unadulterated Book of Common Prayer. Excellent, excellent. You'd think time hadn't moved on in centuries. As long as it's the product of a long tradition it's fine by me. Don't you agree?'

'Don't know. All this is new to me. I fear the Amiss family went in for a dreary Low-Church austerity. Our local church was chilly, bleak and without any architectural merit and the vicar's cassock sported no flounces.'

'His chasuble fell short on the orphrey front, I infer.'

'Whatever you might find a turn-on we were definitely short of in St Joseph's.'

'Too bad. I hadn't realized how deprived was your childhood.'

'You know, I wouldn't have associated you with religious carry-on. Stupid of me, really. I should have realized you'd be attracted by excess in any form. I'm surprised you didn't go over to Rome.'

She shook her head. 'Alas, I couldn't do that. The trouble with Rome is they expect you to take it seriously, believe in God and obey all the ghastly rules stopping you doing anything you want especially if they haven't had it themselves, and what's more, they disapprove of you only turning up to services when you want to.

'Roman Catholic prelates look good, but sadly they're mostly life-denying misery-guts. And what's more they've got rid of their greatest glory – the Latin mass. Now that was something that used to carry me away – a sung Latin mass.' She bellowed 'Kyrie Eleison' a few times. 'In any case Rome is Rome and I'm not going to be pushed around by a crowd of wops. The Church of England is right for England.'

'You mean full of dottiness and doubt and tolerance and the rest of it.'

'Absolutely. Fortunately' – she stopped and pointed towards the cathedral – 'we've got all the grandest buildings. The papists haven't anything to beat that. Look at it. Nigh on a thousand years of faith and hope and Englishness.' There were tears in her eyes. 'Isn't that magnificent?'

'Englishness is pushing it a bit, isn't it? That's surely a Norman tower.'

She hit him a painful blow with her handbag. 'Stop being such a fucking pedant. We Anglo-Saxons absorbed those buggers in no time at all. Anyway, while I grant you the tower and those superlative spires, what makes Westonbury one of my favourite cathedrals is all that Gothic exuberance. No other cathedral can beat that explosion of naturalistic carving.'

'L'excès, toujours l'excès.' He dodged another swing of the bag. 'OK, OK. It is wonderful and I am moved by it. It's just

that I get embarrassed and English about admitting such emotions.'

'You'll come to love it.'

'Jack, I have explained to you in words of one syllable that I am shaking the dust of Westonbury off my feet after today and going home for good. I was not taken in by that cock-and-bull story about your needing to be protected from David's advances. Maidenly delicacy is not a problem with which I associate you.'

'Not even maidenly indelicacy?'

'Shut up!' Grimly he continued. 'I know very well that you wish to maroon me down here to act as some kind of undercover agent. As I told you on Friday night, it is out of the question. Do I make myself clear?'

'You're so hysterical. Calm down. It'll all work out. Now come on, it's time we turned back. David will be looking for me. I think I'm supposed to be gracing the top table.'

'You'll fit in. In fact the more I look at you the more I think you resemble not just a bishop's wife, but an archbishop's. You have that indefinable air of righteous authority.'

'Jolly good. Just the effect I was aiming at. It'll put the fear of God into them.'

'Into whom?'

'Never you mind. Now off we go.' She accelerated. 'Oh, and by the way.'

'Yes?'

'We're not dining alone tonight. David wants to see us privately after all this is over, so I promised him we'll have dinner with him in the palace. Just the three of us.'

'What's going on, Jack? Surely he should be dining with all sorts of visiting dignitaries – archbishops, and so on.'

'No. He pleaded weariness caused by his bereavement. It worked like magic. They all backed off instantly from sheer embarrassment.'

Amiss shook his head in wonderment. 'It's really amazing. Even the clergy in this country can't cope with death.'

'Aha. That's because when it comes to a clash between their essential Englishness and their religiousness the

Englishness wins. And that,' she added, with a smirk of satisfaction, 'is as it should be. First things first.'

'Get her!'

Following the gaze of his neighbour, Amiss focused on a willowy man in a beige linen suit whose clerical collar appeared incongruously above a yellow shirt and a red waistcoat with an oriental design.

'It's not fair. That's Gladys. She's just trying to show us all up, silly old queen.'

Taken aback at this explosion of camp from a scholarly-looking, orthodoxly clad cleric, Amiss said nothing.

His companion sniffed loudly. 'Honestly. Some people! See if I care. She's just vulgar, she is.' He looked at Amiss appraisingly. 'Who are you anyway?'

Amiss put his hand out. 'Robert Amiss.'

'Yes. But who?'

'I'm here accompanying a friend of the bishop.'

'Which one?'

Amiss felt a fit of pomposity coming on. 'You have the advantage of me. You are?'

'You mean you don't recognize me? Most people do. Haven't you seen me on television? Father Cecil Davage, known to my friends as Beryl.'

'Sorry, I don't see religious programmes.'

Davage tossed his head. 'Just because I'm a canon doesn't mean I haven't any other interests. Haven't you heard of *Forgotten Treasures*? Five past seven on Fridays.'

'I'm afraid not. I don't see television much. What kind of treasures are these?'

'All kinds of treasures.' Davage sounded irritable. 'Pictures, antiques, architecture, artefacts of all kinds. What they all have in common is that they are glorious pieces of Victoriana which were cast aside during the wicked, philistine postwar decades and only recently restored to their glory. I'm surprised you haven't heard of me. I'm a bit of a national institution now. Like the queen.' He tittered. 'Anyway, who'd you come with?'

'Lady Troutbeck.'

'Oooh, you are lucky. I've seen her on television getting up left-wing noses.' He craned his neck around the lunchers. 'Where is she?'

'Up there beside the bishop. Hard to miss.'

Davage spotted her, took in the sartorial splendour of her herringbone suit and purple frills, and tittered again. 'Looks my type.'

'You mean she looks like a Victorian monument?'

'Don't be silly. I mean she's flamboyant. If you've got to have women, at the very least they should cheer things up.'

'She certainly does that.'

'So what's she doing with you?'

Amiss repressed the desire to rebuke this little wretch for impertinence. He was after all the guest of a guest. 'Lady Troutbeck and I are old platonic friends.'

'What do you mean old?' Davage looked him up and down. 'You've hardly a line on your face. Either you're under thirty or you're on the monkey glands.' His gaze shifted back to the cleric in the beige suit. 'Now who *is* she talking to?'

'Is that a colleague of yours?'

Davage sniffed again. 'I suppose that's what you'd call her. She's a canon called Fedden-Jones – though the Fedden bit is bogus. Myself I call her a silly old tart.'

Unable to think of an appropriate response, Amiss fell back on the banal. 'A very beautiful cathedral if I may say so. I'm only sorry that I didn't get a chance to look at the inside properly.'

Davage beamed. 'Now there's a place that's full of hidden treasures. Maybe you and your friend would like me to show you round later on?'

'How very kind. But wouldn't that be a nuisance?'

'No. I'd like to. No one else appreciates that place the way I do, not since poor dear Daisy died. Well, even before that . . . not since she went gaga.'

'Daisy?'

'Our darling dean, Reggie Roper.'

At this moment the empty chair to Amiss's left was pulled back. A slim thirty-something blonde in a neat navy dress and jacket sat down and smiled at Amiss. 'I don't know you.'

'I'm a visitor from London – a friend of a friend of the bishop's.' He extended his hand. 'Robert Amiss. And this is Father Davage.'

'I know Canon Davage.'

Davage turned away from Amiss and began to prattle to the woman on his right.

'And you are?'

'Tilly Cooper. I am privileged to be the dean's wife.'

'The new dean?'

She smiled sweetly. 'The late dean would have been a little old for me.'

'I beg your pardon. I wasn't thinking straight. And he wasn't the marrying kind either, I gather.'

'Let us not talk of the past. I forget what is behind and run towards the goal in order to win the prize of being called to heaven.'

Amiss was gripped with dread. 'Quite. Er . . . have you been here long?'

'Only two weeks. That's why nothing has yet changed. There is much to be done, but the Lord has given us the strength to face every challenge. Are you saved, Mr Amiss?'

Amiss's nerve deserted him. 'Er, um, ah, no, um, that is, well, I'm just ordinary Church of England.'

She smiled her saintly smile and took a sip of water. The waiter came up behind her and offered wine. 'No, thank you. I need no stimulants.'

'I do,' said Amiss faintly. 'White, please.'

'It is wonderful to know that God has shaped you for a divine purpose. And that is what he has done for Norm and I . . .'

'Me,' said Amiss automatically.

She was puzzled but polite. 'Norm and you? Well, yes of course you are welcome to help with God's work.'

Amiss blenched. 'Which is?'

'To drive out the Antichrist,' she said darkly.

'Who is where?'

She shook her head. 'This is a joyful day and we must dwell on what is joyful. How often do you go to church to praise the Lord and where do you go?'

'I've been on the move a bit. Haven't got a regular church.'
'Where do you live?'
'London.'
She clapped her hands. 'Thank you, Jesus! Now you see what I mean about the divine purpose. We have just left our Battersea church, but it is in the best of hands. You must go there and hear the good news. When Norm took over four years ago few people came to the church, for the people had lost their way. When I joined him in matrimony there were many hundreds. By the time we left there were thousands of worshippers praising Jesus. And Bev Johns, who helped Norm with the great work and is our friend in Christ, is Norm's successor and full of the holy spirit.' She put her hand on Amiss's arm. 'I must introduce you to him. Look over there. Do you see him? The vital figure sitting close to the door.'
Amiss obligingly craned round. 'Do you mean the chap with the ponytail?'
'Yes, yes. That is Bev.' She gazed earnestly at Amiss. 'Bev saves souls from hell like a man possessed by God.'
She slid her hand down Amiss's arm and clasped his wrist. 'Promise me you will seek out Bev's church.'
'I'm afraid I'm not a churchgoer.'
'You must not be afraid. Jesus drives out fear. And the Church of St John the Evangelist is into Christianity, not Churchianity.'
Amiss felt sick. 'I'm sure it does excellent work.'
She let his hand go and addressed herself delicately to her melon. 'It is true that we have been the means of bringing people to the Lord. But I say that in no vainglorious spirit. We are but humble vessels and the Lord works through us.'
Amiss looked covertly and longingly towards Davage, who was engaged in animated conversation about a decorated commode he had uncovered in a junk shop the previous week. There was no respite. For the duration of the meal, in her South-London-overlaid-with-irritating-gentility accent, Tilly Cooper praised the Lord, repented of her sins, struggled towards the light and spoke in numbing detail of the manner in which she and Norm and Bev had acted as a team to bring

to God the old, the spiritually lost and those rejected by a materialistic and degenerate society.

By the time the waiter arrived with coffee – which Tilly of course eschewed – she was discoursing on the happiness brought to her by her Bible-story classes for children. 'I write them little songs,' she explained. 'It is a great joy to me that they seem to help them. They clap their little hands and warble along.'

'Splendid.'

'Would you like me to sing you the latest?'

'Now? Here?'

She giggled. 'Very low, of course.'

Anything was better than her conversation, thought Amiss. He tried to look overjoyed. 'What fun! Please go ahead.'

In a low, simpering childish voice she sang:

'If you pray most every day
Jesus takes you by the hand
And leads you to the smiling land
Where even little daisies pray.'

'Delightful,' said Amiss faintly.

'Oh, no. That's only the opening verse. It's the chorus I really want you to hear:

'So smile, smile for Jesus, join his daisy chain.
Say nay unto the devil's wiles
And be a daisy for our Lord
And there'll be miles and miles of smiles
For you and you and me.'

'My goodness. You really wrote that yourself.'

She flashed her excellent teeth. 'All by myself.'

'How wonderful. The children must have loved it.'

While Tilly expanded on just how much they loved her and her little songs, he looked around desperately for release, and to his delight, caught the baroness's eye. He signalled distress and she jerked her head in summons. He swallowed the last of his wine and stood up. 'It has been a great pleasure, Mrs Cooper. But I fear I must leave you now. Lady Troutbeck has need of me.'

'But I must take you to meet Bev, so that he can personally invite you to come and worship with him.'

'I'm sorry, Mrs Cooper, but I must follow the path of duty. Another time perhaps.'

'Then you must promise me you will go to his glorious church to praise the Lord this very Sunday, for you never know the day nor the hour when you may be called to God; you must be ready.'

'I'll try.'

She pressed a card into his hand. 'Take this and go with Jesus!'

Amiss bowed, turned and tapped Davage on the shoulder. 'I'm just off for a word with Lady Troutbeck.'

'I'll meet you both at the cathedral door in thirty minutes.'

'I can't promise she'll be there. But I will.'

'Tell her I'll thcream and thcream and thcream till I'm thick if she doesn't come. I'm just dying to meet her.'

'I will certainly pass your message on.'

'That's a good girl.' Davage smiled a feline smile and turned back to talk of matters Gothic. As Amiss walked joyfully away, he heard Tilly ask the waiter where he went to worship Jesus. It was a small consolation to hear him answer that Mohammed was his prophet.

4

The baroness was waiting impatiently by the French windows. 'Come on. Into the garden. I'm going mad.' She barged out and didn't slacken her pace until they were out of sight of the dining room and sitting on a secluded bench in the corner of the rose garden.

'What about the speeches? I enquire only from curiosity, you understand. I have no desire to hear them, but your absence might be noticed.'

'There aren't going to be any. David persuaded the dignitaries that he wouldn't be able to keep the upper lip stiff if there was any public speaking. Naturally they panicked and agreed to keep their mouths shut.' She pulled out her pipe and assorted paraphernalia. 'I thought there were some old fools in Cambridge and the Lords, but this beats the band. I've just been subjected for more than an hour to some ancient episcopal dunderhead wittering on about the iniquities of ordaining women and thus preventing us from linking up once again with his nibs in Rome.'

'Did you put him right?'

She finished cramming tobacco into her pipe, took out of her capacious handbag a box of extra large matches and – aided by much vigorous sucking and blowing – lit up. 'I was a bit constrained, to tell you the truth. Divided loyalties.'

Amiss looked at her in amazement. 'Good God! Are you trying to tell me you don't know whether you are or are not in favour of ordaining women?'

She threw her right leg over her left and clasped her ankle. 'It's not like me, is it? But, you see, I was against ordaining women because all change is bad where institutions are concerned, but I'm in favour of it because if I were religious I'd be bloody furious if anybody was trying to stop me becoming Archbishop of Canterbury. Or pope, for that matter. Besides, I have a female friend who's been priested and when you like someone, general principles are overthrown.'

'What do you mean all change is bad? In practice you're a fucking subversive. Look at the way you revolutionized St Martha's, for God's sake.'

'That wasn't revolution: it was accelerated evolution with a simultaneous return to old-fashioned scholarly values. Besides . . .' She looked unhappy. 'There's a problem with women. I've a nasty feeling that they're not sufficiently appreciative of flummery. They have a ghastly tendency to be high-minded, austere and proponents of egalitarian claptrap. I would worry that women would be resistant to mitre-wearing and processing around the place in fancy frocks.'

'Female royals go in for that enthusiastically enough.'

'Not the real royals. They do it for duty. The queen's never happier than when riding around in the rain wearing a headscarf and the Queen Mum was to be found wading through Scottish trout streams up to her arse in icy water until she was in her early nineties.' She scratched her midriff moodily. 'Remember the grim austerity in which St Martha's was gripped before I took it by the scruff of the neck?' She shook her head. 'So as I said, I'm ambivalent.'

'Where do you stand on gays and lesbians being ordained?'

'Can't be having that. Not officially, anyway.'

'You rotten old hypocrite.'

'I'm not a hypocrite. I don't mind clerics doing – within reason – what they like in private, but they should shut up about it. Sexuality should not define us. The church shouldn't ask and the aspirants shouldn't tell. I don't want the C of E riven by sexual politics. Sometimes it's right to brush issues under the carpet.'

As Amiss's voice rose in indignant liberal refutation, two polite-looking couples came round the corner. At the sight of a young man haranguing an elderly woman whose vast hat was shrouded in smoke from her pipe and whose knickers were clearly visible under her rucked-up skirt, they were gripped in a community of embarrassment.

The baroness waved at them airily. 'The trouble with you, Robert, is that liberal wetness at times fatally undermines your common sense. Make an issue of sexual orientation, force confrontation over ordination, and one of two things will happen. The conservatives will win and thousands of decent and effective homosexual priests will be driven out of the Church of England or the radicals will win and there'll be wholesale defections of straight clergy and flock. Which do you prefer?'

'I'll reserve judgement. You really have a remarkable gift for portraying liberals as nihilists.' He looked at his watch. 'Fortunately, I can't hang around any longer arguing my shaky and ill-informed position, for I must run. One of my lunch companions wants to prance me round the cathedral. And he's dying for you to come too.'

'Nothing doing. Far too much to get on with. I'm off to the hotel to make phone calls and order people around.'

'He'll be very disappointed.'

'Tell him I'm playing hard to get. Enjoy yourself. And pick me up around seven.'

'Sorry,' said Amiss coldly. 'I forgot to pack a crane.'

'Come in.' She was lying on her bed in a silk paisley dressing gown watching the news and sipping what looked like a whisky and soda. 'Grab a drink.' She waved towards the fridge.

Amiss helped himself to a gin and tonic and fell into the armchair. She pressed the remote control. 'Nothing to worry about. The world appears to be in no more of a mess than it was this morning, despite my absence from the centre of things.'

Amiss closed his eyes.

'You're looking a bit dazed.'

'You'd be dazed if you'd had the Father Davage tour.'

'Smart of me to avoid it. What's the matter? Aggressively queer, is he?'

'Coots run from him.'

'He wasn't making passes at you in the cathedral, was he? Even I would think that in rather poor taste.'

'No, no. He's not like that. It's not what he does that bothers me. It's what he says. And worse, what he showed me.'

'I beg your pardon.'

Amiss screwed up his antimacassar and threw it at her. 'This is serious. That cathedral is completely over the top.'

'What's bothering you? Too many candles for your austere tastes? I admit those cartwheel chandeliers are a bit of an eyeful. Marvellous, though.'

'An eyeful? Did you realize they each have a candle for every day of the year?'

'Really? Bit of a maintenance problem, I should think.'

'To Father Davage's deep distress they're lit only on great occasions. No, the candles don't bother me, even though I was taught they had something to do with selling indulgences. Nor was I upset by the highly decorated tabernacles in front of which Father Davage kept prostrating himself. What rocked me was the unProtestant worship of the Virgin Mary.'

'You've got this wrong. Even Catholics don't worship her. She's prayed to as an intermediary.'

'Tell that to Davage. He gives every impression of treating her as a goddess – or rather, as goddesses.'

'You speak in riddles.'

'He took me to this extraordinary shrine – otherwise known as the lady chapel.'

'Nothing wrong with that. Lots of cathedrals have lady chapels.'

'I would be surprised if other cathedrals sported a representation of the mother of Jesus which bears a striking resemblance to Bette Davis.'

'Don't be silly. You're imagining things.'

'I'll take you there en route to dinner and you can see for yourself. Besides, Cecil – we're on first-name terms now – told me all about it.

'Apparently the artist was a protégé of the late dean. I'm told that among the treasures of the deanery – now mostly in Cecil's possession – were a rather nice Boy David and a rather rough and macho John the Baptist. He is, incidentally, very bitter that the Boy David was left to his colleague, Dominic Fedden-Jones, whom he loves to hate. The implication was that Fedden-Jones was for a time the dean's catamite, but in later years failed to look after the old man as Davage thought he should.

'Two years ago the dean and chapter commissioned this youth to provide a painting to hang at the back of the altar of the lady chapel. So here, in amid the canopies of blue, white and gold – which are bad enough – we have this extraordinary piece of art which is intended to show Mary the cosmopolitan. As Cecil explained, she appears in various guises to demonstrate how she would be represented in different parts of the world. Thus, though a dark-skinned Jew, here she has traditionally been represented as a blue-eyed blonde. So the artist wanted to show that she was all things to all races.'

'Sounds a bit modern to me, but otherwise inoffensive.'

'In this substantial canvas there are perhaps twenty small alternative faces of Mary, all surrounding the major central representation – a pouting Miss Davis.'

'What do the other Marys look like?'

'I easily identified Judy Garland, Marlene Dietrich, Marilyn Monroe – and I think the black one was Diana Ross and the Indian, Indira Gandhi.'

She looked puzzled. 'I don't understand. What's the attraction of these for queers?'

'Don't you know anything about gay icons?'

'Certainly not. Just because I'm catholic in my sexual tastes doesn't mean I know about homosexual popular culture.'

'The more camp type of homosexuals have a particular passion for legendary female stars, whether waiflike and vulnerable like Garland and Monroe, glamorous like Dietrich, melodramatic like Joan Crawford and Bette Davis or brassy and vulgar like Mae West and Bette Midler. I fancy it is your resemblance to Ethel Merman that explains why little Davage was so keen to meet you.'

'Beats me. Why should you fancy someone you don't want to fuck?'

'This is a philosophical matter for another day. Let us concentrate for now on the implications of the New Testament according to Hollywood.'

'Didn't the locals go mad?'

'Davage did mention that there was a bit of screaming – or rather thcreaming – but that it died down after a bit. He expects the same to happen over the controversial memorial to the late dean.'

A happy anticipatory grin spread over the baroness's face. 'Whatever that is going to be, I think I'm going to enjoy it. Tell me all.'

'Can't. He said he couldn't do justice to it without having the drawings to hand. Apparently they're with David at present, so we'll see them tonight.'

'Well there's certainly enough going on to take David's mind for a while off grace and sin.'

'Huh?'

'He's refighting the battle between Augustine and Pelagius at the moment. I'm sure you'll remember all about that from your youthful exploration of fifth-century theology.'

'Not my period, old girl.'

Her attention had wandered. 'Never mind. You'll pick up whatever's necessary about the Early Fathers of the Church during the next few weeks.'

'No, no, no, no, no, no, no!' Amiss followed up this fusillade by consciously setting his face in an expression of inflexible grimness. To his irritation, all his effort appeared to be wasted on the baroness, whose eyes were focused on the middle distance and whose face wore an expression of rapt concentration as she exhaled a mighty mouthful of pipe smoke.

'Did you hear me, Jack?'

'What? No. Thinking.'

'Get it into your fat skull that I am not going to become the bishop's nursemaid, nor, after tonight, get involved in any way whatsoever in his little problems in Westonbury. I don't mind lending a sympathetic ear over dinner, but that's it.'

'Relax, my lad. You really must not allow yourself to become so overwrought.' She heaved herself off the bed. 'Now have another drink while I tart myself up. One must always look one's best for one's old flames.'

'I thought you were trying to deter him from getting any ideas.'

'Between showing my knickers, smoking a pipe and dropping in the occasional profanity, I've successfully disabused him of the notion that I'd make a good wife. However, I'm keeping an open mind about any other job vacancy.' And winking salaciously, she shot into the bathroom.

5

'Shall we move to my study for coffee? It's cosier there.'

The baroness cast an appraising glance around the dining room. 'Cosy certainly isn't the word I'd choose for this. Baroque, maybe. Or do I mean rococo?'

'It rather passed me by at lunch time,' said Amiss, 'but it certainly comes into its own at night.'

'It's the lighting,' said the bishop unhappily. 'It points up all the gilt on the cornices . . .'

'Not to speak of those fetching little cherubs peeking out of the corners . . .' put in the baroness.

'And that striking frieze of gold tassels,' added Amiss, gazing in awe at the red velvet curtains.

'Stick in a four-poster bed and it'd pass for an up-market whorehouse,' pronounced the baroness as she stood up. 'Not quite your style, David, I'd have thought.'

'I hate it. Mostly I eat in the kitchen.' He led the way down a long corridor, up a staircase and ushered his guests through a door on the left. 'This is quite pleasant, don't you think?'

'By your predecessor's standards, it's positively minimalist,' said the baroness, making a beeline for the chaise longue and draping herself along it.

'Please make yourselves comfortable. I'll be back with the coffee very soon.'

'Can I help?'

'No, thank you, Robert. Keep Jack company and pour yourselves some brandy.'

As Amiss removed the bottle she yowled.

'What's the matter?'

'I don't like stingy measures.'

'That wasn't a stingy . . . Oh, what's the point of arguing?' He poured her another healthy double, helped himself to a modest portion and wandered around the book-lined room inspecting furniture. 'Why do you think he's got a lectern in his study?'

'He works standing up. It's no wonder he's so straight-backed.'

Amiss wandered over to the mantelpiece, picked up a large photograph of a substantial and cheerful woman and showed it to the baroness. 'Cornelia?'

'Yes.'

'David's tastes clearly tend towards the Amazonian.'

'But with brains.'

'And bossy to boot.'

'But benignly so.'

She took a healthy swig and sighed gustily. 'I feel quite nostalgic for my sporty youth.'

'You are speaking of David?'

'There was more to my youth than sex, I'll have you know. You didn't know I was a rowing champion, did you?'

'I certainly did. How could I forget that you were one of the foursome who won the Winifred Wristbardge Ladies Rowing Challenge Cup? I remember poor Dame Maud speaking of it.'

'Um, not bad, young Robert. Do you know aught else of my exploits?'

He shook his head.

'Clearly I haven't been bragging enough. That year I also pulled off the Hortense Tottman-Hocker Cup for individual sculling, and took seven wickets in the Oxford-Cambridge ladies' match.'

'I didn't realize you were a cricketer, but had I known, I'd certainly have guessed you'd be a demon bowler.'

'I was no mean batsman either, I'll have you know. Five sixes in that match and I'd have been top scorer if I hadn't absent-mindedly hooked a googly to long leg.'

'You're so predictable, Jack.'

'I will admit, however, that my achievements were as nothing to David's: there wasn't much female competition in cricket, or even in rowing, in which David got his blue. And we weren't allowed to play rugger, in which he got another.'

'So you shared more interests than nooky.'

'Don't be coarse. The trouble with you is –' She broke off as the bishop entered with the coffee.

'You can't put it off any longer, David. Tell us all about what's worrying you.'

The bishop tugged his hair energetically. 'Oh, Jack, if only I could. I know hardly anything. I was never very good at reading character or understanding politics. I relied on Cornelia for all that. I've only ever really related to people through games or teaching.'

'H'm.' The baroness sighed. 'That ruled out a lot of the human race, didn't it? Especially women.'

The bishop went pink. 'I don't know if you remember, Jack, but we actually met on the river.'

'I remember very well.'

Amiss broke the silence. 'Why don't you start with the bare facts? A who's who in the cathedral. The dean, for instance?'

Relieved, the bishop leaped up and took a book from a shelf beside his desk. 'They'll all be in *Crockford's*. Let's see. Norman Cooper was born in 1944, educated Queen's University, Belfast, College of the Resurrection Theological College in Yorkshire, curate in Lancashire and then London, vicar in Grimsby and then for the last four years in Battersea.'

'Doesn't sound like the kind of chap who gets made a dean.'

'You're absolutely right, my dear Ida.' He caught her eye. 'Sorry, my dear Jack. But Cornelia had heard that he had tremendous success in both his parishes in increasing attendance and straightening out finances, which, I suppose, helped him to become a member of the General Synod's Board of Mission and later the Decade of Evangelism Steering Group. I suppose he was thought to be a good administrator and just right to wake Westonbury up a bit.'

'What's he like to speak to?'

'I haven't seen enough of him to say. As you saw, he's rather large and rough looking. A bit like Ian Paisley, in fact.'

'Face like a tombstone, a voice like an angry corncrake with laryngitis and an accent like a hacksaw, you mean.'

'Really, Jack. That's a little unkind. We must never judge by appearances. I will admit his accent is a little rasping, but he's been perfectly civil to me so far. But you must understand we've only met a couple of times and that on business.'

'What's the gossip?'

'I don't hear gossip. I've never been a member of the General Synod and I'm just not interested in ecclesiastical politics. Cornelia used to pick up whatever information she needed from wives, but all she mentioned to me was that Cooper was known to be on the evangelical wing and given a bit to demotic preaching. Oh yes, and a bit strait-laced. But there was no suggestion that he was a fanatic.'

'Did she mention his wife?'

'Just that his first wife died some time ago, and he only acquired this whatshername . . . ?'

'Tilly,' said Amiss.

'. . . Tilly, a year or two ago.'

'From my lunch-time experience, I have to tell you that she is a lady whose religious fervour would be more suited to the American Bible Belt than an English cathedral town.'

'Wall-to-wall fundamentalist claptrap in other words,' said the baroness. 'Robert certainly had an instructive lunch wedged between her and the little Davage woofter. Oh, yes. And we've seen the lady chapel.'

'You're beginning to get some idea of what I'm up against. I can't bear even to think about that picture. When Cornelia explained the significance of it to me I couldn't believe it. She said it would be one of our jobs to have it quietly removed.'

'I can't imagine Davage letting it go quietly,' proffered Amiss. 'And since he's a public figure he'll be in a good position to kick up a stink.'

'It's all too much for me,' said the bishop. 'Much too much for me.'

The baroness waved her empty glass. 'More brandy,

Robert. Now, David, stop whinging, pull yourself together and tell us about the rest of the gang.'

The bishop sat up obediently. 'Obviously the key people are the members of the chapter.'

'You'll have to spell all this out to Robert. He's next thing to a pagan.'

'I do apologize. How parochial I am! The cathedral is run by the dean and the chapter, which in Westonbury consists of five residentiary canons. You don't want to be bothered with the twenty-four honorary canons, who don't really count and most of whom I don't know from Adam.'

He consulted his book. 'Cecil Davage is sixty-two, educated at Cambridge, Chichester Theological College, then back to Cambridge as a college chaplain, fellow and lecturer in fine art. Arrived here ten years ago as treasurer.'

Amiss was puzzled. 'Isn't that more an accountant's job?'

'No, no. In fact in most cathedrals it involves few duties, but here, where we are very traditional, he's in charge of looking after all the cathedral's valuables.'

'He showed me what's on display. Absolutely marvellous – particularly, of course, that magnificent diamond-studded gold crozier.'

The bishop sighed. 'Ah, yes. St Dumbert's Staff. I worry about it, you know. These days it's asking for trouble to have such a valuable object in a public building. Not to speak of everything else – all those exquisite rings and reliquaries, for instance. But it would be wrong to put such things in a bank vault: they belong to the people. Remember Auden's lines?

> *'Cathedrals,*
> *Luxury liners laden with souls.'*

'The cases seemed pretty impregnable,' said Amiss soothingly. 'And Davage seemed very happy with the alarm system.'

'I suppose so.' The bishop looked back at his book. 'Then there's the precentor, Jeremy Flubert, who is in charge of the music.' He consulted his book. 'He's forty-seven, went to King's, Cambridge, then the Royal College of Music in

London; his theological college was Wescott House, Cambridge, and from there he came straight here as organist and Hubert's domestic chaplain until fifteen years ago, when he became precentor. As you'll have heard today, Westonbury's music is sublime, and it's said to be mainly his doing. He's a great organist and a marvellous inspiration to the boys.'

'What's he like?'

'What's he like?' The bishop threw his hands wide. 'I don't know. He seems perfectly nice.'

'Woofter?'

'I don't know, Jack. He's not married. But then none of them is.

'Then there's the chancellor, Sebastian Trustrum. He's the chap in charge of the services, Robert. A rather acerbic little man. I suggested a small liturgical change in the service for my consecration, and he was very short with me. Very short indeed. Of course, he's getting on a bit.' He fumbled through the pages. 'Sixty-six, according to this.'

'That's young.'

The bishop smiled. 'Not everyone bears his years as easily as you, Jack. Anyway Trustrum has had a more conventional career: university and theological college in London, a couple of country curacies, then became a vicar in this diocese, an honorary canon and twenty years ago, chancellor.' He riffled through the pages. 'Ah, here's Dominic Fedden-Jones. Forty-two, Exeter University, Cranmer Hall, Durham, curacies in Guildford and Gloucester, then oddly came straight in here as a canon residentiary. I can't think of anything to tell you about him. Spends quite a lot of time away, from what I can gather.'

He lapsed into silence.

'That's four,' said the baroness in a surprisingly patient tone. 'Who's the fifth?'

'Oh, sorry. How could I forget? Alice Wolpurtstone.'

'Alice Wolpurtstone!' exclaimed both his listeners.

'Oh, my goodness, didn't you know? First female canon in the country, in fact.'

The baroness sat bolt upright and slammed her glass heavily down on the table. 'In this haunt of misogynistic woofters you have a female canon? I thought they were violently opposed to even the ordination of women.'

'I do realize it's a little surprising. In fact when Cornelia first heard about Canon Wolpurtstone, she said, "Mark my words. Some deal has been done here." But that was just when she became ill and I haven't given it any further thought.'

'Frankly, David, you don't seem to have given anything much thought.'

He looked stricken.

'Sorry,' she said. 'Thoughtless of me. Considering what you've been through, you've done well just to survive the last few months.'

'Do you know anything about the Reverend Alice?' enquired Amiss gently.

The bishop's brows knitted. 'Seems a nice woman.' He delved back into Crockford's. 'Thirty-five, educated Bristol University. A three-year gap, then studied at theological college in America; she came back here seven years ago and was ordained deacon, then priest two years ago and then a canon just a few months ago.'

'America indeed. Oh, oh,' said the baroness.

'Oh, really, Jack,' said Amiss. 'Curb your prejudices just for once. People can have studied in America and still be sane, you know.'

'Only Mary Lou. What else do you know, David? What qualifications did she have to secure such a ground-breaking appointment?'

'I've no idea. But Cornelia heard she was elected to replace a canon who defected to Rome last year because of his opposition to women priests.'

'That was a splendidly bitchy revenge, I have to say,' observed the baroness. 'What are her ecclesiastical politics?'

'I don't know. I can't understand any of it except that it's all going to be awful if Dean Cooper starts the crusade he's threatening.'

'Which is?'

'To weed out what he calls depravity, indulgence and Romanism.'

'Crikey. That'll keep him busy.'

'It's not funny. I'm afraid of what he'll want to do to the services and the music.'

'Why did he allow today's service to go ahead in that form? I'd have thought he'd at least have cut the incense ration.'

'It was all set in stone before he arrived, Robert. And with the archbishop coming he couldn't have risked a row, I suppose.' He rocked back and forth. 'It's going to be dreadful. My auxiliary bishop is not very sympathetic, and pays no attention to what goes on in the cathedral. And I don't even have a domestic chaplain in whom I can confide. When I told him last week that I was glad we now ordained women and could see no argument against female bishops, he marched straight upstairs, packed his bags and left. His last words were that he was going over to Rome.'

The baroness got up, went over to the bishop and put her arm around him. 'You poor old thing. You must be very miserable.'

'I would feel completely desperate if it wasn't that Robert's going to help me.'

'I'm not.'

'You're not?' The bishop's voice was agonized.

'I just can't.'

'Of course you can,' said the baroness. 'It's only temporary.'

'Look, David, it's not that I wouldn't like to be of use, but what you need to help you in Westonbury is a holy hit squad – not an atheist who doesn't know the difference between a cathedral and a synagogue.'

'My dear young man, above all other attributes I require someone with no ecclesiastical axes to grind. From what I've seen of you and from what Jack's told me, you're ideal – intelligent, discreet and honourable. Surely a job as a temporary researcher-cum-personal assistant will help you financially while you seek permanent employment.'

'But . . .'

'And you're understanding.'

To Amiss's horror, the bishop began to cry. 'Without a confidant I will go mad.'

The baroness pulled his head onto her ample chest and patted him on the back. 'There, there.' She glared at Amiss. 'How could you be so heartless?'

'Oh, God,' he said. 'I give in. When do I start?'

6

'It's all very well for you, you double-crossing . . .'

'Son of a bitch?' suggested the baroness affably. 'Oh, shut up whining. You know you'll enjoy it. You've been secretly pining for something interesting to do. Stop griping and look over there and marvel.'

Amiss's gaze climbed slowly up the opulently lit exterior of Westonbury Cathedral to where – several hundred feet up – darkness fell just beyond the top of the highest spire. Further up again was an expanse of star-studded darkness. There was no sound except faint lapping from the distant weir, until the baroness murmured, '"By night an atheist half believes a God,"' and they began walking again towards their hotel.

'I suppose I might enjoy the peace of it all.'

'Of course you will. Besides, Plutarch needs a change of air.'

Amiss's serenity was shattered. 'Oh, bugger, I'd forgotten about her. Wouldn't she be better off with you?'

'This is a much better environment. It might have a lasting spiritual effect.'

'I can't just import her into the palace. She might tear its fabric apart.'

'You misunderstand that animal. It's confined spaces and sudden shocks that make her cross.'

'Cross is not the word I would have chosen. How about vindictive? Vicious? Destructive? Murderous? I've seen her lay whole rooms waste and make grown men cry.'

'*You* made a grown man cry this evening.'

'Not by scratching him.'

'No, by refusing him succour – temporarily, at least. And that's typical of you. Plutarch is a passionate creature whose sins are sins of commission. You, on the other hand, tend towards the cold-blooded, so yours are sins of omission.'

'That's preposterous crap.'

'It is not. Take, for instance, your treatment of Plutarch. You deny her love. Admit it, you hardly emanate affection. Poor little thing feels unwanted.'

'She is bloody well unwanted. And highly inconvenient and expensive to boot. I am dutiful towards her and she treats me, at best, with disdain. Anyway, all this is bollocks. I grant you she gets on well with you, but even when billeted at St Martha's she still creates mayhem from time to time.'

'Only through an excess of youthful high spirits.'

'The high-table salmon?'

'Healthy appetite and discerning palate. No more than I'd have done myself in her shoes.'

'"*Rem acu tetigisti*", as Jeeves would say. You get on so well with her because you are two of a kind.'

'Anyway, I've already squared it with David. He likes her. Said she'd be company.'

'But . . .'

'Stop arguing. Tell you what. I'll deliver her personally on Sunday when I come down to hear Norm the Noodlehead preach. I'm in need of a good laugh. I look forward to enjoying the occasion with you.'

'I won't be here.'

'What do you mean you won't be here? You said you were coming back tomorrow.'

'Yes, but I'll be going back to London on Saturday evening, so as to be ready the next morning to attend festivities in Battersea *chez* Bev.'

The baroness looked blank.

'Norm's successor. He sounds potentially very entertaining. Davage met him this morning and squeaked apoplectically about his awfulness. Apparently he likes to be known as the Rev. Bev.'

The baroness began to protest volubly, but Amiss cut her short. 'Just shut up, Jack. I've a long-standing date to spend

Sunday next with Ellis Pooley. He and Jim were so tied up with the Wimbledon serial murderer that we haven't had a chance to meet for ages. I have absolutely no intention of welshing on the arrangement. You should be patting me on the back for combining business with pleasure by persuading him to suss out Norm's past.'

The baroness chuckled. 'So be it. I would give a lot to see young Master Pooley leaping around being saved.' She sighed. 'In fact you now make me envious: I expect you'll have much more fun than is likely to be on offer from Norm's Old Testament ravings.'

'I expect so too. From what Tilly told me, the Rev. Bev is not to be missed: charismatic, joyful and ready to heal at the drop of a cassock, apparently.'

The baroness yawned. 'Good, good. Norm looks a bit dour by comparison. Still, I will extract from the occasion what entertainment I can and trust you to do the same.'

They turned into the hotel grounds. 'Now how do you suggest I square Rachel?' enquired Amiss. 'She's becoming increasingly tired of what she calls my Flying Dutchman approach to life.'

The baroness stopped and looked grimly at him. 'Tell her to accept you for what you are. If she doesn't enjoy your adventurousness, ingenuity and dash, then she doesn't deserve you.'

He went to bed comforted.

'So now to the matter of the dean's memorial,' he wrote to Rachel.

'I am told that the major inspiration for this was an immense monument in Winchester Cathedral to one of its Victorian bishops, who was clearly a chap with ideas above his station and whose memorial includes four sizeable angels carrying the bier and a vast eagle poised at the great man's feet – presumably to carry his soul to heaven.

'Plans for Dean Roper's memorial were drawn up three years ago by his protégé, the perpetrator of the lady-chapel picture. The sketches show a marble effigy of Dean Roper clad in full ecclesiastical regalia, coloured in where appropriate with purple and gold, his body being borne by six winged youths in extremely brief togas. At the dean's feet is a representation of the martyrdom of a hunky St Sebastian, who seems these days to be the patron saint of gays. The underside of the canopy is painted with murals of what were presumably the dean's favourite biblical events, many of which seem to involve an excessive amount of romping of the David and Jonathan kind, a few more martyrdoms (was the dean into S&M I wonder?), and what the bishop said were the apostles skinny-dipping in the River Jordan, while John the Baptist and Jesus – turned out for decency's sake in posing pouches – get on with the baptism in the corner.

'Not surprisingly, English Heritage emitted a scream of anguish and refused to countenance having such a monstrosity in the cathedral, whereupon the dean and his chums took legal advice and discovered that there was nothing stopping them from erecting it in the garden of the deanery. So the decision was made to put this gay grotto in a reasonably discreet spot in the northwest corner. The foundations were laid, the plinth was put in position and the sculptor got to work.

'Dean Cooper found out about it, saw the plans, denounced it as satanically inspired and then discovered that his predecessor, a scion of a major brewery, had left to his successor a bequest of a million pounds to be spent on whatever improvements to the cathedral he wanted; the loot would not be released until this gay grotto was in place. That news caused Norm to cave in, so he's not completely incorruptible.

'So you can see that there is much to interest me. Try and look upon what I'm doing as a form of paid social work. I promise the post has been redirected, and my calls diverted and I won't pass up any interviews for real jobs.'

He reread the long letter, grimaced and typed:

'Do I hear words like "pushover", "feeble" and "Troutbeck's office boy" rise uncharitably once more to your lips? Pshaw! That is just because I have become too accustomed over the last few years to apologizing and pretending that I am being pushed into that which secretly I really want to do. So please disregard any wimpery in this letter, any suggestion that I am a piece of flotsam tossed hither and thither on the tide that is Baroness Troutbeck's will (what a fucking awful metaphor!) and accept instead that I am willingly grasping the opportunity to help prop up a great national institution. And at the very least it'll be a lot better than moping at home.

'I must end now. I'm off to Westonbury tomorrow, so this is the only opportunity to assuage my curiosity by visiting Norm and Tilly's old church; Ellis, my anthropological companion-in-arms, is due to pick me up any minute.'

Pausing only to add endearments, Amiss put his letter in an envelope, addressed it to Rachel care of the Foreign and Commonwealth Office for forwarding in the diplomatic bag and stamped it just as the doorbell rang.

Amiss and Pooley arrived at St John the Evangelist's ten minutes early to find that there was no parking space within several hundred yards. By the time they entered the vast Victorian church, there was only just standing room: the nave was chock-a-block with worshippers singing lustily along with a male guitarist and three women with tambourines. The man wore sandals, jeans and a flowered shirt, and the women floaty smocks of the kind that went out of fashion when Flower Power died in the seventies. The tune was Dylanesque and the voices poor – but what really horrified Amiss were the words of the refrain:

'When they come and listen to us sing to God aburve,
They'll know we are Christians by our lurve, by our lurve.'

He avoided Pooley's eye.

This song appeared to be the culmination of the superannuated hippies' gig; when they finished, the lead singer raised his guitar towards the heavens and called, 'Praise the Lord.'

'Praise the Lord,' yelled the congregation.

The Flower Children scampered off into the well of the church and were instantly replaced by a West Indian steel band, which danced onto the platform. Although they were more to Amiss's musical taste, their sound – augmented by even more tambourines – was so deafening as to cause him actual pain. Unable to identify any more than occasional words like 'Lord', 'suffer' and 'save', he let the sound wash over him, wriggled himself into a better vantage point and watched for audience reaction.

Tilly had been right. There was no denying that this was a wildly enthusiastic congregation. And what was more, there was nothing uniform about its members. Middle-aged, middle-class trendies, washed-out teenagers, down-and-outs and clean-cut Mormonesque types were all singing along lustily, their faces full of joy: Amiss and an increasingly tight-lipped Pooley seemed the only spectres at the feast.

The din ceased, the band dispersed and a single light shone onto a youngish man in a bright yellow tunic who had just materialized in the pulpit. Amiss recognized him as the Rev. Bev by his black ponytail and the three rings in his left ear.

'Brothers and sisters! God is love!' He threw his arms out and motioned to his congregation to respond.

'God is love!' they parroted.

'Hallelujah!'

'Hallelujah!'

'Louder, louder. Hallelujah!'

'Hallelujah!'

As the din died away, a hulking skinhead with spots gazed so threateningly at Amiss and Pooley that on the next round of 'Hallelujahs' they participated enthusiastically.

Bev's voice fell several decibels. 'Hey,' he crooned. 'Hey, hey, hey.'

'Hey, hey,' shouted the congregation.

'How do we know that God loves us?' he enquired. There was a dramatic pause. His voice rose. ''Cos he's told us so, that's how! In his very own story!' And in a crescendo: 'In his very own – his very own book!' At which he picked up a volume from the edge of the pulpit and waved it over his head. 'And this is it. The Holy Word of God! God's own book! The Bible!'

He put the book down and looked sternly at the congregation. 'Now why did God give us this book?' They gazed back expectantly. 'So we would read it, of course! Not to leave lyin' there! He gave it us so we could build up the muscles of faith.'

He moved his head slowly from left to right and surveyed each section of his flock sadly. 'But you're just not building up those muscles the way God wanted, are you? You're lazing about. Your muscles are all flabby.' He shook his head vigorously. 'That's not what God wants.' He bunched his fists and flexed his impressive pectorals. 'This is what God wants from you. He wants you all to build big muscles and be champs!

'You know how a wrestler gets to be a champ?' Again he surveyed his listeners slowly, this time from right to left. 'I see you all know the answer. First he works out to build up those muscles. And then he practises wrestling against ever stronger and stronger opponents. He's always preparing himself to meet the next one.'

He brandished the Bible again. 'This is your own private work-out equipment – a present from God to you. Exercise, exercise, exercise. Build up those big faith muscles. And then you'll be ready to wrestle with sin.'

His voice fell dramatically. 'When you're strong enough, you'll be ready to take on the great enemy himself. Yes, brothers and sisters, when you've got the faith muscles of a Mr Universe, you can throw the Great Satan himself!' His voice rose. 'And if we're all champs and we wrestle him together, we'll be able to put our feet on Satan's neck and count him out!

'That's our holy mission! That's what God wants us to do. That's why he gave us the equipment.' He gazed round. 'Now, you know how you feel when you give someone a present and they're not grateful enough? It bugs you, doesn't it? And it bugs God too when he looks down and sees you leaving the exercise bike of faith gathering dust in the corner of your soul.'

The congregation shuffled in a shamefaced way.

'But this isn't just bugging God. It's committing suicide. 'Cos if you ignore God's exercise bike you won't have the muscles to climb into heaven when you die! Think of that! You'll be looking at the staircase and you won't have the strength to climb up to God! Jesus will be standing at the top with his arms open to you, and you won't be able to reach him.

'There'll be a place for you somewhere else, though. You don't need muscles to tumble down the mine shaft to hell. And as you fall towards the devil and the lake of eternal flames, you'll be crying out in despair. "Oh, God," you'll be crying, "I'm sorry I didn't work-out when you gave me the chance. Save me."'

He shook his head gloomily. 'But God won't hear you. 'Cos when you fall down the mine shaft to hell, you're not on line to God any more. Only to Satan.'

Even Amiss was feeling rather guilty and depressed by this time. So, like the rest of the congregation, he was relieved when Bev Johns decided to lighten the tone. 'OK, OK. That's enough of the' – he raised his index fingers and mimed quotation marks – '"Bad News". Now for the' – he repeated the business with his fingers – '"Good News".' Then he leaped in the air. 'Jesus is our friend!' He motioned to his hearers. 'Let's hear it for Jesus!'

'Jesus is our friend!' they cried.

'Jesus loves us!'

'Jesus loves us!' they shrieked.

'Show you love your brothers and sisters! Hug each other for Jesus.'

Apprehensively, Amiss looked sideways at Pooley, who was standing as rigid as a young officer at Rorke's Drift waiting to be overwhelmed by the Zulu hordes. As Amiss made a feeble gesture in his direction indicating that they might be better off hugging each other than awaiting the attentions of perfect strangers, he was grabbed by a large black woman in a cartwheel hat, who enveloped him in her capacious arms and squeezed him painfully. As soon as she put him down, she was replaced by a haggard man in a woolly hat who smelled of unwashed clothes and yesterday's whisky. Amiss tried not to flinch and to return the hug with the appropriate pressure. It cheered him somewhat to see that a horror-stricken Pooley was being pawed by a couple who looked like terminally ill vegans.

Bev, who had been jumping about in the pulpit urging them on, called the proceedings to order. A hunched and twitching Pooley moved close to Amiss. 'I may never forgive you,' he whispered.

'A singularly inappropriate response, if you don't mind my saying so.'

They were drowned out by a holler from Bev, who plucked the microphone off its stand and began to croon with the assistance of an electronically enhanced guitarist who had leaped onto the altar:

'Where on earth is Jesus?
Is he at the bar?
Is he out there raving?
Going much too far?

'Taking dope and drinking,
Kicking up a fuss,
Is he in a harlot's bed?
No! He's here with us!'

The beat induced most of the congregation to bop along enthusiastically and the applause was such that the Rev. Bev went through the performance again with redoubled élan. 'That was a song for Jesus,' he yelled at the end. 'Let's hear it for Jesus, now, brothers and sisters. Save me, Jesus!'

'Save me, Jesus!' screeched his flock.

'Save me, Jesus!'

'Save me, Jesus!'

He motioned them into silence. 'Every week I give you new hope that Jesus wants to save everyone. No one is too wicked or depraved for him to love. Make ready now to greet your new sisters and brothers and help them to Jesus, our Lord.'

He stabbed his right forefinger towards the main entrance and the double doors were pulled open simultaneously. There was a tremendous din of revving engines and then, in a thunder of sound, down the aisle came a vast black-and-silver motorbike with two black-clad riders. It drew level with the platform, juddered to a halt and as it fell silent another bike came through the door, to be followed by another and another until seven stood silent. The dramatic effect was slightly lessened by the outbreak of coughing brought on by the exhaust fumes.

The coughing died down, and in well-choreographed symmetry, the riders propped their bikes against the south wall, strode to the front of the platform, turned their backs on the congregation and raised their arms towards the preacher.

'Praise the Lord!' he cried.

'Praise the Lord!' was what Amiss presumed they shouted in return; the sound was muffled by their helmets. Picked out in silver studs on the back of each black leather jacket was the legend:

HEAVEN'S ANGELS

BIKERS FOR JESUS

'Hallelujah, hallelujah,' cried the preacher. There was a lusty chorus of hallelujahs in response. He tore off his tunic and revealed a T-shirt with the exhortation: 'Jump for Jesus!' Leaping up and down he cried, 'Now, jump for Jesus.' Feeling like a complete idiot and avoiding Pooley's eye, Amiss obediently followed the example of the bikers and his neighbours, until after a couple of minutes exhaustion overtook the crowd.

The bikers removed their helmets and raised their arms again towards the pulpit. 'These were bad people,' shouted Bev, 'but they've seen the light and with the help of Jesus they're going to drive out the devil.' There was an expectant hush, and from the ceiling there descended a fluorescent red cross. 'Come on, now! Shake out the devil! Shake him out! Shake him out!' He descended from the pulpit – revealing his bottom half to be clad in jeans and trainers – rushed towards the bikers and knocked each of them over until they all lay prostrate. 'Down, down, all of you down for Jesus,' he screamed, and the congregation obeyed as quickly as infirmity and clumsiness permitted.

As the entire congregation began noisily expelling the devil, Pooley grabbed Amiss's arm; together they set off, with considerable difficulty, to crawl towards freedom. When they reached the side door and stood up, Pooley strode out immediately. As Amiss took a last half-wistful, half-relieved look back, a sobbing Bev Johns was clasping the bottom of the red cross crying, 'Strike him, Jesus. Save us all,' and the bikers were writhing and alternately screaming and groaning. Various members of Bev's flock appeared to be trying with some success to speak in tongues.

Amiss caught up with Pooley and jerked his head towards the pub on the corner. 'Hold on. I need a drink.'

'I don't. I'll wait outside. I need fresh air.'

Amiss tottered into the bar like an old man, ordered and paid for a large whisky and downed it in one. 'Bad night?' enquired the barman. 'Same again?'

Amiss shook his head. 'No, thanks. Get thee behind me, Satan.'

7

After the brisk walk on which Pooley insisted, they repaired to his flat, where, with the help of some restorative gins and tonic, they put together a hearty lunch of steak, onions and mashed potatoes.

Amiss cleared his plate and washed it down with some more rioja. 'Gosh, I did enjoy that, Ellis. And to think I feared you might think quiche more suitable for *dejeuner à deux hommes nouveaux.*'

'Life in the Met is not conducive to New Mannishness, I can tell you.'

'So what's been going on? I think we've exhausted my affairs. Now give me the lowdown on that case you've been hinting darkly about. And omit no salacious detail, however disgusting.'

Pooley burst eagerly into the account of the perplexing and grisly murders which during the previous couple of months had so much occupied him and their mutual friend, Chief Superintendent Jim Milton. It had been cracked, it turned out, through a great deal of patient investigation, culminating in the discovery of a call girl who had witnessed a crucial encounter from a doorway in which she had been loitering.

'Has this done much for your reputations in the Yard? Jim seemed a bit gloomy about his personal standing last time we met.'

'He's been pretty gloomy generally. All this is-she-isn't-she coming back from the States?/will-he-won't-he join her there? hasn't been helping his morale. Certainly I had some pats on the back and I suppose Jim must have too. But he's been so busy we haven't had a chance to talk as friends and he took off the other day for their long-overdue holiday. Won't be back for almost a month, I think.'

'I hope to Christ they resolve things this time.'

Pooley shrugged. 'I see no happy endings. I just can't see Jim throwing up his job and –'

The telephone shrilled; Pooley picked up the receiver. 'Hello. Ellis Pooley.'

The voice coming down the line was so loud that Amiss could hear it distinctly. 'So how was it?'

'I beg your pardon,' said Pooley. 'Have you got the wrong number?'

'It's Jack Troutbeck, you idiot.'

'Oh, fine. Good afternoon, Jack. How nice to hear from you. Where are you?'

'At the other end of the bloody line is the answer, trying to communicate with you in the couple of minutes I've got. Is Robert with you?'

'Yes.'

'Pass him over.'

'Good afternoon, Jack,' said Amiss genially. 'Feeling like a jolly gossip, are we?'

'Stop horsing about. You and young Ellis had better apply your minds to the fact that the dean appears to be a raving lunatic. Much madder than we thought. God knows, I didn't expect much from the Northern Irish, but there were moments when this guy made Ian Paisley seem like a papist.'

'A bit seventeenth century, was he?'

'Cromwell would have applauded loudly. Call me ecumenical, but I think remarks about the immorality of nuns' men and monks' women, not to mention whores of Babylon, are going a bit far in a High-Church cathedral in Westonbury in the mid-1990s. If I had my way, I'd sentence him to two years in a priest's hole listening to Gregorian chant.'

'Went down well with the audience?'

'David nearly fainted and half the congregation walked out. You really missed something.'

'So did you.'

She ignored him. 'However more important is that

somebody – mind you, quite rightly in my opinion – seems to me to be out to get him. When he had done slavering and foaming at the mouth and left the pulpit, he ended up at the bottom of the steps on his arse: it was a delight to behold. Such was his popularity by then that the congregation uttered nary an "oh dear" but merely tittered. Nice, charitable David picked him up.'

'But what makes you think somebody's out to get him?'

'Instinct. When I got back to the palace I made an excuse about having lost a valuable handkerchief and thundered back to the cathedral. Turned out all the pulpit steps were dangerously highly waxed: going up would be safe enough; going down could have been lethal if he'd fallen earlier and awkwardly.'

'But that would be a crazy thing to do. It's so obvious.'

'No, it isn't. It could easily be blamed on an absent-minded cleaner too cowardly to own up. Anyway, that's what I think. Now chew it over. I'm off.' The telephone went dead.

Amiss looked at Pooley. 'Did you hear that?'

'Of course.'

'Old girl's getting a bit fanciful.'

'You don't expect me to agree.'

'Oh, of course. Sorry. What a thing to say to Mr Fanciful himself.'

'You have to admit your dean seems to be a bluebottle in the Westonbury ointment.'

'Why don't you come down and snoop around with me? Didn't you say you were taking a fortnight's leave in a week or so?'

'Ah, yes, but I have things to do. I've been earmarking this fortnight for a long time to sort out things domestically. Now that I've bought this house I can bring more books and furniture from home: there's a lot to be done. Then I'm having a week walking in the Highlands.'

'Alone or in company?'

'Alone. I get enough company at work.'

'Sounds perfectly foul to me,' said Amiss. 'Boring domestic claptrap followed by getting wet and cold and tired.'

Pooley smiled gently. 'We are not compatible in all respects, you know.'

'Too right. I'll go and open another bottle.'

The telephone rang as Amiss reached the kitchen. 'Hello. Ellis . . . Oh, right, Jack. I'll tell him.'

He put the phone down. 'Robert. Jack says you'd better get back fast. She'll be leaving shortly and reckons Plutarch will be fully conscious in a few hours.'

'Oh, God, no. I'd forgotten she was to deliver her.' He looked at his watch. 'I must run if I'm going to catch the four-thirty.'

He grabbed his coat. 'Thanks for everything. And remember, if you change your mind, you'll be welcome to visit. The bishop has already said any friends of mine would be honoured guests. He's even claimed Plutarch will be a valued companion.'

Pooley shuddered. 'There's no accounting for tastes.'

The bishop looked on with pleasure as Amiss gingerly patted the stirring marmalade form. 'How nice to see you, Robert. You must be very pleased to be reunited with Plutarch.'

'Yes, indeed.'

'Oh, and Jack left you a present.'

Amiss looked suspiciously at the bishop. 'I don't like the sound of that? What kind of present?'

'A portable phone. Wasn't that kind of her?'

He handed it to Amiss; attached was a note written in the baroness's huge and almost unintelligible scrawl, which from long experience Amiss managed to decipher swiftly: 'Programmed: 1) my direct line; 2) my car phone; 3) St Martha's switchboard. Keep me posted.'

Crossly, Amiss jabbed his finger on the first button.

'Yes?'

'Jack, it's me, and I have no intention of using this foul device. I hate mobile phones. They're the mark of complete and utter prats and I have some pride.'

'Calm down, calm down. A portable phone maketh not a prat. You do not need to use it prattishly: it is purely to make it easy for you to keep in touch with HQ.'

'If by HQ you mean yourself . . .'

'Of course.'

'. . . what you mean is vice versa.'

'That's as maybe, but in any event I'm sure you'll find it preferable to having me hound you via David and whatever chums you make in Westonbury. Now stop being such a sourpuss, and remember I want the line kept clear for me.

'See you.'

As the phone went dead, Amiss swore and then saw the bishop looking at him worriedly. 'Sorry, David,' he said, suddenly feeling ashamed, 'it's been a long day and I fear I was being irritable.'

The bishop's face cleared. 'I quite understand. Come down to the kitchen and let us prepare something to eat and tell each other about our day. Mine, at least, has not been uneventful.'

The bishop was a man of regular habits, and within only a few days so was Amiss. Never by choice an early riser, he left the bishop to his own devices for his early-morning prayers and the run on which he was frequently accompanied by Plutarch. The growing friendship between bishop and cat had begun unpromisingly, when – on her first morning in residence – she had pursued her host as he began running, had hurled herself between his legs and brought them both sprawling and intertwined to the ground. She had then compounded her offence by clawing at him savagely through his rather thin tracksuit. Their mutual cries of pain brought Amiss – still in his dressing gown – running from the palace just as they succeeded in wriggling out of each other's embrace. As he shouted 'Get thee to a cattery,' after the fleeing Plutarch, Amiss met firm resistance from the bruised and slightly bleeding bishop. 'Nonsense, my dear fellow. Just an accident. Could happen to anyone. I'm sure tomorrow she'll have learnt her lesson.' And indeed, bizarrely, she seemed to have done so, for on succeeding mornings she accompanied the bishop, if not quite like a well-trained dog, at least without evincing any signs of feline blood lust.

Plutarch was not a slave to routine. If the weather was unpleasant she let the bishop run alone, but wet or fine, she joined them in the kitchen at 8.30 as they made and ate breakfast – muesli and fresh fruit for the bishop, boiled eggs and toast for Amiss and sardines for Plutarch.

Unfortunately for Amiss, too much exposure to the baroness's hospitality had given Plutarch a discriminating palate. She had become contemptuous of all brands of tinned cat food and now created merry hell if not supplied with human food – and good human food at that. These days when he shopped for himself and the bishop, he had to bear Plutarch in mind, and it was necessary also to keep an emergency supply of up-market cans of the kind of food she was prepared to tolerate: sardines, pilchards, tuna, hot dogs, beef stew and so on. A couple more visits to St Martha's, thought Amiss sourly, and she would refuse anything other than rare roast beef and best new season English lamb, washed down with a rather piquant little claret. '"Eat, drink and be merry," as Ecclesiastes recommended,' the baroness had told him she'd instructed Plutarch as she deposited her in Westonbury. When Amiss had retorted that Ecclesiastes wasn't thinking of cats, the baroness had accused of him being a life-denying specieist.

If the bishop was free, they shared a cold lunch and in the evening cooked something simple. The bishop was a novice cook, but he was keen, and he took simple pleasure from preparing a meal which they both enjoyed. Amiss never saw him happier than when he managed to produce a spaghetti bolognaise where the pasta was *al dente* and the sauce delicious.

Breakfast over, Amiss would clear the table and wash up, Plutarch would go about her business and the bishop would disappear to dress for daily duties like services, diocesan management meetings, listening to local pressure groups, attendance at ecclesiastical committees and visits to parishes within his diocese. Amiss would then settle down to his administrative and research duties, for it had rapidly become clear that the bishop badly needed help on both fronts. Amiss's main job might be to hold the bishop's hand and try to make sense of what was going on in the cathedral close, but he had much to do as a substitute for Cornelia. There were the bishop's domestic affairs – such as the payment of bills – and on the research front checking references and footnotes, posting off to, and requesting books from, the London Library and typing up whatever scholarly scrawl the bishop had produced standing at his lectern early in the morning or after dinner.

Even more important was Amiss's role as soother and distracter when the bishop was distressed by ecclesiastical scandals (a married vicar running off with his deaconess, an archdeacon found fiddling his expenses, a General Synod committee wondering if in a very real sense sin existed at all, or some new vulgarization of the liturgy) which elicited squeals of pain and a flood of oh-dear-oh-dear-oh-goodness-gracious-how-distressing-how-dreadfuls.

Amiss was pleased to feel that even if he were to fail absolutely on the cathedral front, he would still earn the £300 a week the bishop had insisted augment his free board and lodging – a sum which came from the bishop's own pocket and which Amiss later discovered represented about two-thirds of his pre-tax earnings.

As a bonus, Amiss began to enjoy reacquainting himself with aspects of early and medieval history to which he had not given a thought since Oxford, so as to be able to – if not maintain a sophisticated debate with the bishop – at least ask reasonably intelligent questions about the performance of this or that pope or about what it was that particularly upset Tertullian about bringing philosophy into theology. It was, he realized, a useful part of his job to act as a surrogate pupil: he could see that losing his students had been almost as terrible a blow to the bishop as losing his wife.

Being both enthusiastic and humble, the bishop was a good teacher. There were moments when Amiss thought he almost cared about St Augustine of Hippo and when one evening, over the shepherd's pie, they got into a dispute about the ontological proof of the existence of God (that than which no greater thing can be thought exists not only in the mind but in reality) – a concept which Amiss had always regarded as a prime piece of theological claptrap – the bishop was so lucid and eloquent that over the next few days Amiss wondered a few times if St Anselm might not have had a point.

Amiss always allowed himself a prelunch stroll around the close and the cathedral. Initially this was to take the opportunity to get to know another part of the building well. He had always tended to be an impatient visitor to great and beautiful places and things – one of those who gets around a building of great architectural interest in twenty minutes while the Louvre or the Uffizi takes no more than an hour and a half. But as the gentle pace of Westonbury had its effect, he found there were great pleasures to be had from applying himself to quiet contemplation of the sunlit rose window or the intricate carvings on the choir stalls.

This period of soothing the spirit was frequently necessary in order to calm Amiss's soul after he had attended to Plutarch's perpetrations and desecrations, for she had taken to demonstrating her fondness for the cathedral by bringing it gifts of dead wildlife. It was only because she liked to take a well-earned nap beside the remains of the rat, water vole or blue tit that had the misfortune to cross her path, that Amiss was able to locate the corpse most mornings before anyone else did. It was once again the bishop who saved her from being ignominiously exiled when Amiss found her lying on the altar asleep beside a well-chewed pigeon.

He spent a great deal of time alone, for the bishop was required to attend, reluctantly, numerous working lunches and welcoming dinners, but Amiss enjoyed the opportunity to read, think and amble by the river – sometimes with Plutarch – and occasionally he went to the cathedral for evensong. Perhaps his greatest and most unexpected pleasure – for he had never particularly liked organ music – was sometimes after dinner, when the bishop was at his lectern, to go over to the cathedral to listen to Jeremy Flubert practising and go back to his little house in the close for a glass of wine.

A week or so after he settled in Amiss had caught up with Flubert after evensong just as he was unlocking his front door. 'You're the precentor and organist, aren't you?'

'And you're the mysterious assistant. Come in and have a drink.'

Flubert had waved Amiss to a brown leather winged armchair which proved to be wonderfully comfortable and crossed the room to switch on his CD player; Chopin came on quietly. 'You don't mind the music, I hope. I fear I've become like one of today's wretched children – hardly able to function without music in the background. I'm almost on the point of succumbing to one of those dreadful Walkman things, though I'm sure it's the worst kind of self-indulgence.'

'Seems pretty harmless as self-indulgence goes.'

'What a comforting thing to say. You're probably right; there is somewhere buried within me too much of the Calvinist spirit. I am an escaped prisoner from the Plymouth Brethren. Every day I thank God for my luck and for giving me the chance to create what I have created here. Sherry?'

What was it about the British Establishment and sherry, wondered Amiss fleetingly. 'Thank you.'

Flubert filled two small glasses, passed one to Amiss and sat down opposite. 'So tell me why you have moved into the palace. My colleagues are agog.'

'Dr Elworthy needs someone to organize him a bit and help him with his academic research. I'm an historian by training and an administrator by profession – at present between jobs – so it's an excellent temporary job for me.'

'I'd be inclined to guess you're adding a little bit of espionage to your activities.'

Amiss adopted his bewildered look. 'Come again?'

'Oh, now, come on. Our bishop is an innocent, there is no dean to hold his hand and we are a rum lot in the chapter. I should think he needs help to understand what is going on.'

'And what is going on?'

'You've come to the wrong person. There is nothing I care about except music.' He smiled. 'And a few creature comforts.'

Amiss looked around the room. Three of the walls were lined with books. Directly in front of him was a long row of volumes of *Grove's Dictionary of Music and Musicians*, to his left were biographies and memoirs of musicians and to the right was music criticism, while the bottom shelf around all three walls was packed with what looked like sheet music.

The fourth wall was covered from ceiling to halfway down with tightly packed portraits. Amiss recognized two Bachs, Beethoven, Mozart, Liszt and Vaughan Williams. Below them was a long refectory table with the sound system and rows of CDs, tapes and records.

In the centre of the room was a Bechstein; beside it were three music stands with sheet music, towards which Flubert nodded. 'An informal chamber-music group. It's not really my forte: I'm essentially a soloist. But it's fun sometimes in the long winter evenings.'

'Who do you play with?'

'A friend from the town and two masters from the choir school. I'm an obsessive, I'm afraid. I mix almost exclusively with musicians.'

'So you don't socialize with the other canons residentiary?'

'No. We are not a chummy bunch. However, let us not indulge in gossip. Tell me about yourself.'

Amiss set himself to win Flubert's trust by the time-honoured English method of humorous self-deprecation. By the time he had given an amusing though heavily censored version of how and why he had quit the civil service and a few of the dead-end jobs that followed, he could feel his host warming to him.

Flubert reached for the decanter. 'More sherry?'

'Yes, thanks.'

'So you are, as it were, still resting?'

'Yes, but it's not as bad as it sounds. I'm enjoying myself here, for instance. I've never encountered such serenity before, you see, not even in Oxford.'

'Hm. It's not as serene as all that. At times it can be pretty poisonous here. A small compound dominated by a gay mafia is not a healthy place, as you might imagine. Under dear Dean Roper, blood was spilled about issues of such staggering consequence as the colour of the new curtains in the vestry. No, we really should have families here – though I admit I would hardly be grateful for the noise. But children might give us some sense of perspective.'

'You aren't inclined to invest in a family yourself?'

Flubert laughed. 'What a discreet way of asking if I too am homosexual. I will say merely that my inclinations are neither here nor there. As a recent bishop put it, my sexuality is a grey area: I am a celibate with no need to parade his sexuality.'

'Unlike some of your colleagues?' ventured Amiss.

'I infer you have been exposed to the vulgarity of Cecil Davage.' He sighed. 'He was an especial trial to me in earlier days, until Dean Roper persuaded us all to sink our differences. Funny old fellow – dreadful misogynist – but quite wise in many ways. Pointed out that since we agreed on so much – liturgy, music and so on – we should as much as possible leave each other alone and turn a blind eye to each other's failings and excesses. It's worked for most purposes.'

Amiss raised an eyebrow. 'Excesses?'

'The fag-hag chapel, for instance. That would darken every day for me, but I choose never to go near it and to block it from my mind.'

'How did it get through?'

'A trade-off. In exchange for my dropping my opposition, Cecil agreed to the appointment of another assistant choirmaster, and anyway he gives me total support on our programme of music. At least no one can fault us for vulgarity in that area.'

'Is there any pressure for change?'

'Nothing to speak of. There are occasional squeaks from local burghers that we should be more popular and less cerebral – a bit more of "Oh, for the Wings of a Dove" and a bit less of Byrd and Tallis – but with the help of Cecil, who is the cleverest politician among us, I see them off.'

'Aren't you worried about what Dean Cooper might have in mind?'

'Not really. He's got to get three members of the chapter on his side before he can do anything. He might do something with that nice earnest woman, Alice Wolpurtstone. But he'll never get a majority with a clever clogs like Cecil against him. And from what I've seen, he's dim. I expect he'll be bought off with a demotic service every Monday or something similar.'

He lay back in his chair and stretched luxuriously. 'I'm indifferent, really. A bit like the bishop. We're two of a kind. He sits in his study wanting to be left alone with Pelagius: I sit in mine poring over a recently discovered variation to a fifteenth-century vesper.'

'What should I know about your colleagues if I'm to smooth the bishop's path?'

'Don't cross Cecil. Get him on your side. You can ignore Trustrum: he's about as effective as the dormouse at the Mad Hatter's tea party and goes sleepily along with whatever Cecil tells him to do. By instinct he's a clerical equivalent of a particularly bureaucratic railway clerk – the "can't-do-this-if-it-isn't-in-the-rule-book" brigade. Which doesn't bother me. It keeps the liturgy intact.

'Then there's Dominic Fedden-Jones. He's quite a little plotter too. Just remember he's an absolute Narcissus – little interest in anything except his own appearance and smarming up to the well-born. Sort of chap you used to find fluttering around Princess Margaret and these days worshipping at the feet of Diana. Loves hobnobbing with Italian cardinals. Ideally would like to be RC and chaplain to the Duke of Norfolk. You know the type.'

'Why hasn't he gone over to Rome?'

'Two reasons. He was Dean Roper's blue-eyed boy and wouldn't have upset him by jumping ship. And then there was the usual problem. His Holiness is too much of a homophobe even for a wannabe papist. In his snobbish soul Dominic wants to float around the Vatican kitted out as a Supernumerary Privy Chamberlain of Sword and Cape or something similar, emerging only to dine with princes and contessas; but he knows that his carnal appetites would interfere. Better to stay with the dear old tolerant C of E than be unfrocked by Il Papa.'

The telephone rang. 'Jeremy Flubert. Ah, Dominic . . . Yes . . . Yes . . . Yes. Certainly, ten a.m. will be fine . . . Thanks . . . Oh, before you go, have you met the bishop's assistant yet? . . . Robert Amiss . . . Look out for him. You might have mutual friends . . . Well, I know his last job was in the House of Lords . . . Yes . . . Yes, I get the impression he's a bit lonely. It might be kind to look him up . . . Right. Goodnight.'

He replaced the receiver and smiled at Amiss. 'Expect an urgent invitation to lunch – and don't spare the name-dropping.'

8

As a host, Dominic Fedden-Jones had the pleasantly condescending air of a minor royal graciously entertaining in his grace-and-favour residence a stranger of unknown stock. However, a casual reference from Amiss to his friend the Duke of Stormerod won his interest immediately. Over sherry they found they had two or three peers in common. And over lunch – smoked fish and 'a jolly little wine from a friend's vineyard' – Fedden-Jones chattered happily of earls and baronets and country houses and society balls and charity functions.

As Amiss drew him out it became clear that his host was next thing to an absentee canon. Preoccupied as he was with his excursions with well-placed friends and acquaintances, he had little or no interest left over for Westonbury. Questions about holidays and foreign travel drew trilling reminiscences of a fortnight here in a Tuscany farmhouse with Contessa Somebody and fun and frolics there in a Bordeaux chateau with the Duc of Something. Amiss was rather dazed by the torrent of foreign titles, but drew the strong impression that at home Fedden-Jones's happy hunting ground was among the Roman as well as the Anglo-Catholic fraternity: happy titters accompanied some story about the conduct of the Papal Nuncio at the birthday party of some titled Monsignor.

Lest a sceptic might have thought he was making it up, Fedden-Jones had taken care to fill his little house with signed photographs of himself in clerical evening dress – sometimes in a striking opera cloak – beside a variety of bejewelled women of a certain age. The sheer volume demonstrated to Amiss that the fellow must be an exceptionally attractive social asset – a kind of cultivated court jester with excellent table manners whom one could take anywhere. After all what could be more respectable for a contessa or a principessa than a clerical walker who could be relied upon to show them the respect they felt their pedigrees deserved?

'You might like to see this.' Fedden-Jones plucked a large silver-framed photograph from an occasional table. Hiding his antipathy to the lady, Amiss assumed a treacly expression at the sight of his host bowing obsequiously to Princess Diana. 'Charming girl. Charming. We had such a giggle at the opera.'

Opera cropped up a great deal in stories of the highborn and famous, but not simply as a backdrop. Interspersed among the social bragging were lines like, 'Domingo was in striking form that night,' or, 'Best Tosca for a generation.' Amiss had a hunch that what had started as a method of extending his network of glitterati had developed into a genuine enthusiasm.

While his music collection was not on Flubert's scale, Fedden-Jones had a very respectable collection of grand opera; his books included a couple of shelves of what Amiss judged to be books for middle-brow opera buffs. As the stories continued, Amiss recognized Fedden-Jones's social gifts: he would be the ideal companion for those who attend opera to be seen rather than to listen. Fedden-Jones would leave you equipped with the correct opinions on the production and the quality of the singers, amused by funny anecdotes about great opera disasters or crazy modern productions, and able to opine after the debut of a new talent that not since Callas – Patti even – had Aida been sung with such passion and brio.

A reminiscence about a weekend at a Venetian *palazzo* was interrupted by the telephone. 'Yes, he's here. Who shall I say is calling?'

He handed the phone to Amiss with an expression of some distaste. 'A person of indeterminate sex states he or she is "Troutbeck".'

'Who's that poncy bloke? The double-barrelled canon himself?'

Thankful that long experience of the baroness had caused him to clamp the receiver tightly to his ear, Amiss answered, 'Good afternoon, Jack. Is there something I can do for you?'

'I said who's that poncy bloke?'

'Canon Fedden-Jones is kindly entertaining me to lunch.'

'Why didn't your phone answer? I had to track David down via his secretary to find out where you were.'

'I switched it off.'

She chortled. 'As you've now discovered, that doesn't do you any good. Only causes David trouble. Look, I've had a thought. That female canon is the one you should be working on. New and insecure, probably, and aching for a lusty male. Get to it.'

When in a position to retaliate with abuse, Amiss endured the baroness's presumption with reasonable equanimity. When – like now – hamstrung by social convention, he could do little but respond coldly – though he knew it was pointless, since she wouldn't even notice. 'Very well, Jack. I shall see what I can do. Goodbye.'

It was obvious from his host's face that his rude caller had somewhat lowered his stock. 'I'm so sorry,' said Amiss. 'I fear Lady Troutbeck can be a little abrupt. She's a busy woman.'

Fedden-Jones wriggled with excitement. 'Lady Troutbeck. Of course. How could I have been so dense. I've seen her on television. Should have recognized her voice.' A faraway look came into his eye. 'Do you think she and you would be free to come to the opera tonight?'

'Sorry?'

'I've been charged with finding a stand-in couple. The Thrupcott-Wintles have had to cancel at the last minute. And though I've left a few messages, no one's come back to me yet.'

Amiss tried to keep the panic out of his voice. 'It's very kind of you, but I can't imagine she'd be able to get up to London at such short notice. She's mistress of a Cambridge college, you see.'

'You must ask her.'

'Hardly worth it.'

'My dear boy, tickets for a box at Covent Garden are like diamond-studded gold bricks. Not to be had unless you're a Greek shipping magnate. I'm sure Lady Troutbeck would recognize that.'

'Oh, I'm sure she'd be thrilled to be invited. As, of course, I am.'

Fedden-Jones smiled. 'I wish it were possible for you to come on your own. Unfortunately I've been charged with producing a couple, so I fear a couple it must be.'

You old hypocrite, thought Amiss. I am welcome only if accompanied by my titled friend. 'Well, I could try her.'

'Ring her up now. I insist. You know she's there.'

Amiss tried and failed to think of a way of getting out of what he feared had the potential to be an exceptionally embarrassing evening. With a sinking heart he fished out his phone and called her direct line.

'Troutbeck.'

'Robert.'

'Looking for further instructions?'

'No.' Gabbling to avert any more loud indiscretions – for Fedden-Jones had moved closer – he continued, 'Canon Fedden-Jones has kindly asked if we'd care to accompany him to the opera tonight. Two of his friends have had to drop out. I've told him it would be impossibly short notice for you.'

'What's the opera? I don't want any modern crap.'

Amiss turned to Fedden-Jones in embarrassment. 'I'm sorry. What opera is it?'

'*La Bohème*.'

The passing on of this intelligence earned a bellow of delight. 'Bugger me, Myles has done everything bar breaking and entering to try and get tickets for that.' There was a pause while she consulted her diary. 'It's a cinch. I can take the architect back to town with me and we can finish our meeting in the car, straight to Myles to change into gladrags, and back to Cambridge tomorrow early in time for the college council.'

'Are you sure, Jack? It sounds very hectic.'

'Balls. Don't be such an amoeba. Seize the moment.'

Amiss knew when he was beaten. He essayed some damage limitation. 'The rags should be very glad, Jack. We'll be in a box, and I should think Canon Fedden-Jones's friends are likely to be very formally dressed.'

'Excellent. If you want me in fine fig, you will get me in fine fig. Time?'

'I'll pick you up at Myles's at seven.'

'That's white of you. Saves me from being groped by the cab driver.'

'More likely to be the other way about,' he said truculently and put the phone down.

Fedden-Jones was looking surprised. 'You seemed a little reluctant.'

'No, no, just a little wary. Lady Troutbeck is a remarkable woman, but I have to warn you that she is socially somewhat unorthodox.'

'That doesn't worry me, Mr Amiss . . . May I call you Robert? Why I remember an evening with Lord Emmott when he took such exception to the food that he seized the bread basket, charged into the kitchen and threw all the rolls at the chefs . . .' And Fedden-Jones moved smoothly into another tale of privileged people at play.

'It's not, you understand,' confided Amiss to the bishop, 'that I am ashamed of Jack. I am indeed devoted to her. It's just she sometimes makes me nervous in strange company.'

With some difficulty the bishop addressed himself to a nontheological problem. 'You mean that she can be a little unpredictable and boisterous?' His attention wandered back to his lectern. 'I expect,' he said, as he returned to St Augustine, 'that it will all be fine.'

Amiss raised his voice slightly. 'I'll have to be off now. I've only just got time to get back to my flat and change into a dinner jacket. Will you be all right with Plutarch?'

The bishop looked up. 'Of course, of course. We will be company for each other.'

Plutarch – who was stretched proprietorially along the chaise longue – grunted when he patted her on the head, turned over onto her back and waved her paws in the air in the peremptory manner which indicated she wished to have her stomach rubbed; it was a task which – as ever – Amiss performed with little pleasure.

Neither bishop nor cat seemed to notice his farewell and departure.

In speculating on what Jack Troutbeck might think appropriate for the Royal Opera House, the one thing of which Amiss had been confident was that she would not go in for understatement. He was right. Admittedly her velvet trousers and satin jacket were black and well cut, but the latter was completely covered in sequins, and the baroness's neck all but hidden by an enormous silver necklace with huge yellow and olive beads and matching dangling earrings.

Myles Cavendish looked proudly at his beloved. 'I'm jealous that you're taking this magnificent creature on your arm tonight in my place. What do you think?'

'She certainly won't be overlooked.' Amiss laughed. 'Sorry, that's ungracious. Jack, as ever when you go completely over the top sartorially, you seem to get away with it. I haven't seen you look so splendid since I saw you in your baroness's robes.' He waved at the jewellery. 'Amber, I see. What are the rest?'

'Peridot,' said Cavendish. 'It's a favourite of mine. Can't afford to deck the old girl out in diamonds of the size she would like, so I stick to the semiprecious and get her plenty.'

'I like plenty.'

'Come on, Jack. The carriage awaits.'

The baroness gave Cavendish a smacking kiss, flung a feather boa around herself and presented her arm to Amiss.

Amiss – who had attended the Royal Opera House only twice and then in humble seats – was looking forward to the evening with mingled pleasure and dread: pleasure at the thought of sampling the high life and dread at what the baroness might do to a gathering of the glitterati.

'You will please behave,' he entreated her in the taxi.

She looked at him innocently. 'I don't understand.'

'You understand all too fucking well. You're required this evening to indulge in polite social chitchat, not to offend anyone, and so to endear yourself to our host that my cachet will rise and I'll be able to worm myself further into his confidence.'

'I'm to suppress my personality, you mean?'

'Yes, please.'

'No good ever came of that.' She sounded genial, but his heart sank.

Fedden-Jones awaited them in the lobby and swept them up to a corner of the crush bar, where champagne was being distributed. For the first few minutes with Fedden-Jones, his walkee (the Contessa di Milano, who was something big in perfume), Sir Elwyn Wainwood, the banker whose institution was footing the bill, and his wife (whose name Amiss didn't catch), the baroness hardly opened her mouth. When introduced she bared her teeth insincerely; when spoken to she produced the minimum response. Lady Wainwood's rhetorical enquiry as to whether she didn't think the weather cold was met with, 'No,' which so disconcerted the woman that she couldn't think of anything else to say.

The Wainwood party – confronted by what they must have concluded was a rude, monosyllabic dullard – made a tacit agreement to ignore her and proceeded without any apology to talk about common acquaintances, the latest crisis afflicting the Opera House, and their plans for visiting Glyndebourne.

The baroness stood apart, champagne glass in hand and bottom lip pushed out in the manner of a sullen toddler on the edge of a tantrum. Amiss looked at her imploringly. 'I said behave,' he hissed in her ear. 'Not clam up.' There was no response. His nerve broke. 'Oh, all right. Sod you. Do it your way.'

The baroness smiled broadly, ceased sipping her champagne in a genteel fashion and took a mighty quaff. She moved closer to her host and bent an ear to the conversation. 'How are things in the financial markets, Elwyn?' asked the contessa. Wainwood smiled sleekly. 'Not bad. Not bad. I think I might go so far as to say that prospects are rosy.'

'I don't like rosy prospects,' interrupted the baroness. The group turned and gazed at her. Wainwood struggled to be polite. 'Sorry?'

'I don't like rosy prospects.'

'Why not?'

'Me – I like rosy present.' She looked at them solemnly. 'The trouble with rosy prospects is that she promises a lot and usually lets you down. Bit of a prick teaser, young rosy prospects.'

As the baroness was complacently to remark later to Amiss, this remark certainly broke the ice. After a momentary stunned silence, Wainwood guffawed and the others followed suit with appreciative titters. 'A wise word of caution there, Lady Troutbeck. The lady to whom you refer has certainly disappointed many of us in the past.' He reached for a bottle. 'Let me give you some more champagne.'

'Are you an opera lover, Lady Troutbeck?' asked the contessa.

'What I like, I love. Puccini and Verdi. I only like Italian. Apart from Bizet, that is. Can't stand the Krauts.'

'Not a Wagnerian, then?'

'Boring bastard. A few good tunes, I grant you. But take away the overtures and what have you got. Pure balls.'

Lady Wainwood looked at her gratefully. 'My sentiments exactly. The worst evening of my life was at *Götterdämmerung*.'

'Except for Harrison Birtwistle,' pointed out her husband. The contessa and Fedden-Jones joined in with a few esoteric candidates and the baroness looked at Amiss and winked. At last at ease, he winked back.

'Hope you're not disappointed it's not Pavarotti tonight.'

'Not in the least. Pavarotti hasn't been the same since he started screwing his secretary.'

The gathering found this equally arresting. 'You feel,' suggested Fedden-Jones, 'that amorous engagements take a singer's mind off his arias?'

The contessa protested. 'Surely not. After all, Pavarotti has been a byword for liaisons.'

The baroness shook her head impatiently. 'You've missed

the point. Of course it's only right and proper that an opera singer should have frequent affairs. How else can a twenty-stone millionaire manage to keep in touch with the feelings of passion and lust which he is paid large sums of money to express.' She drained her glass. 'No, what is alarming is that this time he appears to be trapped in an exclusive relationship. His wife had the sense not to accompany him on his travels and left him free for amorous escapades. This little bint is a clinger. He'll be singing like a bank manager before we know where we are.'

Wainwood grinned. 'That would certainly never do. We're a boring bunch.' Completely unabashed, the baroness proceeded to fly in the face of etiquette by grabbing the bottle from the ice bucket, filling her glass and shoving the bottle towards Wainwood, who smiled and attended to his guests. Not bad going, reflected Amiss. After only twenty minutes with total strangers, she had succeeded in dominating the conversation and changing normal social rules to her own satisfaction without incurring any resentment. Indeed the whole group was focused benignly upon her.

Wainwood replaced the empty bottle in the ice bucket. The baroness jerked her head towards Amiss. 'Get us more champagne, Robert.'

Wainwood shook his head. 'No, no, I insist,' and he scurried away towards the bar.

The baroness nodded approvingly. 'Good. Got to be well tanked up to appreciate opera.' She turned to the contessa. 'At least we English do. You lot are all right. Wops don't have our regrettable inhibitions.'

'I had not thought that you...' The contessa stopped. 'Please, what is your Christian name? I am Gloria.'

'Jack.'

The contessa's eyebrow rose only slightly. 'I have not thought you inhibited, Jack.'

The baroness clapped her on the back. 'Everything's relative, Gloria, old girl.' Although this was fortunately one of the baroness's more restrained expressions of good fellowship, the contessa's shoulders were bare and it caused her to jump. However, by now the baroness's stock was so high, thought Amiss sourly, that she could get away with putting lighted matches between their toes.

English inhibitions were certainly in retreat. As Wainwood returned with another bottle, apologizing with, 'Sorry, I found it hard to push my way in,' the baroness's genial, 'As the bishop said to the actress,' caused the whole gathering to collapse in giggles.

'I do like your baroness,' whispered Fedden-Jones to Amiss. 'What a' – he searched for the *mot juste* – 'jolly lady.'

Once Amiss had fully relaxed, like everyone else in the group he played the evening by the baroness's rules and enjoyed himself enormously. Her exuberant delight in the occasion communicated itself generally. Although it turned out she had seen *La Bohème* more than half a dozen times, she hung over the side of the box gazing raptly at the stage in the manner of an awe-struck neophyte. It was clearly only massive willpower that prevented her from singing along with the best-known arias.

The interval consisted of smoked-salmon sandwiches, more champagne and scandal and a return to the box in even higher good humour. There was an abrupt change of mood during the lingering death scene, for the baroness became immersed in the unfolding tragedy and sobbed piteously. As the curtain went down, she blew her nose loudly, leapt to her feet applauding vigorously and shouted, 'Bravo, bravo!' Flinging what remained of their inhibitions to the wind, her companions followed suit.

As they left the box, Wainwood extended his arm skittishly. 'May I?' and escorted the baroness merrily down the staircase. Amiss and Lady Wainwood brought up the rear.

'Interesting woman. I didn't quite gather what she does?'

'Ex-civil servant. Now mistress of a Cambridge college.'

'Good heavens. You surprise me.'

'What would you have guessed?'

'Difficult. Lion tamer perhaps. Or impresario.'

'I see her rather as an international smuggler.'

'Actually she looks rather like an old-fashioned character actress. Margaret Rutherford or someone. But a sexy version, of course.'

'Sexy? You think she's sexy?'

'You're too young, I expect. But I saw the way Elwyn was looking at her. There's no accounting for these things. I think it's got something to do with pheromones. Anyway, I bet she's quite active in that department.'

'I'm not taking the bet,' said Amiss. A vision of the beautiful, black, silky body of Mary Lou Denslow swam past his eyes and filled him with suppressed desire and resentment. 'You don't know the half of it.'

9

Amiss was roused by the telephone.

'Enjoyed that, didn't you? Bloody good supper, too.' The baroness smacked her lips. 'I like lobster.'

'Wha . . . what . . . what time is it?'

'Late. It's very late. Six-fifteen and I've only just begun the drive to Cambridge.'

'Jack!' Amiss's wail was heartfelt. 'I didn't get to bed till after two. And then Rachel rang and we talked for half an hour.'

'Lazy lie-abed. Get up and get going to Westonbury. And don't forget. *Cherchez la femme.*'

'What are you talking about?'

'The bird. Whatshername. Alice Thingummy. You've got to charm her.'

'Is that what you woke me up to tell me? Have you forgotten that you told me that last night at some length.'

'You might have forgotten. You had a lot to drink.'

'I had a lot to drink! That's rich coming from you.'

He had lost her. 'I'm off. It's time I gave Mary Lou her alarm call.' Her voice rose several decibels. 'Halfwit!'

'Who?'

'Can't talk. Got to teach him a lesson.' The phone went dead.

Amiss groaned, rolled over and tried unsuccessfully to go back to sleep.

'It's very nice to have you back, my dear Robert. Plutarch and I missed you. But I'm pleased you had a pleasant time. Did Jack behave?'

'In her own fashion, brilliantly. Fedden-Jones is mad about her and I'm shining in her reflected glory. It's saved me a great deal of time trying to win his confidence by sucking up to him.'

The bishop beamed. 'There you are. She can be very good when she wants to be.'

'Which is insufficiently often.'

The telephone rang. 'Dr Elworthy's residence,' said Amiss.

'Have you seen her yet?'

'For Christ's sake, Jack . . .' Amiss saw the bishop's worried face. 'I mean, for goodness sake, Jack, I've only been back five minutes.'

'Get on with it. Stop lounging about.'

'Car phones should never have been invented,' remarked Amiss as he put the receiver down. 'Or at the very least they should never have been made available to Jack. She seems to be unable to drive anywhere these days without bombarding half the world with instructions.'

The bishop smiled gently. 'I expect the novelty will wear off. What is she so anxious about?'

'Wants me to get to know Alice Wolpurtstone. Seems to think she might be a key player in the chapter. Being new and all that. They could do with a conciliator.'

'She might well be that. She seems a pleasant girl, from the little I've seen of her.'

'Cecil introduced us in the close last week. She looked a bit like a startled faun.'

The bishop's eyes had strayed back to his book. Amiss left him to it and went off to extract information about Alice Wolpurtstone from his new ally.

'What I can't understand, Dominic, is how you came to elect a female canon. I'd have thought the late dean and the rest of you would have died resisting the monstrous regiment.'

Fedden-Jones looked a little embarrassed. 'I was myself not in favour of female ordination, I have to admit. But it wasn't a huge matter of principle with me. In fact . . . oh, I suppose I might as well tell you the story. Now that we're friends.'

Amiss smiled encouragingly. 'Good. I'd rather get the story from you than from Cecil.'

Fedden-Jones wrinkled his nose with distaste. 'The only thing Cecil is a good source for is Cecil. Oh, and Victorian bric-a-brac, of course.' He poured them both a second cup of tea. 'Two reasons. I wanted to rub Paul Newman's nose in it . . .'

'Sorry? I'm not with you.'

'Paul Newman. The canon who decamped to Rome over female ordination. Miserable little wretch. It really upset dear old Reggie. And then we needed a dramatic gesture. You see there was a lot of rumbling in ecclesiastical circles about the gay image of Westonbury.'

'I'm not surprised.'

'Yes. Exacerbated by that ridiculous lady chapel. That wouldn't have got through if I hadn't been away and poor Reggie hadn't been getting a bit gaga.'

'Why didn't you get the picture moved to somewhere more private? And that daft canopy?'

'Oh, because I was more concerned to get Alice elected to the vacant job and I did a deal – the lady chapel would stay as it was in exchange for Cecil's vote for Alice.'

'And why did you want Alice?'

'I thought it would be good for our image – muddy the waters a bit.'

'I suppose that's logical. So what were Alice's credentials for the job?'

Fedden-Jones fidgeted. 'She's the daughter of a friend. Actually she's Lady Alice Wolpurtstone, though she doesn't use the title.'

Amiss had some difficulty in suppressing his grin. 'So you knew her well?'

'No, I didn't. But I knew her parents well. And I thought, well, with such good breeding, you can't go wrong.'

As some recent tabloid headlines about heirs to great titles floated through Amiss's mind, he suppressed yet another grin.

'I was staying with Toby and Cathy Wolpurtstone one weekend when Cathy happened to mention that she wasn't at all happy with Alice's state of health. Apparently she'd been in one of those awful inner-city parishes as a team vicar, living in squalid quarters with drug addicts turning up before breakfast. Cathy was anxious that Alice be transferred to somewhere more salubrious. That's when I got the idea. Two birds and all that.'

'Had you met her?'

'She came down for a brief visit that weekend to conduct the christening of a neighbour's child and she seemed just right. Not like one of those awful women priests in Crimplene suits speaking in estuary English. She was nicely turned out and she officiated well – had the vain pomp and glory of the world renounced in great style. Nice voice too.'

You mean right accent, thought Amiss. 'You weren't worried about how she might react to the ethos here?'

'Oh, you mean in case she turned out to be homophobic. No, I had no worries there. Cathy had mentioned with some distaste that Alice had spent far too much time helping out at an Aids hospice.'

'Married?'

'No. That was another plus. It leads to trouble. Priests' husbands don't know how to behave. Anyway, I went back and did the deal with Cecil, so that was two to one. Jeremy didn't care and went along with it after some musical bribe or other. Then Trustrum woke up and for once tried to fight it on the grounds that there was no precedent for female canons, but he gave up when he realized everyone was against him. Reggie was horrified at first, but I managed to calm him down and convince him he'd hardly notice her. Anyway he was beyond caring much about anything but his memorial plans.'

'It was all surprisingly painless, then.'

'Except for Alice, who didn't like the idea at all.'

'Why not?'

Fedden-Jones sighed. 'She's an idealist.'

'Ah, yes. I can see how that must have been a bit of a blow. Thought life here would be too easy, I suppose. So how did you crack that problem?'

'Toby Wolpurtstone made a point of running into the

bishop – Elworthy's predecessor, that is – in the Lords and told him he was worried she might crack up. Toby's been helpful before now on the fund-raising side of things, so Hubert was minded to help and use his influence. He called her in and told her she was to take this offer. She was upset, but he told her he gathered she was being moved from her inner city in any case and indirectly threatened her with what Toby had told him she dreaded most: a prosperous suburb with few contemporary problems.

'He told Toby she was pretty obdurate, but he finally sold it to her by telling her she would simultaneously strike a blow for women, awaken the chapter to the need for greater social responsibility, and indicated she might be able to provide spiritual comfort to the New Age travellers who – as I'm sure you've noticed – infest Westonbury. That clinched it.'

'And is she happy?'

'I don't really know. I don't see her round the close much and she's never opened her mouth at chapter meetings. But I'm afraid I don't think so. She looks a bit depressed. Of course it didn't help that up to now she's only been allowed to celebrate mass in a side chapel. Reggie just wouldn't tolerate a woman officiating at high altar, and since he died, Trustrum and Cecil have kept her there.'

He looked a little guilty. 'I've probably not done what I should for her. She might be a bit lonely. Obviously I had her round for sherry, but frankly she turned out not to be my type. She talked very seriously about witness and ministry and that sort of thing and I didn't know where to look. No appetite for gossip.'

'But her presence has helped on the PR front, presumably?'

Fedden-Jones shook his head. 'Not yet, I fear. You see it turns out that she's an enthusiastic member of the C of E Gay and Lesbian Association.'

'She's a lesbian?' Amiss began to laugh but checked himself at Fedden-Jones's evident distress.

'It's not very helpful, as you can imagine. I can't bear to think how the dean will react if he finds out. There was a very embarrassing moment at the lunch after the enthronement when some innocent asked him what he thought about ordaining gays and he rather excitedly began to quote Leviticus.'

'Sorry, Dominic. I'm not up to speed on the Old Testament.'

'It's about how men lying with men is an abomination.'

'It would seem that one knows where one is with the dean.'

'I'm trying not to think about him. Now, would you like me to ask Alice over for a drink?'

After spending an hour in her company, Amiss was little wiser about Alice Wolpurtstone, though he could detect her unease at Fedden-Jones's questions about mutual friends and cousins of cousins. She was polite but unforthcoming; it was not clear whether she was contemptuous, embarrassed or simply very shy. Amiss made a little headway when he asked her about her previous job and she spoke haltingly about the sense of purpose she had found in working in an inner city. However Fedden-Jones clearly found this conversation both boring and unpleasant, so it was abruptly curtailed. Alice made her excuses as early as was decently possible and departed, leaving Fedden-Jones shaking his head and complaining that she had taken after neither of her delightful parents.

There was no sighting of Alice the following day, and she didn't answer her telephone, so instead Amiss found a spurious reason to ring Canon Sebastian Trustrum and received an invitation to call. 'Come at three-forty-five for an hour. That's my time for seeing people.'

Trustrum's home was a shrine to order, a house in which no object was ever misplaced, let alone mislaid. It was short on possessions, other than a few shelves of books and some photographs of Trustrum with various ecclesiastical notables. But in its own way it was a little gem, for in its furniture and appurtenances it was frozen somewhere round the 1890s.

Trustrum, it emerged, was extremely proud of his establishment's imperviousness to change. 'I'm pleased to say,' he explained, 'that for the last few generations this house has been inhabited by people who understand about tradition. None of this mad modern passion for changing things. I never know why people want to do that.'

Much of the fixtures and furniture proved that one of the great advantages of not changing anything was that fashion had a tendency to come round and embrace the old again. Trustrum's Victorian bathroom, which would have been a laughing stock in the 1950s and '60s, was full of artefacts now much sought after. All over smart London the well-to-do were rooting out modern plastic bathroom suites and installing porcelain lavatories and old iron baths with claw feet. And these days too, many people were coming to regard fitted cupboards as rather naff. Admittedly, Trustrum's refusal to instal central heating kept him in a minority, but his Georgian fireplace and blazing fire would have gained many admirers.

'Would you care for a cup of tea? I always have tea here at four o'clock. Except in summer, that is, when I have it fifteen minutes later.' Trustrum, it rapidly became clear, was a man whose passion for routine would have been understandable in someone who had clocked up fifty years in a particularly strict jail.

It wasn't just his timetable that was rigid; so too was its content. Coffee could be taken only in the morning, tea only in the afternoon, beef was reserved for Sundays, chicken for Mondays, fish for Fridays and so on. The dishes were specific too. The fish was always plaice, the lamb always cutlets, the chicken always grilled.

Trustrum was a man determined to ensure that in his life there were as few surprises as possible, so it was no wonder that he was in a state of advanced neurosis about the changes in the chapter. Before the first cup of tea had been finished, Amiss's sympathetic manner had had its effect, and a well-timed question about whether the dean was likely to be an innovator got his host going. 'Why was he appointed? Why should they do such a thing? We were getting on fine. We did no one harm and we kept custom and practice intact. That's what a cathedral is for, isn't it? What is it, if it isn't about passing tradition on unaltered to the next generation?'

Amiss muttered sympathetically and was rewarded with a second cup of tea. 'We're not here to get involved in silly new fads or to keep making changes that years later are recognized as having been all wrong,' continued his increasingly impassioned host.

'Look at those horrid tower blocks that they put the poor in. They said all those nice little artisans' cottages were passé, but now they say they were all wrong and they're tearing down the high-rise monstrosities and building nice little houses on the old model with a little bit of garden instead of those awful open spaces.

'And look at all those so-called reforms in education in the 1960s when they got rid of the old grammar schools and brought in those dreadful comprehensives. And they stopped teaching tables and spelling. And what have we got now as a result? A nation of illiterates, that's what. I could have told them what would happen. And now they're going back to basics in teaching and trying to recapture the spirit of the old grammars.'

He paused for breath. Amiss nodded in agreement.

'What did they do to the monarchy? Tried to make it relevant. I could have told them. Just as Walter Bagehot said more than a century ago, the monarchy has to have its mystery. But they started making television programmes about it and telling people what went on behind the scenes. And what do we have now? An institution that's almost been destroyed by the consequent intrusion. As the Duke of Cumberland said, "All change is bad." Wouldn't you agree?'

'I'd make an exception for dentistry.'

'I grant you that.'

'And plumbing.'

'Yes, yes. And I will even admit to enjoying the wireless. But in most areas of life we should stick with what we've got. For heaven's sake, look at how so-called progress has destroyed travel. Once it was a pleasure, but now . . .' He cast his eyes heavenwards. 'We've replaced ocean liners by nasty aeroplanes, so almost the whole population of the world rushes around it all the time, wasting petrol, ruining the environment, and ensuring that nobody ever enjoys actually travelling and everywhere one goes is overcrowded.'

Not that Trustrum was exactly an expert on this, it turned out, for he rarely travelled. Although he stoutly maintained he was not afraid of flying, he had never done it and did not propose to start now.

The tirade reminded Amiss of the baroness in a particularly reactionary mood; he found it quite familiar and soothing. Besides, Trustrum was not as withdrawn from the world as Amiss had expected. He seemed to keep in touch with current affairs and trends like a prosecuting barrister. He spoke learnedly about large areas of life – from agriculture to politics – where change had spelt disaster. On the question of the European Union he became almost incoherent with distress.

However, if Trustrum was a keen observer of the world, he was not a student of character. Amiss gleaned little more about the other canons residentiary than he already knew. Trustrum spoke approvingly in general terms of his colleagues for their championing of old values, though there were disparaging remarks about Davage for becoming a television performer and about those who had a hand in commissioning the Marian picture. All his colleagues – even the late Dean Roper – were anathematized for having appointed a female canon.

Brooding on the radicalism and foolishness of this move led Trustrum into an assault on the whole notion of coeducation, women's liberation, feminism, and all the evils it had brought to both men and women. He dwelt on young males, deprived of work, denied responsibility as providers and unmanned by aggressive women and again showed himself impressively up to date on the latest controversies – his information gleaned, he explained, from the papers he'd been reading since puberty, the *Telegraph*, the *Spectator*, and the *Church Times*, and of course from Radio Four, which he still called the Home Service.

'And all that modernizing of religion has had the same effect. They've taken away most of the mystery and the magic. The Catholics destroyed themselves by replacing Latin with the vernacular. And what are we doing but replacing the glories of our King James Bible with nasty new rubbish?'

'You mean like the *Good News Bible*?'

'No, no. Much, much worse. You have no idea.'

He jumped up and fetched two books from his shelf, out of each of which stuck dozens of slips of paper. He opened one at the first slip. 'Right. Now this from the King James version of Genesis. "And the Lord God formed man of the dust of the ground, and breathed into his nostrils the breath of life; and man became a living soul. And the Lord God planted a garden eastward in Eden; and there he put the man whom he had formed." Poetry. Sheer poetry.'

He picked up the other volume. 'Now let us see how the *Contemporary English Version* improves on this. Ah, yes. "The Lord God took a handful of soil and made a man. God breathed life into the man, and the man started breathing. The Lord made a garden in a place called Eden, which was in the east, and he put the man there." Ugh! Ugh! Ugh!' Opening the offending Bible randomly at another marker, he snorted, 'Here's a moving passage: "You lazy people can learn by watching an anthill." Obviously a vast improvement on: "Go to the ant, thou sluggard; consider her ways, and be wise."'

He put the books back on the shelf. 'I can read only a few extracts at a time: I get so angry.'

'I don't blame you. It's like comparing a great claret with Diet Coke.'

Trustrum looked at the grandfather clock near the door.

'I've enjoyed talking to you, Mr Amiss, but you must forgive me if I bring our meeting to an end: from four-fifty to five-twenty-five I read my newspaper, and then I go to evensong.'

He ushered his guest to the door.

'Thank you for the tea and the interesting conversation, Canon Trustrum. As a newcomer to your congregation, I, at least, am very pleased you've kept the services traditional.'

'But for how much longer can we hold out against the barbarians, Mr Amiss? For how much longer?'

10

Harassed by another early call from the baroness, Amiss determined the following morning to hunt down his quarry. He sat in a window seat overlooking the close, listened to the radio and watched for Alice Wolpurtstone. Just after ten o'clock her front door opened, and she set off at a brisk pace towards the river. Amiss hared out of the palace and followed her down the towpath and then left into Canon's Leap.

As he watched her swinging athletically along in front of him, he realized that she was much more attractive than he had thought, for at their brief meeting her shyness had been off-putting. And although there was nothing provocative about her clothes, they had none of the depressing churchiness of so much female clerical garb. Her black trouser suit and white polo-neck jumper were well cut and suited her slim figure: presumably Mummy Wolpurtstone had had a hand in kitting her out.

Amiss followed her into Parson's Ride and towards the centre of the city. As ever, when he went into Westonbury, Amiss yearned to take to the town planners the bulldozers they had taken to the old town. Here and there were traces of happy architectural evolution; in side streets, little bits of Tudor were interspersed with some Gothic Victoriana and some charming Edwardian artisans' cottages. But in the centre the planners' philistinism had turned Westonbury into a 1990s shopping precinct dominated by chain stores and indistinguishable from a hundred other English towns.

He caught up with her as she turned down a lane: 'Good morning, Canon Wolpurtstone. I wonder if I might persuade you to join me in a cup of coffee?'

The strong graceful woman instantly gave way to the peerer-under-eyelids and presser-of-arms-to-torso-to-protect-against-wanton-assault he remembered from their first encounter. 'Oh, gosh, how very kind of you. But I really can't. I've got to make a visit.'

'Please do. You'd be doing me a favour. I get very lonely in the close and today I could really do with some company – just for a few minutes.'

She melted immediately, stood upright and let her arms and hands relax by her sides. 'Oh, of course. I'm so sorry. How selfish of me. I'd love to. But please call me Alice. I hate titles.'

'Oh, good. An ally. All these grand formalities get me down. I've never understood why people get such joy from being called by silly names.'

He looked up and down the street. 'Now where shall we go? If you don't mind, I'd like to avoid one of those high-street coffee shops. Do you know of anywhere down here?'

'Not for coffee. But if you're happy with tea . . . ?'

'Of course.'

She led the way into an establishment outside which dangled a sign full of obscure mystical symbols surrounding images of waxing and waning moons. On the walls were posters of goddesses, elves, witches, druids and various other pagan icons along with images of earth, sea and sky and signs of the zodiac, while on the tables covering most of the floor were jars of herbs, bottles of oils, books and tapes, heaps of crystal jewellery, flints, stones and other odds and ends all jumbled up together. In the corner was a rack of long shapeless psychedelic robes. The strong smell of incense made him feel rather nostalgic.

As they sat down at an empty scrubbed pine table in the corner, a bare-footed skinny girl with purple hair and lipstick, huge dangling crystal earrings, silver symbols attached to several orifices and a green T-shirt and leggings covered with orange dragons arrived to take their order. It emerged that all that was on offer at that time of the morning were herbal infusions, so, miserably, Amiss followed Alice's example and ordered camomile tea, which proved to be quite as foul as he had expected.

'This certainly makes a change from the cathedral. Except for the incense, of course.'

Encouragingly, she managed a little smile, so Amiss continued to babble unthreateningly about the claustrophobia of living in such a small community. 'I find it very odd. Very odd indeed.'

For the first time she looked at him with some interest. 'How do you mean?'

'It's so insular, so privileged, so little in contact with the real world – with ordinary people. I've been amazed to find clergymen who never seem to have anything whatsoever to do with the needy.'

She nodded eagerly.

He leaned forward confidingly. 'To tell you the truth, I'm not very happy. You see, I took this job because I wanted to add a spiritual dimension to my life and I've been very, very disappointed. I suppose it's different for you, being a canon and having a role in the cathedral.'

'Oh, but I haven't. I expect I've less to do than you. I might as well not exist for all the use I am at Westonbury.'

'What a waste. And I can't understand it. What is the point of having people dedicate their lives to God if they aren't serving the poor and the despised and the rejected? Isn't that how wisdom is acquired?'

He gazed earnestly at her. 'I know that what I have learned from friends of mine with Aids has added a huge and rich dimension to my life.' As he lobbed this in, Amiss tamed his protesting conscience by reminding it that, yes, he had one friend with Aids, yes, Peter was bearing up courageously, yes, he was in his own way a bit of an inspiration and yes – cynic that he was – he would chortle at being trotted out piously in such circumstances.

It was a bull's-eye. There was a catch in her voice as she said, 'I've never found anything as rewarding as my work with Aids victims. I didn't want to leave and come here.'

The dam broke and Amiss found himself in the middle of every man's nightmare – escorting a crying woman in public.

'All I've ever wanted,' she sobbed – so violently that the assistant, who had been sitting behind the till vacantly stroking a black cat, livened up and showed some interest – 'is to look after people. Sometimes I wish I were dead.'

Following immemorial male custom, Amiss looked embarrassed, passed Alice a clean tissue and muttered a few 'there, there's'. When she had wiped her tears, he decided on a policy of distraction rather than confrontation. Woo the filly first, as the baroness, in her helpful way, had once put it to him; some of them take fright if you try to corral them too early. So when she calmed down, rather than pressing her to talk about herself, he confided in her about his rootlessness, his striving for the worthwhile life and any other relevant problems he could manufacture: she brightened up in no time, clearly thrilled to be viewed as a sympathetic ear.

'I so much like Bishop Elworthy,' he confided. 'A good and kind and Christian man – and of course I'm glad to feel I can help him a little, but somehow I feel that I would like also to be assisting more materially deprived people.'

He shook his head sadly. 'Of course, not being myself a believer, I couldn't bring anyone religious comfort, but I might be able to offer a little practical help.' He sighed. 'In another time or another place perhaps.' He decided to play a long shot, leaned back in his chair and waved vaguely at a pile of coloured rocks. 'I suppose I'm very typical of my generation. I look around a place like this and recognize it is a Mecca for people similarly engaged on a spiritual quest . . . Not,' he added, in response to her slightly worried expression, 'that I think this New Age business is for me, but I have a curiosity about these people and about what they believe. One can always learn from others, don't you find?'

Alice could hardly contain herself. She gazed at him with such glowing excitement that it was a relief to him to remember that she was, after all, a lesbian; he had enough troubles without incurring the devotion of doe-eyed clergywomen.

'How strange,' she murmured, 'for that too was part of the attraction of Westonbury for me. I had heard about it as a centre for these people and I knew that somehow they too were in search of spiritual grace.'

'And have you managed to meet any of them?'

'Yes, a few. I didn't get anywhere for a long time. None of them was welcoming at first. Of course they thought I was trying to convert them, or being patronizing, and anyway most of them didn't need any help. And there are as well so many varieties of pagans dotted around the outskirts of Westonbury, it's very hard to know what they actually believe and to avoid offending them. I'm afraid I put my foot in it with the Satanists particularly.' She winced. 'But I have managed to get to know two groups a little.

'The separatist feminist witches have been quite welcoming, and also there's a small encampment of shamans at the bottom of the town where I go quite often now and they let me bring them groceries and play with the children.'

Amiss said hesitantly 'I don't suppose . . . ?'

'You mean you would like to visit too?' She ventured a little smile. 'I'm afraid the witches wouldn't welcome you, but I don't see why you shouldn't just come along with me to the shamans. I'll just say you're a friend and with you wearing jeans and so on they won't see you as a threat from society.' She lowered her voice. 'And, obviously, you won't mention the dope to anyone.'

Amiss looked solemn. 'Of course not.' He looked at his watch. 'My goodness, it's eleven o'clock already. Can we manage a quick visit now, do you think? I said I'd be home for lunch.'

'I felt a complete and utter bastard.'

'Stop being so sensitive. You've a job to do. You can't be a good spy and indulge in a tender conscience.'

'I didn't want to be a spy, Jack. I just keep getting pushed into it.'

'Bollocks! It's in your nature. You were born to be a spy and a seducer – in the nonsexual sense, that is, for most purposes, more's the pity. You persuade people to blab like no one I've ever known. If it makes you uncomfortable, you'd better have a conscience transplant. Now will you please tell me what you found out?'

'She's a walking bleeding heart, guilty about her background, guilty at having had a loving family, guilty about having money in a world of inequality. A missionary by instinct, of course. A hundred years ago she'd have been preaching Christianity to African natives, but that's not PC any more. And of course rebellion against family values requires her to champion the cause of every section of society which her father no doubt daily denounces at the breakfast table.'

'Why did she let herself be appointed to Westonbury then?'

'Good old-fashioned emotional blackmail by her family – "Mummy's heart" – in addition to the bullying by David's predecessor. As well as that it emerges that she was optimistic about the new dean, who she thought would shake up Westonbury and bring in the marginalized. Gays, lesbians, travellers – the lot. She's a bit rattled since she heard him preach.'

'She seems very wet and a real silly-billy. I'm no expert on these matters, but I wouldn't have thought that Bible-thumpers were very keen on homos of either sex.'

'Unless repentant, of course. Anyway, she's planning . . .'

'Damn! Have to go. Trouble.' The phone went dead.

'I don't want to be a sneak.'

The bishop looked worried. 'Why then, of course, you mustn't be, my dear Robert. More cheese?'

'No, thanks.' For the first time in their burgeoning friendship, Amiss felt like hitting Bishop Elworthy. He imagined that the late Cornelia must occasionally have been similarly tempted. How very Church of England he was, with his propensity to allow tolerance to spill over into moral abdication.

'However, I have little option, since my real job here is to keep you abreast of what's going on in the cloister.'

'Oh, but my dear Robert, you must not in any way allow that to sway the dictates of your conscience. Think no more about it and let me instead tell you about my happy visit this morning to the Centre for Ecumenical Debate.'

'No, David. That would be an evasion of responsibility by

both of us. My duty is to you, so here goes. I have to tell you things I'd rather not tell you and that you'd rather not hear.' Ignoring the dread gripping the bishop's features, he continued, 'It's Alice Wolpurtstone. She's mixing in very undesirable company and is so frustrated by the pointlessness of her life in the close that she's almost certainly going to precipitate a crisis.'

'Oh, dear. Of what kind?'

'First, she's meditating moving in with a crowd of dodgy New Age travellers.'

'That wouldn't be a problem, would it?'

'Perhaps not for a good Christian like you. Or even for a mad evangelist like Dean Norm. But I have a feeling she's too innocent for such a world. I've seen this crowd. They call themselves shamans . . .'

The bishop put down his knife and fork. 'My goodness me. How amazing to find devotees of a religion which goes back to before the Bronze Age. Well, well, well. Gods, spirits and souls, eh? I'm not at all surprised Canon Wolpurtstone wishes to study them more closely: it would be a great anthropological treat.' He jumped up. 'I must rush upstairs and look them up to see by what migratory routes they have arrived here.'

Amiss spoke firmly. 'Please sit down, David. These people are no more shamans than I am. They're hopheads, acid-droppers . . .' He observed the incomprehension on the bishop's face. 'Sorry, they smoke cannabis all day and take LSD by night. As well, they are idle good-for-nothings and probably petty criminals. And yes, I know I sound sixty rather than thirty, but I do know an idealist from a layabout.'

The bishop threw up his hands. 'But we can't stop her. Why don't we leave her alone to help them if she can. She seems a girl of good heart who must be allowed to follow her instincts.'

'It could all end in tears and excruciatingly embarrassing tabloid publicity. Besides, from what I've seen of the leader of that group – a charmer called Tengri – I wouldn't be surprised if he wasn't asking her to join them because he'd like to rape her.'

The bishop's jaw dropped open. 'Oh, how terrible! Surely you're wrong. No one could be so wicked.'

'Of course they could. Now, in addition, she's involved in some sort of lesbian witches' coven, and the result of her attempts to minister to them in an ecumenical manner is to bear fruit in a coming-out ceremony in the lady chapel on Thursday night.'

'A what?' As always when he was particularly alarmed, the bishop tugged his hair in an agitated fashion.

'On Thursday night she's holding a coming-out service in the lady chapel for a group of lesbian witches.'

'Witches!'

'Good witches, I understand, who want to hold hands across the divide that divides pagan from Christian.'

'How can she? Who would give her permission?'

'She has the right to hold services in the lady chapel and only in the lady chapel. Who is there to intervene? The dean is still away, Trustrum refuses to have anything whatsoever to do with her, Cecil Davage – presumably from sheer mischief – has encouraged her and neither Fedden-Jones nor Jeremy takes any interest.'

'But the dean hates homosexuals and lesbians. She will get into fearful trouble if he finds out about it.'

'What I'm trying to convey, David, is that she doesn't care. She's a kind, dutiful woman who feels she's wasting her life here and has reached that point of desperation where she's prepared to take any risks. She would like nothing more than to be drummed out of the cathedral and released for what she thinks is real work – helping those in trouble.'

'So you don't think you could persuade her at least to postpone the service?'

'Absolutely not. I'm still trying to win her confidence – not alienate her. In fact she's given me permission to observe the ceremony discreetly. I can't participate, fortunately, because they're separatist feminists.'

The bishop slumped back in his chair. 'The poor girl. Is there anything that can be done?'

'Well, for a start, you might take a bit more interest in her.'

'How?'

'I don't expect you to be her confessor, but you could chat to her a bit about religion. For God's sake, she seems to be the only one of the canons with any interest in it.'

'But if I ask to see her, she'll know you've been . . . sneaking.'

'I could ask her over here for a drink and you could arrive accidentally. I might even propose that you take each other on at tennis. Fedden-Jones tells me she used to play at county standard before she turned to higher things.'

'Tennis. Oh, my goodness, I'd give a lot to have a tennis partner. Running gets very lonely – even with dear Plutarch.'

Amiss snorted. 'Running isn't having much effect on Plutarch's figure.'

'Well, I suppose in truth the dear thing doesn't actually go very far along the route with me. I do detect a tendency to accompany me for the first fifty yards and then lie down until my return. And of course she has a hearty appetite.'

'And all those snacks in the cathedral must add on the pounds,' added Amiss bitterly. 'Although I have to admit they've diminished since I cut off what you might call her takeaway service. I discovered she was getting most of her prey by lying in wait on top of the north tower for the kestrel to drop a juicy corpse into what it considers its larder. Since the door's been kept shut she's been on short rations. All she's caught since last Tuesday was one fluffy yellow duckling. Removing its mangled remains was yesterday morning's treat.'

'Oh dear, oh dear. How very unpleasant for you. But we can't blame Plutarch. She is, after all, feline and it is in her nature to hunt. To criticize her for following her instincts would to be question divine providence.'

'Perish the thought. Now can we get back to Alice? Do I have your agreement to arrange for you to meet accidentally?'

'Well . . .'

'Please. No one here has been looking after her. You could at least offer some interest and support and see if you could find her some less risky good works, couldn't you?'

'You make me feel ashamed, Robert. I fear I am still emotionally so feeble I am dodging all but my formal responsibilities. Poor girl, I shall make a point of seeing her just as soon as I can.' He pulled out his diary. 'I could be here at around six next Monday evening.'

'Is that the earliest you can do?'

'Truly it is. I have no free time between now and then, what with the visiting Africans, the address to the archdeacons' conference and that frightful fund-raising committee.' He looked at his watch. 'And now I must run. I'm sure you will do your best for Alice in the meantime and at least prevent her from moving out before the dean returns on Friday. And let us hope that the . . . the ladies' ceremony passes off successfully without attracting any attention.' Addled and worried, he ran out of the kitchen.

11

Just before dawn the following morning, Amiss was awakened by the sound of engines in the close. Unable to think of a rational explanation, he tried to block out the sound and will himself back to sleep, but eventually he was driven by curiosity to get up and creep down the hallway to the great window that overlooked Bishop's Green. There he found the bishop wringing his hands.

'I don't quite know what's happening, Robert, but I fear it must be something terrible. Why should people be surrounding the palace? Could it be protestors? Or even terrorists?'

'I can't think there's anything to protest about and terrorists are usually keen to be quiet.' They stood for a few minutes watching lights swinging around the close. 'They seem to be moving onto the lawn. Should we find a torch and go out and warn them off.'

'Surely there may be a perfectly innocent explanation for all this.'

'Like what?'

'Tradesmen, perhaps? Anyway, dawn is about to break. Let us wait for a few moments so as to see what really is going on.'

Within a couple of minutes the objects on the lawn below began to take shape. Suddenly Amiss banged his hands together in fury. 'Shit! It's the fucking shamans! Sorry, David. But this is serious. Alice hasn't moved in with them. They've moved in with us!'

At Amiss's insistence, the bishop agreed that in the absence of the dean it was his job to take the initiative. 'But, my dear

Robert, what is to be done? Why, Bishop Moputowke and his colleagues are due here at nine-thirty and we cannot be involved in altercations then.'

'Get dressed. I'll call a council of war. We need to know at least how the law stands.'

By 7.45, all seven inhabitants of the close were gathered in the drawing room in varying moods of apprehension and anger. The first twenty minutes consisted mainly of squeals of rage from Cecil Davage about vandalism, enlivened by a long monologue from Sebastian Trustrum about how such an event was without precedent and how in addition these people were a very low and degenerate form of life and vastly inferior to gypsies, who were at least rooted in tradition and not given to peddling ersatz philosophies. Fedden-Jones said that decisive action needed to be taken, although since he had to catch a train at 10.15 and still had to pack, he would be unable to be of much assistance. Flubert suggested that perhaps they might just go away if left alone and Alice timidly suggested that perhaps the role of the canons was to welcome them into their midst and offer them material and spiritual help. The cacophony of outrage that broke out in response to that caused the bishop for once to exercise his authority and call for silence.

'Thank you, Canon Wolpurtstone, for that inspiring suggestion. I acknowledge the depth of your feeling and the great-heartedness of your desire for putting Christianity into practice. However, the chapter has the duty to safeguard the fabric of the cathedral: in the absence of the dean it is entirely your responsibility. We must seek to balance our duty to love our neighbour against the need to protect this great institution for subsequent generations.'

Davage glared at him. 'And how do you suggest we reconcile those irreconcilables?'

Amiss came in smoothly. 'Perhaps before we devise a plan of campaign, we should know how the law stands. Is the close private property?'

'Yes,' chorused the male canons.

'So we can just throw them out,' said Davage.

'I doubt it,' said Amiss. 'You can ask them to leave. But

to the best of my knowledge, you can't use force on anyone, even in your own home, if they've come in peacefully. It'll be a matter for the police.'

Alice interjected with a timorous squeak. 'Excuse me.'

'Yes, Canon,' said the bishop encouragingly. 'You have some light to shed on this matter?'

'The shamans had been living on private land for a few weeks and I know they'd had an eviction order served on them a week ago. Tengri –.'

'Who is Tengri?' snarled Davage.

'Their spiritual and temporal leader. He's the one with the beard and the necklace of hooves and trotters and things.'

'You know these invaders? They're friends of yours? Perhaps you invited them here.'

Alice's recognition of the hostility in Davage's voice made her voice quaver slightly. 'I know them and I'm friends with some of the children. But I didn't ask them here. I wouldn't have done such a thing.'

'You were saying, Canon Wolpurtstone,' said the bishop encouragingly. 'About the eviction order.'

'Tengri mentioned it yesterday and said the local police only implemented these orders when they had to. When there are children involved, they get such bad publicity when there are pitched battles and damaged property that they avoid confrontation as much as possible.'

'What does that mean for us?' asked Fedden-Jones.

'That for the moment, at least, persuasion is our only course. It would take days to go through the legal route, and even then . . .'

Flubert groaned. 'I can just imagine the headlines!'

'CLERGY BANISH NEEDY?' offered Amiss.

The bishop was looking increasingly woebegone. 'I have a lot of sympathy with Canon Wolpurtstone's point of view. I keep thinking of Jesus saying, "Suffer the little children to come unto me." And yet, and yet . . .' He wrung his hands.

'Bishop,' whispered Alice. 'May I just say . . . ?'

'Of course.'

'I don't think you should get upset because you believe

the shamans shouldn't be here. I know I said that maybe we should welcome them, but we can't really. It's not fair to the people who use the church or even to anyone living here.' She hesitated. 'They make an awful lot of noise and they won't do the grass any good. I think we should try to persuade them to move somewhere else. Maybe to one of our fields on the other side of the river.'

'A good idea,' said Davage. 'At least as a halfway measure. Isn't Chancellor's Meadow fallow at present?'

The gathering agreed it was and that this was a sound move.

'Excellent, excellent,' said the bishop. 'Now since this is a cathedral matter, may I leave it to you, Canon Trustrum, as the senior canon here, to deal with the negotiations.'

'Not me,' said Trustrum. 'It should be Canon Davage's job – he's treasurer.'

'Excuse me,' said Alice hesitantly. 'Tengri can be violent. I think it would be better if there was a delegation.'

'I appreciate that warning, Canon,' said Davage grimly. 'I would be grateful for some able-bodied accomplices. Preferably His Lordship and Robert. Sebastian seems disinclined to be involved, Dominic has to catch a train and we'd better not put Jeremy's hands at risk.'

Amiss and the bishop nodded.

'I'll go too,' said Alice. 'At least they know me.'

As Davage began to object, the bishop smiled at her. 'Thank you, Canon. Very well, shall we proceed now? And let us remember that a soft answer turneth away wrath.'

Amiss noticed that Alice looked rather unconvinced.

'It was awful.'

'I wish I'd been there to deal with them,' said the baroness.

'And how precisely would you have done that?'

'Thrown them out bodily, if they refused to go.'

'No doubt you would, Jack, but then you're a pugilist, not a bishop.'

'So what happened?'

'Alice performed the introductions sweetly, but when Tengri, the shit in charge, leered at her and said he'd be happy to get off the lawn if he could get onto her, she disappeared and went to talk to some of the children and keep them away from the aggro. Davage then addressed Tengri quite reasonably, but when told to sod off, he became apoplectic. David dear-me'd a few times and asked that matters be conducted in a civilized manner, which led Tengri to explain graphically that he had little use for civilization and that what was camping on the lawn was a group representing a high and ancient civilization beyond the understanding of a shower of fat, greedy clerics. At this stage Davage shrieked that he would get the police and Tengri grinned unpleasantly and wished him luck.

'"Take you weeks," he added, "the speed they move in Westonbury. That's what that git Farmer Scott discovered and why on the quiet he paid us handsomely to fuck off." He then excused himself on the grounds that it was time to roll another joint – though he thoughtfully said that, if we'd like to wait, we were welcome to a quick drag.

'On our way back to the palace, tails well between legs, and the sound of triumphant drumming coming from our conqueror's quarters, Davage had a momentary hope that a drugs bust would solve the problem. But, of course, all that would mean would be that a couple of them would be bailed; it wouldn't actually get them off the land. And the bad publicity remains a difficulty.'

'Do you mean you're just going to leave them to mess up the place?'

'I'm not that pusillanimous, Jack. But it occurred to me – and my colleagues agreed – that when the dean comes back on Friday refreshed from his religious adventure in the States, it will make a challenging task for him. We will take no further steps except to register our complaint with the police.'

'You're hoping he'll foul up and be fatally undermined?'

'What an unworthy thought! I would in fact prefer that he win. But this way, at least we win either way.'

'I'd still have preferred you all to wade in and throw the blighters out by force majeure. But full marks for constructive cowardice, which can, I admit, often be a better course than blind courage.'

She rang off before Amiss could tell her about the lesbians.

The next few days were miserable for the inhabitants of the close. Tengri was clearly determined from the beginning to show who was boss. He took every opportunity to demonstrate contempt for his unwilling hosts, particularly delighting in drumming at maximum volume at daybreak, for he and his community rose with the sun and like crowing cocks ensured that those around them awoke too. Evensong coincided with another drumming session, during which the entire community danced badly but vigorously and intermittently broke into loud chanting. A polite request from Trustrum to keep the noise down during services was met with shouts of rude laughter.

The children were encouraged to regard the whole of the close as their play area. When Amiss entered the cathedral on his morning visit he frequently found two or three toddlers playing naked in the nave. And when one of the vergers attempted to remove the children from the cathedral, he incurred screaming abuse and threats from their mothers to report him for sexual molestation.

As twilight approached, Tengri and his women liked to sit on the steps of their trailers smoking pot and drinking some home-made alcoholic concoction, the effects of which were variously apparent in raucous laughter or loud quarrelling. Tengri's lewd remarks and lubricious glances were so blatant that even Alice – the only person in the close inclined to put out a hand of friendship – was repelled and, like everyone else, avoided the encampment as far as possible.

From the first day, the inhabitants of the close began to use the back entrances to their houses and to the cathedral itself. The only exception was Plutarch, who refused to be browbeaten. On the morning of the invasion, Amiss glanced out the window as she walked past the green and saw Tengri aiming a kick at her. He was about to run out and protest when he saw that Plutarch had the matter in hand. She launched herself at her assailant viciously, and left him a couple of minutes later scratched and winded. Amiss gave her chopped sirloin as a reward.

The shamans were tucked up in their beds on Thursday night when the lesbian witches' service took place. Lurking in the chantry opposite – from which he had an excellent view of the lady chapel – Amiss was torn between horror at the general naffness of the proceedings and sympathy for what Alice Wolpurtstone was trying to achieve. Horror triumphed. Because so intimate, the ceremony proved to be far more embarrassing than even the Rev. Bev's evangelical service.

Alice had confided to Amiss that the form of service was not of her choosing. She had hoped to introduce some material from the Psalms, but the entire Bible had been banned for ideological reasons, being patriarchal and unsound on witches. In the end there was little she could do except provide the location for the ceremony and veto a few blood-curdling anti-male passages. The only Christian prayers allowed were adapted from a prayer book for gays and lesbians.

Amiss could tell that she regretted impulsively inviting him to observe the proceedings, but he headed off any change of mind by telling her how much he was looking forward to seeing how such an imaginative experiment in ecumenism could work.

As he watched from his discreet vantage point, Amiss witnessed the arrival of the dozen or so heterogeneously clad participants. Being temperamentally opposed to the uniform mentality, he applauded spirits so free that they thought apposite a range of clothing from boiler suits to floating white drapery and layers of dangling beads. Several had exotic hair colouring, most had substantial earrings and all of them sported trailing bits of greenery on their heads. Alice was wearing a cassock and looked pretty.

Incense burners pumped out a piny smell as the group formed a circle and Alice switched off the light. There was a long chant which yielded only a few comprehensible words, including 'witch', 'circle', 'magic', 'matriarchy' and 'moon' and then a candle was lit and shone on a book from which someone read a passage about women emerging from desert into garden, darkness into light and denial into affirmation. That led to a lot more chanting, followed by each woman declaring in turn: 'I name myself lesbian and witch. Blessed be the goddesses who made us so.'

At this juncture, the congregation lit their candles from the central flame. A large woman in dungarees threw flower heads vigorously over everyone, a dirge about strength and outness and womanness was sung, an incomprehensible speech was made about sexuality being the seat of relationality and then a wistful woman in muslin began the lengthy prayers to her goddess for those living, dying, fearing and loving in closets. Amiss almost choked as she finished with, 'Oh Goddess, may closets go the way of the Berlin Wall. Alleluia! Amen.' To celebrate this conclusion, she announced a song by k.d. lang relating to sisterness, which was relayed from a small ghetto blaster and lost in the bad acoustics of the tiny chapel.

As a serious young woman with cropped hair began reading a muddled passage about personhood and sexual consumerism, Amiss acknowledged to himself that at heart he was English in the same way as the baroness: the notion of trumpeting one's sexuality in public was anathema.

Waves of words and phrases he hated – 'alienation', 'empowerment', 'mutuality', 'healing hurts' and 'sacred possibilities' – crashed down on him, and as he cringed he became enraged at the notion that expressing one's sexual preference could be transformed into some kind of sacrament. Dammit, he reflected, whither now? Surely, logically, we move on to church ceremonies for bisexuals. He allowed himself briefly to fantasize about an appropriate service for the baroness and Mary Lou Denslow ('Oh God, who loves both male and female, we give thee thanks for empowering us to put it about all over the place'). What about emerging transvestites and postoperative transsexuals? Why not a ceremony for the loss of one's virginity or for healing the hurt of an unsuccessful one-night stand? And while considering ceremonies of loss, what about appendectomies and hysterectomies – not to speak of amputations?

Thought through and developed properly, he decided,

such innovations could give the Church of England a new lease of life: 'Rites of Passage plc' could quickly come to rival counselling as the great growth industry of the 1990s. As he reached this inspiring conclusion and wondered how the bishop would feel about it, the rest of the congregation was commencing a rousing poem about the virtues of intragender love. At that moment, a large figure crashed through the entrance to the lady chapel and in a familiar Belfast accent screamed, 'Mariolatry, you agents of Satan.'

'No, no, Dean,' said Alice bravely. 'What we are worshipping here is love.' He glared at her, looked around at the circle of women holding hands, rushed over and grabbed the multifaced portrait of Mary, raised it up high and brought it crashing down over Alice's head. Pausing only to tear savagely at the gold-and-blue canopy and bring it down all over the company, he strode away, his footsteps ringing in the deserted nave.

Amiss's respect for Alice Wolpurtstone increased markedly in the moments after the exit of the dean, for in the true tradition of the British aristocracy the stiff upper lip came into play. As she and the witches emerged from under the canopy, she calmed and soothed them even as she disentangled herself from her canvas necklace. After a momentary dither, Amiss decided to leave her to her companions. It would, after all, be the height of male arrogance to think that a lesbian with a dozen sisters in attendance was in need of consolation from a man – and a man whom the coven weren't even aware was present.

As he followed the dean and slipped silently out of the north side door, his mind was full of questions. Had everyone got it wrong or had the dean returned early? Had he been tipped off about the ceremony? If so, by whom? Had he gone madder in the States? And if he got that exercised about a little sideshow in the cathedral, what the hell was going to be his reaction to Tengri and his acolytes?

As he began to walk the long way home around the back of the cathedral, an idea occurred to Amiss that made him stop and think hard. If the dean was only just back, could it be that he didn't yet know about the shamans? If so, should he not be briefed? To be introduced to them by their daybreak drumming might lead him in his present mood to run completely amok.

Amiss imagined what that might involve and he found himself smiling. Perhaps a berserk dean was exactly what the shamans needed. But would a briefed berserk dean not be in a stronger position than one jetlagged and sleepy in the early morning who could not know without investigation that the drummers were not simply overenthusiastic seekers after God?

He leaned against the cathedral wall, looking up at the new moon and trying to decide where his duty lay. On the one hand was the dean – a frightful fundamentalist bigot who had just perpetrated a humiliating assault on a good woman. On the other was Tengri, who had so far routed the forces of decency with contemptuous ease.

Put like that, Amiss decided, there was no contest. He turned, retraced his steps and entered the deanery garden by the side gate.

The clock tower was just striking 9.00 when Tilly Cooper opened the door. Her bland, pretty face was becomingly tanned and even the return from the cathedral of a raving husband did not appear to have rattled her serenity. She greeted him warmly.

'Why, Robert, bless you for calling to welcome us home.'

'I saw the light and thought I'd drop by for a moment. I would have waited for the morning, but there's something I should tell the dean.'

'Come in, do.' She led him into the hall and closed the front door.

'Are you just back?'

'Hey, yes. We're ahead of ourselves. We'd always wanted to come back today but hadn't been able to get the flights, but I just prayed hard, and Jesus fixed it. So here we are, fresh and eager to get going on God's work.'

'Excellent, excellent. Now you'll be tired, so I won't hold

you up. Is it possible to have a quick word with the dean on a matter of some urgency?'

'Sure, sure. Follow me.'

She took him into a room whose wonderful Georgian proportions, high ceiling and splendid French windows were constructed for elegant furniture and elegant people. Dean Roper's furniture had already been dispatched to various appreciative legatees; in its place was an array of spartan and unattractive chairs and sofas.

'I'll go and find my husband. May I give you anything? Water? Juice, if we've got any?'

'How kind, but no thanks.'

Tilly went off singing in a low voice about being a twinkle in God's eye, and returned within a couple of minutes escorting her husband, whose tan was overlaid with a red flush. Though he managed a controlled and polite welcome, the dean was clearly struggling to contain his feelings. Amiss gave him a few more minutes to simmer down by asking inane questions about flights and what sort of a break they'd had and had there been any time for a holiday before their studies. As he might have expected, he elicited from Tilly the information that studying Jesus was in itself a rest for mind and body and that no happier month could have been spent anywhere than in the loving companionship in worship experienced at the Bible college.

'And I don't want to boast, Robert, but I have to tell you something happened that's made me very proud.'

He tried to look keenly interested.

'I preached for the first time. I preached – and I think I can say I've found my vocation. Norm was not the only one kind enough to tell me I showed real promise.'

Husbandly pride was restoring the dean's good humour. 'I'm very proud of my wee wife,' he announced. 'She has a God-given gift. I can tell you that at times she moved that congregation to tears. And at the end they applauded as if she was Billy Graham himself.' He nodded portentously. 'And you'll be getting your chance to hear her in the cathedral just as soon as there's a vacant slot in the schedule.'

'I look forward to that very much.'

'Now, young man, I don't want to rush you, but we're dog tired. I understand you have something urgent to tell me.'

'Have you seen Bishop's Green since you got back?'

'No. We came straight to the deanery.'

'You haven't been out since?'

'Only to the cathedral for a brief visit.'

'In a nutshell, the green was taken over a few days ago by an encampment of New Age travellers who have proved exceptionally disruptive. While the chapter have gone through the legal motions, it is clear that these people will leave only if forced. And since there are small children involved, this could produce very bad publicity for the cathedral.'

'What kind of people are these?' asked the dean, his lips set in a straight line and his eyes narrowed.

'There are four trailers, each housing a woman and two or three children; it seems that the commune is polygamous; each family shares the same man – known as Tengri – who is, as it were, husband and father to all.'

The dean's eyes began to flash. Tilly emitted a shocked squeak.

'The reason I came to tell you about it tonight was to warn you that you will almost certainly be woken at dawn by drumming.'

'Drumming?' bellowed the dean, giving the word an emphasis and inflexion reminiscent of Lady Bracknell and the handbag.

'It's a feature of his religion – or at least what he alleges to be his religion, which revolves a lot around drumming and conversations with spirits and' – fuck it, he thought, let's get the bastard well wound up – 'magic and drug taking.'

Veins began to bulge on the dean's forehead. 'And these degenerates are given shelter in a place of worship?'

'Not voluntarily, I assure you, Dean. In view of their immoral behaviour and their antisocial practices, although feeling that to an extent a hand should be held out even to the most despised of God's creatures, the bishop and canons appealed to them to leave.'

'No hand should be held out to degenerates, unless they repent. And certainly not to people who practise wicked superstition and sully the temples that are their bodies with vile substances.'

The dean brooded for a moment. 'Do these people have a name for their degenerate cult?'

'I suppose generically they're pagans.'

'Pagans?' The dean's voice was loud enough to reach Bishop's Green.

'More specifically, shamans. Tengri calls himself a shaman.'

'Shaman! Shaman! Satan is everywhere!' screamed the dean, leaping up and running from the room.

'Jesus save us,' said Tilly as she ran after him; Amiss brought up the rear.

12

For once Amiss had the pleasure of ringing the baroness at a time which suited him and not her. When he reached her at midnight she was deep in what she self-pityingly mourned as her baby sleep.

'She who lives by the telephone dies by the telephone,' said Amiss unfeelingly. 'If you think I'm going to give you any sympathy when I think of the number of times you've woken me at some frightful hour, you can forget it. Now do you want to hear about the dean exorcizing the devil or do you not?'

The baroness's grumbles ceased abruptly. 'Do I just!' She smacked her lips.

'We start with the unfortunate events in the lady chapel.' He took the baroness through the high points of the ceremony, which elicited predictable snorts of derision and condemnation. 'Christ, what a load of bollocks all this sort of stuff is. Why they can't just shut up about sex and enjoy it is beyond me. "Pray for those of us in the closet," my arse!'

'I certainly find it hard to imagine a closet which could contain you for long. However, can we drag ourselves away from you for a moment? I'm trying to tell you about the denouement.'

The story of the dean and the portrait was a great success. 'Magnificent. I wish I'd been there.'

'Have you no sympathy for poor Alice?'

'Certainly not. It might do her a lot of good. She's got to put all this rubbish behind her and get down to useful do-goodery on behalf of the deserving. I hope this deters her from ministering to self-indulgent weirdos.'

'Which leads me to the shamans.' His account of his visit to the dean caused her to pay him one of her rare compliments.

'I hand it to you, Robert. Perfect timing. By morning he might have been calm.' She chortled. 'Ooh, good. I hope the next bit lives up to expectations. So we have him thundering through his front door pursued by wife and *agent provocateur*.'

'Not only – as we were to find out – was his strength as the strength of ten, but his speed was as the speed of light. I hadn't realized that righteous indignation adds wings to the feet, but so it proved to be. By the time we reached the green, Tilly and I – many years his junior – were in some distress, but the run appeared to have taken nothing out of the dean. Even his breathing was unaffected: he gazed at what by that time of night was the silent and apparently innocent quartet of trailers and emitted a thunderous bellow which put the fear of God into me – I can't imagine what it sounded like to the slumbering, doped-up shamans.

'"Come out, you children of Satan!" he shouted. And when they didn't instantly appear, he started racing around the trailers crashing his great fists against the sides and screaming about the fires of hell that awakened infidels. This presumably penetrated the adult brains – for, I suppose, when you live in encampments, your worst fear would be an arson attack.

'From three of the trailers emerged the heads of wary women and from the fourth the great shaman himself scrambled out looking slightly alarmed; a woman and child were silhouetted in the doorway behind him.

'As Tengri ascertained that all that was in front of him was a large clergyman, a thin blonde and me, he reverted to type and began to sneer. Within two minutes the dean had pulled him down the steps, had got him in an armlock and was delivering maledictions of the Old Testament variety. There was quite a lot about the Lord raining brimstone and fire from the heaven down on Sodom and Gomorrah, various references to whetting glittering swords and rendering vengeance to his enemies and some rather incoherent stuff to do with false gods and smiting trangressors. It was pretty unnerving, I can tell you, especially to the women at whom he shouted that if they didn't obey instructions he'd break Tengri's arm. "Up and out," he shouted. "If you're not gone in ten minutes I'll have the water hose turned on you and the insides of your abominable homes." He waved with his free arm. "And take all your filth with you."

'One of the women looked nervously at the wretched Tengri, who incautiously began his response with the word "don't", and for his folly had his arm twisted so far up his back that he screamed like someone on a griddle and said, "Go, go." "Where to?" asked one woman. "Far away from this city," said the dean, "for if I catch sight of any of you again, believe me, this time the wrath of the Lord will be brought upon you and there will be no mercy. Do I make myself clear?" To which Tengri screamed, "Yes."'

'By now, we had been joined by David, Jeremy and Cecil – the others, I learned later, were gazing through their windows afraid to emerge – but no one tried to intervene, for the dean appeared possessed. One would as easily have demurred at his treatment of Tengri as have had a quiet word with the Lord when he was in the middle of laying waste an altar of idols or sending down a plague of frogs. So we watched open-mouthed and silently.

'Not until all the detritus had been removed from the green, the engines had been revved up and the headlights were on, did the dean take Tengri over to the door of his trailer and release him. "Begone, you Satanists and fornicators," was his parting sally. "And never darken the gates of the City of Westonbury again."'

'Compelling stuff. Was that it?'

'That was it. They drove away without a backward glance, the dean and Tilly went off to bed and I came back here and did my best to rid David of his guilt at allowing – and even being pleased about – the expulsion of the people who'd been making his life a complete misery.'

'It would be your guess that they won't be back?'

'Since they don't even know who this mad exorcist was, I can't see them taking the risk of running into him anywhere in Westonbury. No, I think they've definitely gone off to persecute some new community.'

'Good for the dean. He did exactly what I told you to do the morning they arrived, with a few embellishments of his own. As an exorcist, he certainly beats the bell, book and candle merchants any day.'

'He was the right man for the job, Jack. None of the rest of us has such balls.'

'We might have to revise our opinion of him, you know,' she said ruminatively. 'The fellow's only been back ten minutes and he's already put paid to lesbian drivel, fag-hag art and New Age vandalism. Perhaps he should be Archbishop of Canterbury. See to it, will you?'

'I hate him,' said Cecil Davage some days later. 'Hate, hate, hate. He's a perfect example of everything that is nastiest in English life – that hideous puritan streak that took the religious art we had spent centuries perfecting and destroyed it. Look at this.'

He led Amiss to a tiny cell-like chantry, bare except for a stone altar. Davage unlocked the gate, switched on the light and pointed to a square foot of rose and silver paint in a corner just above the altar. 'This whole wall contained a mural of the Nativity, said by the chronicler of St Dumbert to have been the most beautiful ever seen throughout the length and breadth of England – and that at a time when our religious art was possibly the greatest in Europe.'

He gave a muffled sob. 'There's evidence to suggest that this survived the first wave of vandals under Henry VIII and Elizabeth at a time when they were destroying every statue in the cathedral as well as the paintings, and stealing every object of value we possessed except those now in the treasury which the then dean managed to hide. But when Cromwell's barbarians came, they mopped up what the others had missed. That's when our wonderful medieval stained glass went – except for the rose window, which by some fluke they couldn't get at in the time available. They threw some stones at it, but didn't make much impact.

'But they found time to take axes to this little miracle here – our own tiny Sistine Chapel. And so in the name of God they destroyed in Westonbury – as elsewhere – the wonderful fruits of the greatest flowering of English art, designed to worship God and honour his mother and his saints. Here, they didn't rest until they had taken from us every last little bit of beauty and vision and joy except for this remnant of previous glory. I hate, hate, hate that century of desecration. And I hate all those responsible for and sympathetic to that desecration. Dean Cooper is one of them; he's a Roundhead and I wish he were dead.'

'Surely you forgive him much for throwing out the shamans.'

'No, I don't. It doesn't make up for wantonly destroying the Marian picture. He's a desecrating throwback.'

'Oh, come now, Cecil. You can't seriously claim that pulling down the canopies and smashing that frankly not-very-good painting is on a par with Cromwell.'

'It's the same mentality, don't you see? He didn't like that painting, but he could have asked us to move it, or to give it away. And you know he said he'd have Reggie Roper's memorial pulverized if it wasn't that the cathedral needs the bequest. He says he's praying for a bolt of lightning.'

'But is it reasonable to expect him cheerfully to put up with having a gay extravaganza in his garden? I'm not surprised he's complaining.'

'I know the memorial's not in the best of taste, but it is very well sculpted. And it kept Reggie happy thinking about it. Why can't it be treated as an enjoyable folly. That's another thing about puritans; they have no sense of humour. Nowadays they hate even what they helped to construct themselves – the great and wonderful language of the King James Bible: the dean's language is banal.'

His voice rose to a near squeak. 'No, no. I see how it will be. Everything beautiful will go and we will have ugly, ugly, ugly, ugly puerile minds and all will be brought down to the level of idiots and philistines.'

He stamped his right foot six or seven times. 'What great art is about is raising the philistines and the brutish to an understanding of beauty. That was what God wanted. It was Cromwell who was the Satan. Like Cooper.'

'Did Westonbury suffer more than most other cathedrals?'

'No. Everywhere suffered, every little church in the country with its own little piece of beauty. All that survived was maybe five per cent – an altar cloth here and a statue there. Do you know that when they had finished with us our religious artists forgot how to paint and it was generations before any concept of religious art re-emerged.

'Now do you wonder that I'm drawn to Rome? At least pre-Vatican II Rome. Bloody church has been going to pot aesthetically since then. Old Catholicism might have been corrupt, decadent, autocratic and greedy for power and money, but it was greedy for beauty too. Corrupt people were the sponsors for the greatest art to come out of Italy and corrupt people treasured that art and kept it in being.'

His little face took on a malign expression. 'Every year I take some friends and we go and dance on Richard Cromwell's grave. We can't dance on his father's since he was dug up and his head stuck on a spike. But people like that believe in the sins of the fathers being visited upon the children, so we reckon Richard can pay for the sins of Oliver – as well as his own. We curse him to hell – and I don't mean a namby-pamby Church of England hell either, with its consciousness of difference or absence of God or any of that other insipid muck. I mean good old-fashioned lakes-of-fire-for-eternity hell of the kind the dean is so fond of.'

Amiss lay on his bed and told the story to the baroness. 'It's given me a whole new perspective on little Davage.'

'Indeed. Who would have thought the little man had so much passion in him? And of course he's absolutely right. Tell him to invite me to the next Cromwell-stomping session and I'll wear hobnailed boots.'

She brooded for a moment. 'He's not afraid for his treasures, is he? Even if the dean is mildly crazed, he's hardly going to set about the cathedral like a Roundhead. I should have thought he would get a pretty stiff rebuke from the Church Commissioners and English Heritage if he started firing rocks at the rose window.'

'There's something to be said for progress after all, Jack.

Modern vandals are constrained by bureaucracy from physically expressing their feelings of outrage.'

'Pah! It's a pretty poor century that has us trouncing Dean Cooper with a set of regulations. My ancestor, old Alfred Troutbeck, would have known what to do with him. Knock his block off and stick it on one of the spires with that grinny, sappy woman of his along with him.'

'I shall recommend that course of action to David. I'm sure he'll take swift and decisive action.'

'Tell him if he doesn't I'll knock his block off too.'

'I've had the most awful meeting with the dean and his wife.' The bishop was slumped in the chair behind his desk. 'They came, as she put it, for a social call and to chat about their plans, and then began to talk about all kinds of terrible things.'

'Like what?'

'She simpered at me and asked if I would be "people friendly" and stop calling myself either Doctor or Bishop Elworthy and instead call myself Bishop . . .' he gagged.

'Bishop David?'

'No. Worse. Bishop Dave. Or just Dave.'

Amiss's attempt to keep his face straight failed. He looked across the desk at the embodiment of scholarship that was his employer and began to laugh.

The bishop looked distressed.

'I'm sorry, David. I'm truly sorry. But I've never in my life seen anyone less like a Dave. You mustn't think of giving in to that: you'd be a laughing stock.'

'But she told me that titles frightened off ordinary people and that the cathedral must become the meeting place for all God's children. Anyway that's but a small thing; there's much worse. He was talking of closing down the choir school – apparently it's elitist – and getting rid of all traditional music in the cathedral. Henceforward, it's all to be' – he looked at his notes – 'as she put it, "sing-alongs for Jesus", rave music and whatever else is "relevant". Incense, of course, will go, the King James Bible will go, the Book of Common Prayer will go. In will come the *Contemporary English Version* and other dreadful American muck.'

'He can't do that without the agreement of the chapter surely.'

'He said he was certain they would listen to reason and she said she knew that Jesus would make them see the light. Apparently they're asking that Rev. Bev creature to address the next meeting of the chapter to show them how' – he scrutinized his notes again – 'to make Jesus accessible. The dean rambled on a bit about how the Rev. Bev's faith could move mountains.'

'What did you say to all this?'

The bishop smiled. 'I had, I think, a moment of divine inspiration. Anyway they left pretty quickly afterwards. I remembered that piece of advice Cromwell gave the General Assembly of the Church of Scotland which he would have done well to follow himself: "I beseech you, in the bowels of Christ, think it possible you may be mistaken."'

'Will you come back and see me later this evening?'

'Sure, Jeremy, I'd be glad to. When?'

'About tennish.'

'Anything in particular?'

'The dean . . .' Flubert's mouth set itself in a hard line. 'The dean wishes to talk to me about the future.'

'Any hint of what he has in mind?'

'I can't imagine I'll like it, whatever it is. But I don't have to pay that much attention to it. I don't mind making a few concessions here and there, but when the chips are down, he can't enforce any changes without the support of three members of the chapter. And even if he gets Alice on his side . . .'

'I wouldn't worry about that, if I were you. She's being stoical about his assault on her, but she is – for her – very angry. She's decided he's not a good Christian, which is a frightful thing for Alice to say about anyone.'

'Oh, good. I can't see him getting any other support, so I'm not worried. But just in case things get unpleasant it'll be consoling to have you to talk to about it afterwards.'

'Ring me when you get back?'

'Just turn up here. I'll leave the door open. Help yourself to a drink.'

'I hope things go well.'

'Me too, though I fear acrimony when two positions are as irreconcilable as are ours. One of us has to end up very, very dissatisfied.'

The phone rang as Amiss was pouring himself a glass of whisky.

'Hello. Jeremy Flubert's house.'

'Robert, it's Jeremy. If you don't mind, I'd like to meet you somewhere else.'

'Are you all right?'

'Yes, I'm fine. But I don't want to meet you at home. Can we make it a pub. There's one in Meltonian Street called the Dog and Duck that looks pleasant enough from the outside. I'll try to be there about ten-thirty, but I might be late.'

Amiss was compliant but baffled, unable to think of any coherent reason why Flubert – who valued privacy above all and who almost never went near pubs – should make such an odd request. Still, he obediently knocked back his drink and set off on the twenty-minute walk across town to the Dog and Duck, which proved to be an unfortunate choice of venue. The clientele was young and noisy, its taste reflected in the metallic music that blared out over the loud speakers.

By 11.00 the thumpity, thumpity, thump had given Amiss a severe headache; he thought of going outside and wandering up and down, but feared that if he did he might miss a message from Flubert, so he sat miserable and fed up until closing time when, sorely perplexed and rather worried, he walked back to the close. Flubert's door was open, but there was no sign that he had been there. Amiss scribbled a concerned note and went home troubled.

'I've got bad news, Robert.'

'What's the matter?' Amiss looked fearfully at the bishop, who stood in front of him quivering.

'I'm afraid something terrible has happened.'

'It's Jeremy, isn't it?'

'How did you guess?'

'Just tell me.'

'He's dead.'

'How?'

The bishop's legs appeared to give way. He fell into a kitchen chair. 'Hanging.'

'He hanged himself?'

'I suppose so,' said the bishop miserably. 'Although he didn't leave a note so the police are reserving their opinion.'

'Where was he found?'

'Oh, it's too dreadful, too, too dreadful. He's in the cathedral.' The bishop's face was a mask of pain. 'It's a horrifying sight, Robert. I wish they hadn't taken me to it. I fear I lack the necessary fortitude.' He buried his face in his hands for a moment. 'He was hanging off one of the organ pipes. Whatever you do, don't go and look. I don't think I'll ever get that sight out of my mind.'

Amiss put his arm around him. 'Have you said a prayer for him?'

'Oh, yes. I said one as I looked up at his poor tortured face. It's a piece of Tennyson I always loved:

'Speak no more of his renown,
Lay your earthly fancies down,
And in the vast cathedral leave him,
God accept him, Christ receive him.'

That destroyed Amiss's unnatural calm, and for a couple of minutes the two men sobbed like children. Amiss was the first to recover, blow his nose and sit up straight.

'Excuse me for a moment. I must go and ring Jack.'

'Do you think she might come down to us?'

'If she can, I'm sure she will.'

'I'm afraid the mistress is at breakfast.'

'I don't care, Miss Smart. It's Robert Amiss here.' He ground his teeth as she emitted squeaks of delight and welcome, until, able to bear it no longer, he interrupted with,

'I'm sorry to be abrupt, but it's an emergency. Can you please fetch her?'

The baroness came on breezily after a couple of minutes. 'What's up? I had to break off in mid-harangue.'

'Jeremy Flubert is dead.'

'How?'

'Hanging off an organ pipe.'

'Apposite, at least. Suicide?'

'Could be murder. They've found no note.'

'How's David?'

'Very cut up. He saw him.'

'And you?'

'I'd become very fond of him.' There was a silence.

'OK,' she said. 'Clearly you need reinforcements. I can't do much for a couple of days. I've got to speak early in a Lords debate this afternoon and wind up tomorrow. And besides on Friday . . . oh, fuck. It's hopeless.' There was a brief silence. 'I was going to say I'd send you Mary Lou, but of course the person you need is Ellis.'

'It's not fair to Ellis. He's been looking forward to his holiday.'

'Balls. He owes you. Remind him. Get to another phone and start blackmailing him. Now hand me over to David.'

'I'm very sorry, Robert. You must be very upset.'

'Will you come down for a few days?'

'Would you mind if I didn't? I've got so much to do here. A van arrived last night from my parents and it's going to take days to sort everything out.'

'I don't care if the fucking ceiling has fallen in.'

'We can't all live the way you do, Robert. Look, I'll come down for twenty-four hours in a few days when I can see daylight.'

'Ellis, would you be kind enough to cast your mind back – *inter alia* – to a school in Kensington and a club in St James's? Let me remind you that you owe me several very serious favours. I'm collecting my debts.'

There was a moment's silence. 'I'll call you as soon as I know what train I'm getting.'

13

Within a few hours, Flubert's body had been removed from the cathedral, it had been established that the cord that had hanged him came from a dressing gown kept in the organ loft for especially cold weather, the search for a suicide note had been called off and the superintendent assigned to the case had interviewed the bishop so perfunctorily as to give the impression that he was barely interested. Amiss – restless and unhappy and unable to concentrate on anything – had the brainwave of calling on Alice Wolpurtstone and asking her to look after the bishop and leave him free to meet Pooley's train.

They managed a rough embrace without embarrassing Pooley too much. 'I'm sorry, Robert. It was pusillanimous and mean spirited of me to hesitate about coming. I know he had become a friend. You must be feeling like hell.'

Amiss grinned sourly. 'I should be used to it by now, shouldn't I?'

'One never gets used to it. Not as long as one stays human.' Pooley smiled. 'And you're certainly that, aren't you? Are you ready for a late lunch?'

'Am I just!'

'Jack Troutbeck. Thought I'd better bring you up to date on your chap. He's in a bit of a state and will need comforting.'

'Is he ill?'

'No, he'll be fine when he sobers up. Latest intelligence is that he has just been assisted to bed by Ellis Pooley.'

'What's the matter with him?'

'A friend of his just snuffed it.'

'Who?'

'Jeremy Flubert, the Westonbury organist.'

Rachel banged the telephone in frustration. 'Oh shit, no. He's the one he had grown fond of.'

The baroness sighed gustily. 'So it appears. We hadn't realized how close they'd become. What's more he's managing to blame himself in some obscure way for not having been around to save him.'

'From what?'

'Killing himself or being killed.'

'Oh my God, you mean you've let him in for another round of blood and guts.'

'He's a grown-up.'

'But an unusually malleable grown-up.'

'You're just complaining because he's doing what I tell him rather than what you tell him.'

Rachel laughed. 'Maybe, although actually, as he has started to admit, the truth is he does it because he wants to. Unfortunately, he doesn't always enjoy it.'

'Like life.'

'Quite. But in his case, with more horrors than most people will ever experience.'

'Don't worry, he's in good hands. I've press-ganged Ellis into promising to stay until he has to go back to work at the end of next week. Indeed I'm about to instruct him to get himself attached to the local police force, since the word is the rozzer in charge is a lemon.'

'Do you push everyone around?'

'I try.'

'We must meet sometime.'

The baroness snorted in agreement. '"But there is neither East nor West, Border, nor Breed, nor Birth/When two strong men" – or to be strictly accurate, two strong women – "stand face to face, though they come from the ends of earth!" Yes, we must. We might get on.'

'Yes, Jack, he's sleeping peacefully.'

'Good. I've been thinking.'

'Mmm?' Pooley sounded cautious.

'There's no point in you hanging about in Westonbury being a nanny. It's time you and Robert got going on the case. From what David said the superintendent seems to be a waste of space. You'd better get yourself formally assigned to his staff.'

'Don't be daft. That's not the way the system works.'

'Why not? Wouldn't they like an extra hand?'

Politeness began to give way to exasperation. 'Surely you understand about turf wars? They're one of the nightmares of being a policeman. Regional forces are all jealous of each other and everyone hates the Met. We're supposed to be arrogant, patronizing know-alls.'

'Don't be defeatist.'

'Jack, I can absolutely assure you there is no chance whatsoever that on hearing that a police sergeant from the Met – steeped in murders though I may be – is around here on holiday, the local superintendent in charge of the case will tug his forelock and beg me to help. You might as well expect the US Senate to ask you to become a temporary legislator when you next descend on Washington.'

'That's a fatuous comparison. I'm not suggesting you offer yourself to the FBI. Come on, lad, think flexibly. You've got to network. One of your Met pals must know this guy or one of his bosses. Look how Jim Milton got you assigned to the St Martha's little local difficulty.'

'I suppose if Jim were here he might be able to sort out something.'

'Well, he isn't. So you'd better pick up your flat feet and run with the ball.'

'If you insist.' The evident irritation in Pooley's voice was completely lost on the baroness, who had already rung off.

Pooley woke Amiss with a cup of tea. 'How are you feeling?'

Amiss sat up and shook his head vigorously. 'Fine. Slept like the dead.' He winced. 'Oh, God, I'd forgotten.'

'Try this. It'll wake you up. You should get up for a few hours or you won't sleep tonight.'

'What time is it?'

'Almost eight. We're having dinner in half an hour. I know the bishop would be glad if you could join us.'

Amiss took a cautious sip of tea. 'I'd be delighted. Oddly enough, I don't feel hung over. Maybe I'm still drunk.'

'That's the most likely explanation. Now, I've got some good news. I've got myself drafted in to help the local police investigate Flubert's death.'

'Wonderful, Ellis. I was in despair at the indifference of Superintendent Godson. How did you pull it off?'

'Under extreme pressure from Jack I rang around my most friendly colleagues; it turned out that Sammy Pike worked with Godson years ago and they've stayed pals. He just rang him up and fixed up for me to help him. Can you believe it?'

'So what's the deal?'

'Godson says he's short-handed and glad to have me. He thought it might be useful that I'm staying in the close and will have some inside knowledge. It's an informal arrangement. From the point of view of the Met this won't be a secondment: I'll just be having a busman's holiday.'

'No doubt Jack's taking the credit?'

'Need you ask? Mind you, she probably deserves it. I'd never have thought it possible to fix up something like this. Godson must be an unusual copper.'

'And to think he seemed to David and me to be a bit of a jerk. Well, well – a further useful lesson in not jumping to conclusions.'

'Are you all right now, or is there anything else you need me to do?'

'Thank you, Jack. No. You seem to have pushed people around most constructively. Rachel's been sympathetic, Ellis is girding on his metaphorical helmet –'

'You don't gird on a helmet: you don it.'

'– and David has stopped wailing and is doggedly getting on with his duties.'

'Like you, I trust. What news have you for me?'

'Nothing except that I had a most cheering conversation this morning with Alice Wolpurtstone. Between them, the lesbian witches, the shamans, the dean and now poor Jeremy have transformed her from crying hand-wringer to purposeful toughie. She confided that loneliness and the absence of challenge in Westonbury had unmanned her for a time. "I've got my sense of perspective back," she explained cheerfully, sounding like a veritable memsahib. "They can do their worst."'

'Who?'

'The dean, obviously. Though she's got over being mad with him. Says she should forgive him what he did to her because of what he did to Tengri, which apparently she equates with Jesus throwing the money changers out of the temple. We hadn't realized how much she was suffering at Tengri's hands: he used to shout obscenities through her letter box.'

'Whose side will she be on in the chapter, though?'

'Says she's keeping an open mind on the issues.'

'Don't like the sound of that.'

'You wouldn't. Anyway, she's demonstrated her mettle in dealing with the witches. Apparently they arrived at her house in force last night to demand she join them in suing the dean for assault, hurt feelings and the rest of it. When she refused, they accused her of colluding with homophobics. When she explained she believed in turning the other cheek they became vituperative. She was accused among other things of being crone-unfriendly and a sadofeminist.'

'A what?'

'It's a feminist who follows a patriarchal agenda.'

'Well at least they've an original line in insults. So what did she do?'

'Told them to get out and not darken her door again.'

'And did they?'

'Indeed they did. And haven't been seen since. Presumably they're delivering themselves of angry incantations and sticking pins in wax images of her, but if so they're having no effect. She's concluded it's time she went back to looking after people who deserve to be looked after and has put charlatans behind her.'

'Very good. Very, very good. That girl has more spirit than

I'd have thought. We'll make a man of her yet. I'll be in touch.'

The phone went dead.

'To be perfectly honest. . .'

Pooley adopted the interested expression that was the appropriate response to a phrase normally followed by statements like 'I prefer good weather to bad' or 'I'd rather I hadn't broken my leg in fifteen pieces'.

'I'm lazy.'

Pooley looked at Superintendent Godson with new respect.

'In fact I'm very lazy. Very, very lazy. At least as far as work is concerned.' He grinned. 'I'm telling you this, a) because Sammy Pike says you're OK and b) because I don't give a bugger. The only thing I give a bugger about is my garden – more particularly my carnations, which won second prize at the Westonbury Flower Show last year and which I hope this year will scoop first. If they don't, I can tell you it will not be for the want of trying on my part.'

He sank further back into his armchair and took another sip of the coffee with which Pooley had provided him. 'I'll be retiring in eighteen months, so there's now no chance of promotion. And I'm sick and tired of police work and spending my life fighting criminals and bureaucracy.

'Quite simply, my main objective during what remains of my professional life is to get other people to do the work. Of course I take some of the credit, but I give others plenty if it's deserved. Especially if they help me to get home in good time to tend my flowers.' He paused expectantly.

Pooley nodded gravely. 'I understand, sir. I hope I can be of assistance.'

'As far as I'm concerned you're heaven-sent. I've got a thick DC assigned to me on this case who doesn't know if it's breakfast or Tuesday. Several corpses short of a morgue, you might say.' He shook his head in exasperation. 'Can't think how people like that get into the police force.'

He took another sip and smiled genially. 'And now you arrive from nowhere, bright as a button and keen as a whippet, according to Sammy Pike, and anxious to sort out what happened to that canon just for the hell of it. And if this is your idea of holiday, more fool you and lucky old me.

'However we have to observe the proprieties. I don't want to overstep the mark and be drummed out of the force before I've earned my full pension. I'll have to be seen undertaking the basic enquiries, you understand, but you can investigate away like a good 'un with my blessing. Find me proof of suicide and I'll be delighted. And if it turns out to be murder, I'd like the murderer delivered to me, please, in a nice package with a pink ribbon and a bow, preferably with all the paperwork stapled to it.

'Oh, yes. As far as possible, I like my hours to be a maximum of nine to five: if I stay till six I probably won't start until ten next day. You, of course, can ferret away all night for all I care. Just do it discreetly.'

'All that seems fine to me, sir. Just one thing. What will my status be?'

'You'll be what you are – Detective Sergeant Pooley of the Met lending us a hand. None of the clerics will ask any awkward questions: we're all plods to them. So you can attend my interviews and give me some tips where you think they will be useful: I've got no false pride. Just keep remembering that all I want is as little work and as much credit as possible.'

'But what about DC Boyd, sir?'

'DC Plod himself? Don't worry about him. He'll fetch and carry. He can read and write and take notes and run errands, you'll provide the brains and energy and I'll go through the motions.'

'Fine by me, sir.'

'Right.'

He looked at his watch. 'We'd better sit down at the table and look serious. I sent Plod to pick up the dean. They should be along any minute now.'

'Suicide or murder?' asked Godson.

Dean Cooper gazed at him grimly. 'I can give no opinion on that. Though I had not thought that poor wee wretch so depraved as to destroy himself. For suicide is the great abomination in the eyes of the Lord.'

'Spare us the sermon, sir. How did you find Canon Flubert when you saw him shortly before his death?'

'In what sense?'

'Was he in good spirits? Did you have a disagreement?'

'I called him to tell him that there must be changes in the music in this cathedral. He has made it a centre for the elite, for the rich, and often for the decadent and the Romish. It is time we followed the word of Jesus and suffered the poor and the deprived to come to us. It is our duty to save souls and that means we must make this place welcoming. You do not welcome a poor person by playing him music fit only for popinjays. My wife understands all this. She knows how to bring souls to Jesus through uplifting song.'

The superintendent sighed loudly. 'I'm not interested in your justifications, sir. I want to know what happened between you and the deceased.'

'I made my position clear to Canon Flubert and he dissented, which is hardly surprising. However, we discussed this as brothers in Christ and agreed there was room for compromise.'

'How much room?'

'That was to be finally determined at the next meeting of the dean and chapter. I hoped that with the help of a friend of mine I could persuade these people to take the righteous path.'

'Was there acrimony?'

'There may have been a slight raising of voices. No more than that.'

'So nothing took place that would incline you to think that in his distress he went straight off and hanged himself?'

'Certainly not.'

'And you didn't take such exception to his defence of his music that you took him into the cathedral and hanged him.'

Understandably outraged, the dean jumped up and shook a furious finger at Godson. 'How dare you make such an allegation against a man of God.'

'How do I know what you are capable of? After all, you

appear to favour a god of wrath.' Godson laughed gaily. 'Who can be sure that you might not have felt morally obliged to rub out Canon Flubert for the sake of the sinners he was keeping out of the cathedral.'

The dean's cheeks expanded like those of a toad. 'As God is my witness –' he began to shout.

'Cut it out please, sir. I have my job to do; you have your job to do; the unfortunate Canon Flubert had his. We must all do the best we can. That will be all for the moment.'

As the dean stormed out of the room, Godson turned to DC Boyd. 'Fetch that young fellow, Robert Amiss. He should be hanging around somewhere nearby.' He smiled benignly at Pooley. 'What did you think of that then?'

'You were certainly . . . um . . . very direct, sir.'

'I'll tell you what, Pooley, being demob-happy is a wonderful state of mind. I don't have to put up with any shit, because as long as I don't actually break any of the rules there's nothing my superiors can do to me. And, indeed, if I get a reputation for being rather difficult they might be inclined to bring my retirement forward, which would suit me very well if the redundancy money was right. Anyway, what did you think?'

'I didn't really have enough time to form an opinion, sir.'

'Never mind. You'll have plenty of time to suss him out when I'm not around. Ah, right. This sounds like your friend Amiss now.'

'Would it have been in character for Flubert to kill himself?'

Amiss spread his hands wide. 'I've been wondering about that since yesterday morning. Remember I hadn't know him for long. But my guess is it would be possible if he were in despair about his musical life.'

'You mean if the dean was going to destroy what he had created?'

'Yes. But I can't see how he could. He doesn't have the power to order a change in the musical arrangements without the consent of a majority of the canons, most if not all of whom would, in any case, have backed Jeremy.'

'The dean said there was room for compromise. Do you

believe him? You're the last person known to have talked to Flubert.'

'I couldn't say. We only had a few words on the phone. But I can't anyway see him committing suicide without leaving a note. It would be unfair and discourteous and Jeremy was never discourteous. And anyway, why would he change the venue of his meeting with me?'

'Because he was afraid you might come looking for him in the cathedral and find his body?'

'But all he had to do was postpone our meeting until the following day. There was no reason to send me off on a wild-goose chase: again, that would be uncharacteristically discourteous. Suicide seems impossible.'

Godson shrugged. 'So murder seems more likely. But it still doesn't explain why he changed the venue.'

Pooley leant forward. 'Perhaps he needed to meet someone in his house before he saw you.'

'Why would it have to be in his house? Why not in theirs? Or in the cathedral? But why would anybody murder him in such a horrible way and how could they do it without his cooperation?'

'That's straightforward enough,' said Godson. 'All the murderer would need would be a gun. March the fellow up to the organ loft, fix up the arrangement on the organ pipe, put the noose around his neck and push him off the edge. Easy peasy.'

Amiss's face contorted. 'But what possible motive would anyone have to do such a thing?'

The superintendent laughed. 'Maybe the dean felt very worked up about the music business. Maybe Flubert convinced him that he'd never get the chapter to agree. Maybe he goes in for drastic solutions. Search me, I don't know.' He looked at his watch. 'Right. I've got to call in at the office. Then it'll be time for lunch. Boyd, you come with me. Pooley, I'll see you back here at two-thirty.'

Boyd leaped up and rushed to the door to hold it open for his superior. As Godson was leaving, he turned around. 'Oh, and Pooley.'

'Yes, sir.'

'Tell that little TV fellow – what's his name? – to report promptly at two-thirty. And if you want to do any sleuthing between now and then, be my guest.'

Smiling broadly, he vanished from the room.

Amiss shook his head. 'What an extraordinary man.'

'He certainly is.'

'He doesn't seem quite of our world.'

'As far as I can see, in his imagination he's permanently in his greenhouse crooning at carnations.'

'But his attitude to Flubert's death seems one of detachment – even indifference.'

'Come on, Robert. You've met enough policemen to know that mostly they don't get involved and can't afford to. Just be grateful he doesn't care. It leaves me with a free hand.'

Amiss stood up. 'OK, OK. Now do me a favour and come with me to the cathedral. I couldn't face it alone. It's bad enough facing the site of Jeremy's awful death, but if Plutarch has decided to mark the occasion with an ornithological sacrifice, I might be sick.'

14

'Which do you think, then?'

'I don't think,' said Davage. 'Mine is an aesthetic, not a conceptual, mind.'

Godson looked at him irritably. 'Now look here, Mr –'

'Father, please.'

'Father then. I'm a busy man, and I haven't got time to mess about. Do you know anything about Canon Flubert's death?'

'No.'

'Can you think of any reason why it should have been murder?'

'Who'd murder poor old Edna?'

'Who is Edna?'

'Oops! Sorry, Superintendent. Slip of the tongue. It was just an affectionate description of Jeremy.'

'Are you implying Canon Flubert was homosexual?'

'I expect so. But if he was, God knows I don't think he did anything about it. So if you're imagining he was done in by a rent boy or some such instrument of fate, I'm sure you're wrong. Jeremy didn't do much but get on with his job. My guess is that the poor old thing probably topped himself because he didn't like the new dean.'

'But the dean couldn't make him do anything he didn't want to, could he?'

'I suppose he could have made life difficult. Jeremy hated cathedral politics and he might have feared a long-drawn-out war of attrition.'

'But I've been told you are an able politician. Wouldn't you have protected him?'

'I'd have been on his side, yes. But frankly, I've recently been looking round for another job and he knew that. There are other cathedrals, you know, and some of them actually value celebrities.'

'Did you discuss with Canon Flubert your relationship with the new dean?'

He tittered. 'No, not really. Jeremy and I didn't talk much. We weren't each other's types. He was awfully serious.'

'So there's no help you can give us?'

''Fraid not.'

'Thank you and goodbye.' In a tone of heavy sarcasm, Godson added, '*Father* Davage.' As the door closed, he looked at his watch. 'Nearly three o'clock. Pooley, let's take a stroll around the dean's garden and talk about where we've got to. Boyd, write up your notes.'

Pooley was not averse to a sunlit saunter in pleasant surroundings, but his work ethic interfered with his enjoyment on this occasion. As he observed afterwards to Amiss, he had had clever superiors and stupid superiors, but he'd never had one who thought half-an-hour's work called for a long break.

Godson, of course, had no intention of discussing anything other than the garden. The stroll turned into a veritable horticultural orgy, with Godson obsessively pointing out to Pooley plants of which he had superior equivalents at home.

'See that camellia?'

'Yes, sir. It's very beautiful.'

'Not a patch on mine. The thing with camellias is you've got to mulch them, and when you've mulched them you've got to mulch them again and again with peat, leaf mould and hop manure: I'm a great believer in varying the diet. You simply can't overdo the mulching. As I always say to people in the Camellia Society, it's no good complaining if you don't put the work in. And that's what I do rain or shine. It's a bad day when I can't put in my four hours in the garden.'

'I thought carnations were your speciality, sir.'

'Yes, indeed. But there's more to life than carnations. You

should see my roses, for instance. I'm thinking that this year I might show them too.'

For almost an hour they strolled in the sun. Interrupted every few moments with horticultural chatter, Pooley was unable to keep even his own mind on the case. He tried to interest Godson in the matter of the Roper memorial, now completed and under a tarpaulin, but he failed. Godson was far too exercised about the manner in which some of the shrubbery had been damaged by the digging of the foundations to pay any attention to the reasons for this tragedy.

After almost an hour, the garden had been examined thoroughly and Godson suggested a return to the palace. 'You go and rustle up some tea and get Boyd to track down that double-barrelled-name fella. He was told I'd want him mid-afternoon. We'll see him at four-fifteen and then we'll call it a day.'

It did not take Godson long to elicit from Fedden-Jones that he knew nothing, that he couldn't think why anybody would murder Flubert, but that then again he couldn't imagine why he would commit suicide and that he was vague about the politics since he didn't worry too much himself about what happened at Westonbury owing to his concerns being primarily cosmopolitan. The superintendent shrugged as he left. 'Waste of time,' he announced. 'Boyd, we'll look at the final forensic evidence at the station in the morning. Tell that Trustrum fellow to be here at two-thirty and the female canon at three-thirty. With a bit of luck that should wrap it all up. I'm off now. 'Bye.'

'This is so frustrating, I could scream. Godson makes no effort to tease anything out of them.'

'Are you going to have a go?'

'Can you put in a good word for me with Fedden-Jones and Davage? I'd like to see both of them before two-thirty tomorrow.'

'Leave them to me.'

* * *

'Dominic? Hello. It's Robert Amiss.'
'Ah, Robert. Good morning.'
'All this is very disagreeable, isn't it? I mean quite apart from poor Jeremy.'
'Damned inconvenient, frankly. Do you know that young plod had the nerve to tell me I should postpone my visit to Paris for a few days?'
'Do you mean the redhead? Detective Sergeant Pooley?
'Yes.'
'Actually, Dominic, there's more to him than you might think. He's a friend of mine. Staying at the palace at present and just giving the local coppers a hand. And a very unusual background for the police. Doesn't want it known, but his father's an earl.'
'Are you serious?'
'Absolutely.'
'Is he . . . ?' Fedden-Jones sounded quite faint. 'Is he the heir?'
'No, just the younger son. But remember not to tell anyone. Even the superintendent doesn't know. He wants to avoid jealousy. He's told me that if his colleagues knew he was an old Etonian, let alone an honourable, his life would be impossible.'
'Well, well, well. Thank you, Robert. It helps to know one can expect some decent standards of behaviour.' Fedden-Jones put down the phone and rushed away to consult Debrett.

'Cecil? It's Robert Amiss. Please be nice to that young policeman. He's a friend of mine.'
'Do you mean the pretty one with the red-gold hair?'
'Sergeant Ellis Pooley, that's the one.'
'Ooh, it'd be no trouble being nice to her. Do you think she'd like it as much as I would?'
'Ellis is very reticent. I don't know his proclivities. But watch out, Cecil. It doesn't do to proposition the police.'
'I can see you've led a sheltered life if you think one shouldn't proposition the boys in blue. But I can fantasize, can't I? Now let me see. Ellis of the red-gold hair and eyes

of blue. Of course, Elinor Glyn.' He giggled. 'Tell Sergeant Elinor she can come up and see me any time.'

As Amiss put the phone down, his mobile rang.

'Find out what Tilly the Terrible thinks is going on.'

'How the hell do I do that?'

'Christ, I don't know. Flutter your eyelashes, wiggle your bum, do whatever's necessary.' The phone went dead.

Amiss decided on a frontal assault. He rang Tilly, requested advice on a personal matter and was granted an audience over a morning orange juice.

'Since I came here,' he began, 'I've been thinking about the service at St John the Evangelist's.'

She looked excited. 'I hadn't realized you went to that. Were you saved?'

'I can't say I was. It was all so new to me, you know. But I was moved. Very moved. Yet with me these things take time. I have been reading the Bible and trying to see the light, but it's a difficult path.

'But now with this terrible, terrible event it makes one think even more. How could someone who has dedicated his life to Jesus as had Canon Flubert possibly do such a terrible thing? If he could do it, does it not make you question the whole basis of your faith?'

'Certainly not. Nothing could make me do that. In any case, Canon Flubert was not saved. He was not there for Jesus. Canon Flubert was there for decadence and self-indulgence and the sin of sodomy.'

There were limits to Amiss's tolerance for his own hypocrisy. 'I don't think he was. I found him to be a good man who loved music.'

She looked at him darkly. 'You don't understand the forces of Satan. It is Jesus we are supposed to love. Not anything earthly.'

'But surely to love religious music is to love God?'

'Music is a means, not an end as it was for that man. You must try to avoid associating with people like that. Only through the born-again can you find the path to Jesus.'

She leaped up and strode over to a pile of tapes on a shelf beside the television set. Having sorted through the lot and dithered over a couple, she selected one and took it to Amiss.

'You must watch this. It is a compilation of some of the greatest preachers now alive, including the Reverend Oral Roberts, whom Norm and I had the privilege of hearing in his very own church last month. He was awesome. Awesome. Play this tape again and again and he will help connect you to the Internet of God.'

Amiss thanked her, asked some polite questions about their American experiences and then asked artlessly, 'So now that you've had time to reflect, what are you and the dean hoping to do here? Having seen and been impressed – I may say awe-struck – by the vibrancy of your old church, I assume you intend great things.'

'Indeed we do, but don't forget that in Battersea Norm could make his decisions unhampered and we had as well the inspiration of Bev, a man touched by God – yeah, a God-given inspiration. We are all poor vessels, but Bev is stronger than most of us. Jesus speaks through him.'

'You must miss him.'

'We do, but he will find time to help us.'

'So you are becoming clear about your plans for the cathedral?'

'We prayed to the Holy Spirit to help us make holy decisions about how to bring holy government into this place. And we see the way. Our holy task is to make this a place of transformation for all the people of Westonbury.'

'It won't be easy, will it? Not with the forces of reaction that exist here.'

She looked at him suspiciously. 'A strange remark from someone who works for Bishop Elworthy.'

'I am his humble research assistant, Mrs Cooper. I have nothing to do with his opinions.' As Amiss was to remark later, amateur sleuthing seemed to require him unpleasantly often like Peter to deny his friends and like Judas to betray them – or at least appear to betray them. Warming to his role, he added, 'It doesn't seem to me that the bishop is suited for his job.'

'Suited for his job? It is worse than that.' She gazed at him soulfully. 'Do you know the dean said to him, "Do you believe in hell?" and he replied, "In a very real sense, yes; but it is a hell of loss – not a hell of fire."'

Her eyes burned. 'That is heresy.'

'But isn't the Church of England supposed to be a broad church. Tolerant of differences of opinion and all that.'

'There are some things on which there is only one opinion, as God made clear when he struck York Cathedral with lightning because a bishop denied the truth of the resurrection.'

Amiss decided to take a risk. 'Wouldn't you be happier in another church?'

She responded angrily. 'God wants us to bring this church to the path of virtue. We cannot leave it to the infidels, the heretics and the sodomites. He has shown us that by slaying one of those very sodomites.'

'Do I understand you are suggesting that God hanged Jeremy Flubert?'

'He moves in mysterious ways his wonders to perform, doesn't he? What happened to that man will be an example to others like him who might wish to stand in the way of the Lord's work of removing sin from this cathedral and replacing it by grace.'

'Where are you going to start?'

'With God's help we must persuade the chapter to agree to do what has to be done. Out with the choir – instead we will have relevant services and people singing new, vibrant, happy music.'

She clapped her hands gaily. 'And now I must tell you, because you were kind enough when we first met to show an interest in my little creative endeavours, that in America I found new inspiration for my tiny songs. What they understand there is that Jesus is in everything, and that we must not reserve him for the solemn occasions. That truth came to me when I heard a wonderful song called "Drop-kick me, Jesus, through the goal posts of life"!'

'Come again?'

'It's about football, you see. "Drop-kick me, Jesus, through the goal posts of life,"' she sang. 'Isn't that wonderful? If you think positively like that, then Jesus is everywhere. So I made up this little song of my own. Hold on, let me get my guitar.'

This was even worse than Amiss had feared. Dully he awaited his fate, trying hard to look pleasantly anticipatory when she arrived back with an instrument which she commenced strumming vigorously. 'I think I'm ready.'

'Oh, good.'

And to a hippity-hoppity tune she sang in an irritatingly childish voice:

'It takes just a minute to clean your teeth
The mornings and the nights.
It takes just a minute to pray to Christ
And set your soul to rights.

'So clean your teeth for Jesus
And wash away the dirt;
Put the holy brush to work
Scrub, scrub until you hurt.'

She beamed at him. 'Now for the chorus:

'Scrub, scrub for Jesus,
Remove that devil's plaque.
Scrub till there's nothing left that's dark
Scrub, Scrub, Scrub.'

She threw her head back and trilled joyfully, 'I'll play the chorus again, and you can sing along.'

Amiss had reached his limit of tolerance. 'Sorry, I'm afraid I can't carry a tune,' he lied. 'But you sing it again for me.'

Fearful lest she have another up her sleeve, Amiss stood up as Tilly finished the chorus and reluctantly put down her guitar. 'I must get back to my duties, I'm afraid. Are you composing anything at present?'

'I'm working on "I'm going to wash that Mr Devil right out of my hair in a lather of Jesus shampoo".'

'That sounds most promising. Now I'll be on my way.'

She shook her head archly. 'Not so fast. First we must kneel down together and say a little prayer.'

'It's not just that she's mad,' said Amiss peevishly to Pooley as they peeled potatoes, 'it's that she's boring. She's the most boring fucking woman I've ever had to spend any time with. Ten minutes in her company and I'd almost settle for her ghastly husband in preference. "Scrub, scrub for Jesus," indeed. I'm just waiting for her to come up with: "Jesus is my toilet bowl,/He flushes my sins away."'

'I think it's been done.'

Amiss threw another potato into the colander. 'However, I owe her something. I watched a bit of the happy-clappy tape before you came in and it promises hours of fun. My favourite lines so far are: "Mr Devil, don't put your tribulations on me: I intend to prosper right in your face" – as, indeed, all these preachers seem to do.'

The telephone rang. 'Canon Fedden-Jones for you, Ellis.'

'Was it you told him about my father?'

'Of course. You need all the friends you can get here.'

Pooley grimaced. 'You know how much I hate –'

'Now don't be silly. I know you don't want them to know about it in the rozzers' canteen, but this is different. As Jack rightly says, whatever you've got you should flaunt when it suits you.'

'Um.' Pooley sounded grouchy. 'Well I admit it worked. He was all over me. In fact he's insisted we talk over lunch at his house tomorrow. Apparently he knows my brother-in-law and two of my cousins.'

'Excellent. Now, why don't you ring Davage? I'm sure he'll be anxious to see you too.'

Pooley looked at him in deep suspicion. 'What did you tell him?'

'Nothing really. Just that in secret you're as camp as a row of pink tents.'

15

'Why aren't you at lunch with Fedden-Jones?'

'I'm on my way. I just had to call in to see you and get Davage off my chest.'

'H'm! Really? He went that far?'

Pooley flushed. 'Have you ever been in his house?'

'Couple of times.'

'It's extraordinary.'

'I really do not understand, Ellis, how a policeman contrives to live such a sheltered life. What the hell did you expect to see in the house of a camp, high Anglican canon who doubles as an expert on high Victorian art?'

'Well, I wasn't surprised at his drawing room. All those knick-knacks and bits of kitsch. And after the initial shock I didn't mind the way he dresses. If a man wants to wear a purple velvet kaftan in his own house, one must be broad-minded. It's his business. But I was horrified by some of the rest of it. What he's got in his . . . I don't know what to call it . . . study, I suppose . . .'

Amiss grinned. 'Go on, Ellis. Spit it out. I know what it says on the door: "Playroom"!'

'Yes. That was it. I hate to think what he gets up to there. All those divans and cushions . . .'

'Did you enjoy the wall decorations?'

'How could he? All those . . .' – his nose wrinkled in distaste – 'hunks – and in the middle of them that huge portrait of the pope. He's depraved.'

'You sound like Tilly. What upset you so much?'

'It demonstrates an obsessiveness about sexuality which might just be normal in a fifteen-year-old girl – though I may say that if she were my daughter, I would be most perturbed if she had such posters. Some of those men were naked.'

'Did you cop an eyeful of the Chippendales calendar?'

Pooley exhaled sharply. 'I certainly did . . . And, of course, that wasn't all. There were those extraordinary objects he showed me.'

'Go on.'

'The cardinal's hat; the nun's wimple. I really don't know what the Church of England is coming to if you get that sort of stuff in a house in a cathedral close.'

'You haven't mentioned his greatest treasures. Didn't he show you what was in the glass case in the corner?'

'Fortunately, he did not. And I'm probably glad he didn't.'

'Hah! He obviously spotted your panic. And so, my dear Ellis, you've missed a private view of a splendid pair of Queen Victoria's knickers, for which he recently paid a substantial sum at an auction of royal memorabilia. It ranks as high in his esteem as the skullcap of Pius IX, who is the pope about whom he squeals most enthusiastically because he liked his macho stance on infallibility. I trust he didn't lay a finger on you.'

Pooley smiled reluctantly. 'I have a feeling that I disappointed him rather.'

'Did you get anything out of him?'

'No, not specifically. Not anything more about Flubert's death anyway. But I'm pretty convinced now that he knows a lot more than he's telling. It just doesn't ring true that he's talking as if he would walk away from this cathedral without a backward look and not fight the good fight. It makes no sense.'

'Well, get Dominic talking about him. They hate each other's guts. Your difficulty there will be to get him off the *Almanach de Gotha* and onto matters of more pressing concern.'

'I hate all that stuff.'

'I know you do, Ellis. You're an upright, honourable soul and it does you credit. But you must approach these people with a bit more of your sense of humour operating. If you ask me, your trouble is that deep down you're a snob. You're not easily shocked by anything the criminal classes get up to, but you expect propriety from the middle and upper.'

'You may be right. OK, I'll go off now to Fedden-Jones and I'll try very hard to take everything in my stride.'

'One tip.'

'Yes?'

'If he's wearing his monogrammed slippers, make a point of asking him where he got them. It'll save him having to find some excuse for imparting the information.'

'Don't tell me. They were embroidered for him by Princess Diana.'

'Close. Close. At all events, you'll be relieved to hear, neither popes nor naked men had anything to do with them.'

'Got to be suicide. No motive for murder.'

'But, sir. Surely –'

'Look here, Pooley. We've got nothing from anyone, have we? Trustrum and Wolpurtstone were even less use than the others. There's no explanation except that Flubert – being a musician and a bit of a recluse – was so highly strung that he became overwrought by his conversation with the dean and decided to make a dramatic gesture.'

'But I'm sure if we push the canons we'll get some more information. I've only had a chance to talk to a couple of them privately, but I feel it in my bones that there's much more going on than they've talked about. We just need time.'

Godson shrugged. 'It's all the same to me. Tell you what, I won't close the case until Monday. That gives you two days to nose around and see if you find out anything useful.'

'May I have your number in case anything important or urgent develops?'

'My home number? H'm, I suppose so. But I've a great deal of work to do this weekend reducing the straggling shoots on the camellias. Be clear that important means important and urgent means urgent.' He scribbled on the notebook Pooley proffered. 'Understood?'

'Understood, sir.'

'Come on, Boyd. You can give me a lift home.' And pausing only to wish Pooley a good weekend, Godson was gone.

'You look dazed.'

'I'm more angry than dazed,' said Amiss. 'I suppose I just can't believe that any senior policeman would be so irresponsible. How in hell did he get to be a superintendent?'

'Maybe he used to spend on his job the time he now spends on his garden. It's not really true to describe him as lazy; he's just opted out at work.'

'He mustn't be allowed to get away with this. I can't bear the thought that poor Jeremy committed suicide, but it would be even more unbearable to think that there's a chance he was murdered horribly and that no one can be bothered finding out who did it.'

'Well at least Godson's postponed closing the case – though I don't know how much help that is. After all, the only cloak for my activities is as his unofficial assistant. When he stops, presumably I stop. If they wouldn't open up to me when I had the cloak of officialdom, why should anyone talk when I revert to being a private citizen?'

Amiss felt depressed. 'I don't know. Let's go out and get drunk and perhaps some inspiration will descend. David won't be back until late this evening, so nothing holds me here.'

Pooley jumped up. 'Good idea. We could do with a relaxing dinner somewhere. I'll just go and change.'

'Before you do, let me just try Jack. Now where did I put that bloody – ?'

As he spoke, the wall telephone rang. Amiss picked it up. 'Bishop Elworthy's residence.'

'Well?'

'What do you mean, "Well?" About what specifically are you welling?'

'Has Ellis found whodunit? And incidentally, why didn't you answer your mobile? I've rung you several times.'

'Temporarily mislaid. I'll pass you over to him.'

Pooley gave a fluent, comprehensive but economical account of the superintendent's investigations, which came to an abrupt end as he reported that the case would be closed on Monday unless he found some new evidence. There was a pause. 'No. We're going out shortly.'

A moment later he put the phone down.

'What happened?'

'She's starting a meeting in a few minutes and wanted to ring back in an hour, but when I said we were going out she said, "I'll ring tomorrow," and hung up. Does she ever say things ordinary people say? "Hello" or "goodbye", for instance?'

'No. Jack regards such social niceties as a waste of her valuable time. What did she want to ring back about?'

'She didn't say.'

'I expect she's thinking. She *was* listening to you, wasn't she?'

'There was no reaction, except a grunt towards the end.'

'It has to be said in her favour,' said Amiss grudgingly, 'that when she listens, she listens and when she thinks, she thinks.'

'Not making much progress, are you?'

'If there's one thing I hate more than somebody who rings me an hour before I normally wake, it's one who does so in order unreasonably to chide me. Considering the constraints under which Ellis and I are operating, I think we've done as well as we possibly could.'

'Skip the self-congratulation. You have to do better. Got to speed things up. Ellis has less than a week's leave to go, and if we're not careful, it'll end up with the case formally closed, you two having come up with no alternatives and Ellis leaving just at a time when further bloodshed is likely.'

'So you think Jeremy was murdered?'

'I don't know, but I think his violent death is more than likely to be followed by another. Everyone – or nearly everyone – is lying. When the truth comes out it will not be pretty, but we'd better find it sooner rather than later.'

'What do you mean, "we"?'

'I mean, "we". I'm about to take a hand. Catalyst.'

'Who? Which?'

'Me.'

'True. You are frequently a catalyst. Indeed I might go as far as to say far too frequently. Could you be more precise?'

'Got to shake things up. Clearly you two can't sort it out without help. Is David in tonight?'

'Um . . . yes . . . I think so. What day is today?'

'Saturday, you dimwit.'

'He'll be here. The reception for the fund raisers was cancelled as a mark of respect to Jeremy.'

'Good. Are you listening?'

'Yes, yes, I'm listening,' said Amiss testily. He turned over and moved the telephone to his other ear.

'Right. Here are your instructions. "Action this day," as Churchill used to write on memoranda. Tell David he's giving a dinner party this evening in honour of the dean, Tilly the Tosspot and the chapter – oh, and me.'

'Are Ellis and I invited to this?' asked Amiss coldly.

'Yes, of course. After all, you'll be preparing it.'

'What is its purpose?'

'Stirring things up. Put all these people in a pressure cooker, stick the lid on tight and see what happens.'

'An explosion, probably.'

'Quite.'

'And do you expect me tamely to agree to this?'

'Of course.'

'I've done many things for you which I had reservations about, but even you have not until now had the gall to demand that I prepare dinner for ten to satisfy a whim.'

'What do you mean "whim"? This is a strategic decision. Besides, you've got Ellis to help.'

'On what scale would you like this entertainment?'

'Did you ever see a film called *Babette's Feast*?'

'I did indeed. To the best of my recollection, it involved someone spending a substantial legacy and months of organization and preparation on a dinner party for depressed Scandinavians.'

'Well, we'll have to cut the corners a bit, but think in those terms. Push the boat out. We want to seduce them into indiscretion. Got the idea?'

'I haven't woken up sufficiently to know whether I have or not. All I know is that I am lying here feeling cross but resigned.'

'Good. I'll see you at seven. Summon them for seven-thirty.'

Amiss burrowed under the bedclothes, to be interrupted half an hour later by Pooley and a cup of tea. Pooley responded to Amiss's aggrieved account of the instructions from Cambridge with surprising equanimity.

'She's right, Robert. This is not an orthodox investigation, so we might as well be unorthodox. Amateur sleuths have to take advantage of the weapons they've got. Look upon this as Nero Wolfe getting Archie Goodwin to deliver all the suspects to his study.'

'I don't recall Nero Wolfe expecting Archie Goodwin to make them dinner.'

'Oh, stop crabbing.' Pooley took a notebook from his pocket. 'Come now, we'll decide on the menu and make the list. I need to drop in at the station and spend some time on the telephone, so you can do the shopping. But I'll be back in plenty of time to help you prepare dinner.'

'We haven't any guests yet.'

'You're the diplomat. You'll find a way of getting them here.'

Amiss sat up, laughed and took a sip of tea. 'What a shame you were born too late to be sent out to run India. Very well, then. Sit down, Sergeant Pooley, and let's plan the menu.'

As Pooley perched on the end of the bed, the phone rang.

'Caterers by appointment to the Empress Troutbeck,' said Amiss.

'I'll bring all the booze, the cheese and the caviar.'

'Caviar?'

'Someone brought me lots from Iran the other week. We'll have blinis.'

The phone went dead. Amiss laughed again. 'I'm mollified. The old bag has an unerring ability to notice when she's gone too far and you're really fed up with her, and then to put things right in grand style. OK, let's get planning.'

Interrupted by just one more instruction – 'Get little

Wolpurtstone in to help; she must be at a loose end without her shamans and lezzies' – the menu and shopping list proved surprisingly painless. Amiss looked with deep admiration at the list Pooley handed him, written in handwriting as clear as type and divided into five categories of shopping to ensure maximum efficiency. 'I don't know why I'm the personal assistant, Ellis. You'd be any tycoon's delight.'

'But I wouldn't keep him as happy as you would, Robert. You make people feel good, while I struggle not to show my irritation.'

'You mean I'm more of a creep than you. Pity it isn't a more marketable commodity.'

'It would be if you could bring yourself to boast of interpersonal skills. Now stop jabbering. It's eight-fifteen and you'd better get a move on. You're the one that has to break this news to the bishop.'

'Of course I wouldn't dream of going against Jack's wishes. But why does she want this dinner party?'

'She feels that the simple act of breaking bread together . . . I speak figuratively,' added Amiss, remembering the caviar, 'might help ease the obstacles to communication.'

'Of course, of course. I should have thought of this myself. After all none of these people is bad. It is just that the dean is perhaps a little overzealous and the others perhaps rather too set in their ways.'

Amiss smiled at him affectionately. 'You really are a Christian, aren't you, David? Jesus couldn't have put it more charitably.'

The bishop looked worried. 'No, no. You are too kind. Those that say I am feebly well meaning are probably more accurate.'

'Either way, you're happy about the dinner.'

'Very. And it is most kind of you to offer to organize it. Had there been time I would have brought in caterers, but I will of course pay for everything. Now where is my wallet?'

'Don't worry. I promise I'll bill you afterwards.'

'I'm so sorry I can't help. But I'll be back shortly after six and I would hope to be of some use to you then in some unskilled job – chopping carrots or something.' And with a sweet smile and a goodbye stroke to Plutarch, the bishop retired from the kitchen to change from tracksuit into canonicals.

Amiss tailored the invitations to the recipients. To the dean he explained that the bishop apologized profusely for the short notice, but hoped the Coopers would be kind enough to forgive him and agree to be guests of honour at an informal supper that evening to be attended by the inhabitants of the close: it was, he said, a celebration of neighbourliness. The dean sounded positively touched, and agreed immediately.

He announced to Davage the happy news that Lady Troutbeck was coming to stay and His Lordship was throwing a dinner party, which though nominally in honour of the dean, was really for her: the response was ecstatic. Trustrum didn't like the idea for the predictable reasons – he was already looking forward to his Saturday pork chop – but he grudgingly agreed that in the interests of harmony, he should turn up. Fedden-Jones havered for a moment because of his commitment to a supper party in town, but excited at the thought of seeing the baroness again, concluded that he was sure Moira Gloucestershire would understand and forgive him.

When it came to Alice, Amiss simply rang up and said, 'Help.' Her initial eager desire to come to his aid was dampened by the discovery that he wanted assistance in preparing a dinner in honour of the dean which he also expected her to attend. Forgiveness was one thing, she pointed out, but it was a bit early to expect her to forget he had given her a nasty bruise over her right ear and accused her of being a Satanist. However, as Amiss had expected, she was a pushover for an appeal to her better nature. It took him only a few minutes to convince her that the death of Jeremy Flubert required the dean and chapter to sink their differences and work towards the common good: within half an hour he was in her car and bowling along to the supermarket.

16

The day turned out to be surprisingly pleasant. Homely discussions around the supermarket distracted both Alice and Amiss from their apprehensions about the evening, and when Pooley joined them for lunch he found her laughing and drinking white wine without any evident signs of guilt about self-indulgence.

Having heard from Davage that Fedden-Jones had been babbling about the well-born policeman, Amiss had met the issue head-on. 'You remember the red-haired sergeant you met yesterday?'

'Just about. He didn't say anything except "hello" and "goodbye".'

'Well, in his private life he's my close friend Ellis Pooley, who's staying with me at the moment, so you'll meet at lunch time today. You have much in common quite apart from a refusal to use your courtesy titles.' He went on to dilate on the principle and selflessness that had caused Pooley to extricate himself from a background of privilege, hinted delicately at great domestic resentment at his becoming a policeman and did not pass on the information that the reactionary but generous Lord Pooley had forgiven his son sufficiently to set him up financially for life.

'You've met Canon Wolpurtstone,' said Amiss as Pooley arrived in the kitchen. 'Now meet Alice. Alice, meet Ellis. You have in common deep shame about a background for which Dominic Fedden-Jones would have sold his soul.'

They shook hands and smiled at each other rather shyly: Alice actually blushed. But jollied along by Amiss, the two of them relaxed over lunch, gossiped about the ghastliness of county society and then settled down companionably to prepare vegetables.

At 6.30 the doorbell rang long, loudly and several times. 'That'll be Jack,' said Amiss. 'She always rings as if attempting to acquaint the deaf with the news that their house is on fire.'

The bishop put down the cutlery and rushed for the dining-room door. 'Let me greet her.' He returned beaming. 'Doesn't she look wonderful?'

Amiss gazed at the voluminous kilt, the green velvet jacket, the cascade of white ruffles and the enormous Celtic brooch. 'What are we celebrating?'

'Burns Night. Yes, yes, I know it was a few months ago, but I haven't had time to mark it this year so I thought this as good an opportunity as any.'

'I thought you were unrelievedly English.'

'Half Campbell on my mother's side.'

'Suitably warlike. But excellent taste in formal wear, I grant you.'

'I think she looks marvellous,' said the bishop. 'Now, Robert, will you look after Jack? I must change.'

'Put on your purple waistcoat, David. We'll cut a dash together.'

Pooley and Alice were doing efficient things in the kitchen with various pots.

'Smells excellent,' said the baroness. 'Good evening, Ellis. Now who is this?'

'Canon Wolpurtstone.'

'Alice, please.'

The baroness smiled benignly. 'And you must call me Jack.'

She took two large jars out of her handbag and handed them to Pooley. 'Here's the caviar – which we will refer to as fish roe for fear of shocking the dean. Right, what are we eating?'

'Blinis and sour cream with the caviar; a vast leg of lamb with baby leeks, mangetouts –'

'Don't like them.'

'So don't eat them,' said Pooley with a touch of asperity. '– asparagus tips, ratatouille, carrots and Lyonnaise potatoes; followed by Elizabeth Moxton's Posset.'

'Ooh, yummy. I'm surprised your puritan soul would countenance anything so fattening and self-indulgent, Ellis.'

'Just following orders. Besides, all this is very modest by comparison with Babette's feast.'

'True, but she had more time to prepare.'

Alice came in hesitantly. 'I'm a little worried, Robert. Aren't the Coopers teetotal?'

'Yes,' said Amiss.

'But there's a lot of white wine in the posset and you've just poured almost a bottle of red into the roasting pan.'

'Yes, but they're not recovering alcoholics or anything like that. It's not like vegetarians. Teetotallers don't mind alcohol in food: it's just that they don't actually drink. Adding a little wine to cooking is fair enough: it improves the taste and just might cheer them up a little.'

'Quite.' The baroness turned to Alice. 'Stop fretting, my dear. Let us leave the men to get on with the little last-minute feminine touches. Can you help me carry provisions from the car?'

It took two expeditions to retrieve the cheese and the drink. The baroness directed Alice to carry cartons into the dining room and drawing room, while she transported to the kitchen the champagne and white wine, which had been sitting in the boot in a large basin of ice. 'Do something with ice buckets, somebody,' she called, as she sped out the back door. 'I must see to the punch.'

She returned bearing an immense Georgian silver punchbowl, and removed the covering film to reveal within a pile of fruit and fresh mint. 'Courtesy of Mary Lou, who sends her love to you both. I'll take this to the drawing room and add the lemonade.'

'How very kind of you to have gone to so much trouble, Jack,' said the bishop, as the hosts stood in the drawing room awaiting their first guests.

'I thought it the least I could do for the nondrinkers. Oh and by the way, there isn't that much of it, so FHB.'

'FHB?'

'Family Hold Back. We can make do with champagne.'

'My goodness, this really is turning into a feast. It reminds me of high table at a rich college. I hope the dean won't be shocked.'

'We'll just keep telling him it's in his honour. That should draw his sting.'

'I hope you're right,' said Pooley. 'From what I've seen of him one might as well reason with a hornet. Champagne, anyone?'

The Coopers arrived at 7.30 on the dot, he glowering suspiciously, she all smiles and gush. 'What a charming idea this is, Bishop Dave. Most thoughtful. Most thoughtful. Although of course our little celebration cannot but be marred by our sadness over the wicked act of that unfortunate. May God forgive him.'

As she delivered herself of this spectacular piece of crassness, the bell rang again, allowing Amiss to escape the temptation to strike her. At the front door were the canonical trio, all clad as orthodoxly as the dean and all clearly on their best behaviour. He led them through.

The baroness took command. 'Hello, hello. Welcome. Delighted to meet you two,' she said to Davage and Trustrum. She clapped Fedden-Jones on the back. 'What a jolly night out we had last week.

'Now, we have a little wine here for the drinkers and a simple fruit concoction of my own for the others.'

She smiled gaily. 'Hands up the nondrinkers.'

The Coopers obliged. 'Right. Ellis, sort out the others. Now, Dean and Mrs Dean, come over here and examine my lemonade fruit punch. If you don't like the look of it, you can have water.'

The dean, who had appeared ill at ease since he first caught sight of Alice, made a big effort. 'How delicious this looks. My goodness, strawberries. I haven't had any of those since last year. Yes, please.'

'That's both of us, then,' said Tilly with a bright smile.

The baroness ladled punch into two large tumblers as Amiss and Pooley poured champagne for the others from bottles swathed in white cloths to conceal their identity. Davage, Fedden-Jones and Trustrum, who had been looking depressed, seemed to cheer up when they tasted the contents of their glasses; so indeed did the Coopers.

'Very delicious, I must say, Lady Troutbeck. Most refreshing.'

'What is it called?' asked Tilly. 'You must tell me how to make it.'

'We called it Granny's Punch in my family, and I'm afraid I'm honour bound to keep the recipe secret.' The baroness reached for their glasses. 'Have some more, Dean. And Mrs Dean, of course.'

By the time they sat down to dinner the mood was perceptibly lighter. Invited to say grace, the dean restricted himself to: 'For what we are about to receive, may the Lord make us truly thankful.' Offered a switch to water, he and Tilly opted to finish up the punch on the grounds that it would be a shame to waste it. Conversation had begun rather stilted and artificial, as might be expected of people required to be civil in almost impossible circumstances, but the dean's evident good humour caused his colleagues to relax. The blinis were delicious and allowed several minutes of appreciative oohing and aahing and reminiscences from Fedden-Jones of eating the dish in St Petersburg.

'You carve, David,' commanded the baroness, when Pooley came in bearing the splendid leg of lamb.

'Oh, dear. I'm not sure that I'll be able to do it.'

'Nonsense. The host must carve. It's tradition.'

Obediently, the bishop applied the knife uncertainly to the joint and began to cut slightly jagged slices, as Pooley and Amiss fussed around with plates and vegetable dishes. Suddenly there was a squeal, and the bishop stuck his finger in his mouth like a child.

'You've cut yourself,' said Alice, rushing to his side with her handkerchief.

'Doesn't matter,' offered the baroness cheerily. 'It'll mingle with the blood of the lamb.'

It was a tribute to the dean's equable mood that he chose to ignore this blasphemy. The baroness directed Pooley to take over carving, which he did with extreme competence.

Over the main course, Amiss, Davage and Fedden-Jones – the most practised social animals among the gathering – kept the focus on the Coopers, enquiring about their recent travels, their impressions of America and their assessment of the political scene there. There was a momentary upheaval when the dean began to denounce the Democrats as abortionists, but an astute question about the blurring of party boundaries got him back on benign track.

The dean, Amiss realized, was not at all stupid or ill-informed. Indeed there were moments when it was clear that had he not succumbed to the virus of fundamentalism, he might have been good company. Unfortunately – as became clear later on in the drawing room – the virulence of that virus was only temporarily in remission.

After dinner, it was the baroness who started the trouble. 'How much you must miss Canon Flubert. It will be difficult to find anyone to replace him, won't it?'

'I see no practical difficulty,' responded the dean. 'We need less and less of that kind of music and there are always freelance organists available.'

'You mean you're not proposing to replace him with a musician?'

Tilly snorted. 'Certainly not. Norm's mission is to make the church relevant to the world of today and bring souls to God.' She smiled patronizingly at her expectant audience. 'So that is why our dear Battersea colleague, the Reverend Bev Johns, a great fisher of souls, will be the new canon.'

Fedden-Jones's normal cautious mask slipped. He blurted out incautiously, 'You're joking, of course. Make that awful vulgar creature with the ponytail a canon? Why he actually told me at the bishop's consecration that he likes to be known as the Rev. Bev.'

'I have the utmost faith in the Reverend Mr Johns.' The

dean spoke stiffly, although his consonants were slightly slurred. 'He will give our proceedings an energy which they lack.'

'Over my dead body,' said Fedden-Jones. 'We're not having him, are we, colleagues?'

Davage and Trustrum failed to meet his eye. 'Cecil! Sebastian!'

Trustrum continued to look at the floor, but Davage came in bravely. 'I'm sorry, Dominic, but we mustn't rule anyone out. Sometimes one has to compromise.'

There was a long and uneasy silence, broken by Tilly, who moved further up the sofa until her body was touching Ellis Pooley's, giggled flirtatiously, put her hand on his thigh, gazed at him coquettishly and asked, 'And why is a nice boy like you not married?'

Pink with embarrassment, Pooley muttered something feeble about never having met the right woman, eliciting a skittish rejoinder about how different things would have been had Tilly been free, which caused the dean to look thunderously in her direction.

'We are a little gathering of confirmed bachelors and spinsters, aren't we?' tittered Davage, ill-advisedly holding out his glass to Amiss for a refill of port. 'What is it about the air of Westonbury, I wonder?'

The dean scowled. 'It is better to marry than to burn.'

It was hard not to feel that the conversation was deteriorating. Worse followed shortly when the effects of alcohol removed whatever control Davage normally kept on his malice. 'How do you feel about being the only straight in a chapter of queers?'

'What did you say?'

'You know about us. But it must have been a shock to come back from Bible-thumping country to find lesbians affirming in the cathedral.'

The dean stood up slowly. 'Have I heard you correctly? Are you telling me that those women worshipping idolatrously were also sexual abominations before God.'

''Fraid so,' tittered Davage. 'What you hit on there was a coming-out ceremony of the Wolpurtstone coven. And a pretty ghastly bunch they were too. I saw them coming out of the cathedral.' He shook his head. 'What an ugly crew.' He waved his glass in Alice's direction. 'I can't understand, I simply can't understand, Alice, why you don't leave those dreary, dumpy, frumpy dykes and hang out with lipstick lesbians.'

He leaned forward confidingly. 'Why don't you just find yourself a little church in London and make it a really chic centre for lesbians who know how to dress?'

The dean's attention had now been completely distracted from the sight of his wife patting the cheek of the increasingly miserable Pooley; he stormed over to Alice.

'Is this true? Were these women perverts?'

'They were lesbians, yes,' she said quietly.

'And are you one of their abominable number and therefore hateful in the eyes of the Lord?'

She remained silent.

'Answer me, woman. I insist on knowing if you are a degenerate.'

She looked him straight between the eyes. 'I refuse to answer such a question.'

The baroness came in cheerfully. 'Come now, Dean. I don't think you're right there. I was looking up the Old Testament only the other day to check on that fellow often quoted these days for his denunciation of homosexuals . . . What's his name?'

'Leviticus,' said the bishop.

'Well, I've scrutinized Leviticus thoroughly and he says absolutely nothing about lesbians. Now he's chock-a-block with prohibitions of a sexual kind – blokes are forbidden to do it with mothers, aunts, step-granddaughters, men and animals among others. His list of no-noes is as thorough as anyone could reasonably expect, but lesbians do not appear. So what's the problem?'

The dean ignored him. 'Answer me, woman.'

The bishop stood up. 'Dean, please. Canon Wolpurtstone is a guest in my house. She should be treated with courtesy.'

'She is a member of my chapter. I must know the answer

to this question. Are you or are you not that abomination – a woman who lies with women?'

She remained silent. The baroness jumped up. 'Oh, for Christ's sake, Dean, don't you realize the girl is as straight as the next man. She's doing her Lillian Hellman before Joe McCarthy's anti-Communist Senate committee – refusing to distance herself from her friends. Don't you realize she pretends to be a lezzie because she thinks they're victims and therefore she feels she must support and identify with them. An honest girl like that would tell you if she was one. The fact that she doesn't, means she isn't. Have you got that?'

The dean's bad temper magically disappeared. He patted Alice on the top of the head. 'That's a good wee girl,' he said. 'I'm glad to hear you're not an abomination.' He sat down again.

'A little more punch, Dean?'

'Why not?'

The port however was working its potency on Davage and unleashing further stores of mischief. He leaned forward. 'Have you had a chance to peek at Reggie Roper's memorial since you returned?'

The cloud chased the sun from the dean's features. 'Is it finished?'

'It certainly is. And I can tell you it lives up to all expectations. Pop down to the bottom of your garden, lift up the tarpaulin and you'll get a treat. It's just as Reggie wanted it.'

The dean began to glower. 'We should get rid of it.'

'Come on, Dean. Reggie paid you handsomely for tolerating his little whim. Think of all the lolly you got to spend on the cathedral.'

The word lolly distracted Tilly Cooper from further pressing her attentions on Pooley. 'Oh, yes. The lolly. And how wonderfully we will spend it on behalf of Jesus. Soon we will have the disco system, the strobe lighting, the pool for total immersion.'

She beamed at everyone, but the dean was unresponsive. 'It may be that we have been tempted by Satan. I must go home to pray. Come, woman.' He grabbed Tilly's hand and hauled her protesting from the sofa, muttered a few words of gratitude for the hospitality and without looking at any of his canons dragged his wife from the room.

The bishop returned from seeing them out to find the room plunged in despair.

'What is strobe lighting?' asked Trustrum.

'Flashing coloured lights as used in taverns where the young dance. You must have seen them on television,' said Davage wearily. 'Oh, sorry, I forgot. You don't have one. What Mrs Cooper seems to want is to have the cathedral full of dancing coloured lights which whirl around the whole area, while a modern sound system produces the sound of thump-thump music at about a thousand decibels – all in the name of Jesus, you understand.'

'She said something about a pool.'

'I expect higher authority may be able to block that, but I doubt if they can do anything about the lighting and the music.'

'Can't we stop it, Cecil?'

'You can try, Dominic. I'm afraid I doubt if we'll be able to prevail.' Davage stood up, staggered and then recovered himself. 'Excuse me, My Lord. Thank you and goodbye to you all.'

Fedden-Jones and Trustrum followed soon after.

'What a strange evening,' said Alice.

'With that mixture it's bound to be,' said the baroness robustly. 'You poor girl, what a ghastly lot of colleagues you've got.'

'In your place,' said the bishop, 'I have to say I would feel like looking for another job.'

'Another job! Oh, Bishop!'

'David, please.'

'David, I'm only here because your predecessor made me take the canonry. Please, please, will you find me somewhere else to go? Somewhere I can be useful.'

The bishop took her hand. 'My poor girl. You should not be here against your will. Talk to me about it tomorrow.'

She gave him a stunning smile. Pooley stood up. 'Let me walk you home.'

* * *

'Why are you blaming me?' The baroness stubbed out her cigar.

'You are being a little unfair, Robert,' said the bishop, visibly fighting the sleepiness brought on by champagne, claret and port. 'Jack has been a wonderful hostess. It's just a little unfortunate that Cecil Davage was so tactless, Dean Cooper so irascible, Fedden-Jones so distressed and –'

'And Tilly so trollopy.' The baroness drank some more brandy.

'You tell her why it's her fault, Ellis. I'm too drunk.'

'Robert may be a little overstating it, Jack. But I have to say that it was perhaps a little unscrupulous of you to slip alcohol to teetotallers.'

'Bollocks. What did you think I was doing, hauling all that punch-making paraphernalia from Cambridge, if it wasn't with a view to getting the dean drunk? Besides, I never told anyone it was nonalcoholic: that would have been dishonest. I merely described it as the punch for the nondrinkers.'

'What was in it?' asked Amiss.

'Pimms, obviously. Vodka-based Pimms because it doesn't taste, beefed up with more vodka, since on its own Pimms is a very mimsy drink.' She thought for a moment. 'Oh, yes, and I suppose it did get a certain extra kick from the alcoholic lemonade.'

'Sweet Jesus,' said Amiss. 'That can only be described as a drink that packed – as it were – a treble punch.'

'He's a big man. He'd need a treble punch.'

'What were those lines of Mark Twain?' asked Amiss dreamily. '"Never play poker with a man called Doc."'

'"Never eat at a place called Mom's,"' offered the baroness.

'To which I would add, "Never touch a punch called Granny's." Oh, yes, and that vital piece of advice I was given at St Martha's, "Never shag a neurotic."'

Pooley came in rather impatiently. 'But why did you lace the punch, Jack? What were you trying to achieve?'

'Sometimes I think you two shouldn't drink: it appears to affect your wits. I told you the purpose of this dinner was catalytic. Your investigations were stuck in a groove, and when you're stuck in a groove, the only thing to do is to bring in a rotovator to agitate everything and see what is churned up.

'Instead of bitching, you should be thanking me for having been the means of uncovering useful new information and some fruitful lines of investigation.'

Pooley – who always drank like a gentleman – poured himself a glass of water. 'She's right, Robert. I have to admit that some things are clear that weren't before.'

'Or unclear that were clear before,' proffered Amiss, amazed at his own grip on the proceedings.

'I'll take these in chronological order, as they emerged.' Pooley put up his thumb. 'One, Davage and Trustrum appear to be resentful allies of the dean.'

'No, no, hold it,' said the baroness. 'The first important thing to emerge was that Alice is not a lesbian.'

'It's not germane to the investigation.'

'Everything is germane to the investigation. Mind you, I could have told you that anyway. She was wholly resistant to my sexual signals. And believe me' – she smirked – 'I usually find nice, well-brought-up dykes melt when exposed to my rough-hewn charms. Anyway, it's now official.' She laughed. 'What a good moment that was!'

The bishop looked distressed. 'I was very worried there for Alice.'

'She's a lot tougher than she looks.'

'Two,' said Pooley firmly. 'As I said, Davage and Trustrum are going along with the dean and seem prepared to sell Fedden-Jones down the river for undisclosed reasons.'

'Three,' came in the baroness. 'Tilly Cooper has the hots for you, Ellis.'

'Four,' said Pooley, clearly anxious to move on, 'we know that Mrs Cooper is more of an ends than a means person, unlike her husband.'

'Five,' said the baroness, 'we now understand much more about the dean's conversion to fundamentalism. He is in sexual thrall to that little tart.'

Amiss, who was almost asleep, perked up. 'Is it common to screw people to bring them to Jesus?'

'A good question. An even better one is how common it is to screw them in the interests of justice. How about it, Ellis? Shouldn't you do your duty and see what pillow talk you can get out of Tilly?'

'I'd really rather not dwell on such a distasteful notion, if you don't mind, Jack. And now, I'm going to bed. Come on, Robert.' He raised his voice. 'What about you, David?'

The bishop awoke from his snooze. 'Oh, sorry. Sorry. Would anyone mind if I went to bed?' He looked at his watch. 'It's after one o'clock and I'll have to be alert tomorrow. Even if I pass up the running, I'll need to be up by seven-thirty. It is Sunday, after all.' He stretched. 'Thank you all for your wonderful work. My goodness, I'm tired.'

The baroness drained her glass and shook her head sadly. 'Puritans, puritans. I'm surrounded by puritans. Very well, then. Off you all go. I'll follow in a moment, when I've checked on Plutarch. Poor old girl. The only other Cavalier in the palace and you keep her consigned to the kitchen all evening. I will take her to bed with me in lieu of anything better.'

Amiss kissed her on the cheek. 'Just don't tell Leviticus.'

17

'Emergency meeting.'

Amiss emerged from a dream of great confusion – which featured *inter alia* the dean dressed in crusaders' chain mail declaring to a congregation of confused Mohammedans that they must convert to lesbianism – to find Pooley standing over him looking agitated. 'Wha . . . wha . . . what emergency?'

'I'll explain everything in the kitchen. Come on. Hurry up.'

The inhabitants of the palace – in various states of dishabille – assembled in the kitchen blearily and irritably to find to their horror that it was only just six o'clock.

'This had better be serious, young Ellis,' said the baroness. 'I may be an early riser, but I draw the line at being dragged out of bed at cockcrow on a Sunday morning when I've been carousing into the early hours.'

Pooley looked at her grimly. 'It's serious, all right, Jack, though not as serious as it might have been. No thanks to you.'

The baroness looked at him warily.

'Stop being minatory, Ellis, will you?' begged Amiss feebly. 'What is it? What's happened?'

'We almost had two more deaths – both drink-related.'

'Who?'

'What?'

'How?'

Pooley raised his hand to quell the agitated questions. It struck Amiss that he closely resembled a scoutmaster who had just taken over an unruly troop. 'Let me take this in sequence.

'I had a call fifteen minutes ago from Superintendent Godson. Tilly Cooper called the police about five to say she had woken up and realized the dean had gone out last night and not returned. A patrol car came round and found Cecil Davage lying unconscious in the cathedral with a broken arm in the midst of the debris of one of the chandeliers, which he seems to have lowered from the beam. There was a big box of matches by his side, so our working assumption is that he was intending to light the candles.'

The bishop went pale. 'He might have burned the cathedral down, the state he was in.'

Pooley held his hand up, this time reminding Amiss disloyally of a particularly autocratic traffic cop. 'They sent for an ambulance and reinforcements, and when Davage had been taken away they searched further afield for the dean. He was discovered unconscious beside the Roper memorial, which he seems to have been attacking with an axe. In the course of his exertions he apparently hit his head and concussed himself.

'He in turn was taken to hospital; the police and ambulance men are sanguine about both.'

Pooley surveyed them sombrely. 'And that's not all. I'm sorry to have to tell you, David, but the treasury's been burgled.'

The bishop had been looking miserable enough, but this news caused his face to twist in misery. 'Not the Great Staff?'

Pooley nodded. 'The most valuable croziers as well, I'm afraid. And all the rings and reliquaries.'

'Bugger,' said the baroness. 'But surely that means little Davage was a victim of burglars rather than being the cause of his own misfortunes?'

'It may be. But then why was he in the cathedral in the middle of the night? And what was going on with the chandelier?'

'Maybe . . .'

'Sorry, Robert. You'll have to excuse me. There's a car waiting outside to take me to the superintendent. I wouldn't have woken you so early if I hadn't had to leave the house.'

Amiss threw himself into a chair as the door shut behind Pooley. 'Shit!'

'Oops,' said the baroness. 'I'm feeling a bit guilty. Maybe I shouldn't have added the vodka. But it seemed such a good idea at the time.'

The bishop put his arm around her. 'You mustn't worry, Jack. Your intentions were of the best as always and we all make mistakes.'

'Besides,' added Amiss, 'whatever happened to Cecil isn't your fault. He, at least, knew what he was drinking.'

The bishop looked solemn. 'We must thank God that both these poor people look like recovering. Perhaps these unfortunate events will have the effect of bringing dean and chapter closer together. Now if you'll excuse me, I'll go and get ready.'

Amiss got up to follow him. 'I hand it to you, Jack. When you say catalyst you sure mean catalyst.' He looked back at her. She was sitting at the kitchen table with her chin on her fist; her hair was dishevelled, her flannelette nightie slightly awry and she bore a dejected expression. He felt sorry for her. 'Don't get too upset about it.'

'Upset? I'm not upset. I was just trying to think of some way of getting out of having to go back to St Martha's today. I hate to miss the fun.' She stood up and sighed. 'It's no good. Duty calls. I've a crowd of ravening scholars coming to lunch and I have to preside. You and Ellis are going to have to get on with things today on your own.'

Amiss – who was feeling decidedly seedy – only just restrained himself from giving her a swift kick as she bounded past him.

Called on by Canon Trustrum at an hour's notice to preach in place of the dean, the bishop was inspired. With no time to draft, redraft, worry or haver, he spoke simply and from his kindly heart. Whereas the dean had been threatening to give a sermon about the wickedness of despair, the bishop took as his text the last verse of 1 Corinthians 13: 'And now abideth faith, hope, charity, these three; but the greatest of these is charity.'

He began with a moving tribute to Jeremy Flubert, whom he told the congregation bluntly had either been murdered or had committed suicide in the house of God. 'Whether terrible violence was done to our brother, or for some reason he yielded to despair, we do not know – and may never know. But we do know as a congregation that we owe him our prayers and our gratitude for what he gave us selflessly through his passion for music.

'It can be difficult for many of us to understand those amongst us who are single-minded in their vocations. For Canon Flubert, as Joseph Addison put it, music was "the greatest good that mortals know,/And all of heaven we have below." For it was through music that he expressed himself as a man and as a priest. And which of us is to say that was wrong? Did not his gifts and his dedication bring priceless inspiration and solace to us all? Great music raises us to another plane. Elizabeth Barrett Browning wrote that "The music soars within the little lark,/And the lark soars." Music soared within Jeremy Flubert, and he brought us closer to God when he expressed it. May he rest in peace.'

Equally bluntly, the bishop informed his audience that more misfortunes had hit the cathedral that very morning in the shape of a couple of – as yet – unexplained accidents, one of which had resulted in the destruction of one of the great chandeliers.

'We have also had a burglary: many of our most prized possessions are missing from the treasury. And while I know that what matters is to lay up treasures in heaven rather than on earth, I still pray fervently that we may recover what we have lost, for we were but the guardians of beautiful objects made by artists to honour God.

'However, it is about people that I want to talk to you today. You will already have seen some speculation in the press about differences among those running our cathedral, and I will not lie to you and pretend it to be unfounded. In any walk of life, problems arise even between people of good will when they differ on the means to achieve the same ends.

The clergy may be known as men and women of God, but they are men and women, and as fallible as their secular siblings.'

He talked for a few minutes of the importance of understanding those with whom one worked, of giving each other the benefit of the doubt. 'Our broad church accommodates rather than accentuates difference, strives to be inclusive rather than exclusive and in so doing properly represents the English people at their best – tolerant, dutiful, well-meaning and with an affectionate respect for their history.

'I admit to being old-fashioned. For me our church is epitomized in all those little villages where for a thousand years the community has lovingly looked after its church, decorated it with flowers every week and has kept its bells ringing to praise God and call the faithful to worship. While on the average Sunday, such churches may contain perhaps only a few dozen worshippers, in times of national fear or disaster as well as national rejoicing they are full.

'English society may be very secular, but it is a secularism imbued with Christianity. The old-fashioned Church of England, the guardian of the noblest of English traditions, still has a great role to play in underpinning our sense of identity as a people and in extolling decent values: it should not be thrown out in the urge for modernization.'

At this moment, to Amiss's horror, an all-too-familiar shape emerged from behind the pulpit, stalked around to the front, launched herself upwards and swung on its edge until rescued by the bishop, who helped her onto the ledge. As she turned triumphantly and surveyed the congregation, a subdued titter broke out, to be followed by a horrified gasp from those close enough to see her drop a dead mouse in front of the bishop. She squatted, raised her right leg and begin washing intimate parts of herself vigorously.

The bishop picked up the corpse, placed it in his handkerchief and put it in his pocket. Then he stroked Plutarch and smiled at his embarrassed audience. 'My friends, in a moment I will try to recover my train of thought. In the meantime let me introduce my friend Plutarch, who bears the name of a great first-century Greek philosopher who mused much on the nature of the soul. Plutarch is rather Old Testament in her thinking, and inclined to favour the slaying of living creatures and bringing them into the cathedral as sacrifices. I have reasoned with her about this, but so far she remains steadfast in her determination to follow her traditional practices.'

Plutarch gave a mighty stretch and lay full-length in front of the bishop, who continued to stroke her absent-mindedly throughout the rest of his sermon.

'Plutarch indeed reminds us that respect for tradition needs to be tempered with reason and an openness to necessary change. There are many advantages in our English slowness and doggedness – not least that we have had perhaps the most stable society in the world during this past millennium.

'But there are deficiencies too, of which we need to be aware. We come under severe criticism for failing to adjust quickly enough to the new pressures of a multi-cultural society, to young people who are little adults before they're teenagers, to the technological pressures which are turning the world of work and leisure upside down and to the desperation of the underclass in parts of our great cities.

'Those young, energetic, evangelical clergy who take near-empty churches and turn them into a cross between a disco and a revivalist meeting are laughed at by many, but the Church of England needs those people too, for without such experiment there can be no renewal.

'Until the day I die I will be a lover of the King James Bible. I think we will do our children a great disservice if we impoverish them by denying them the chance of absorbing the wonderful language of the seventeenth century. I will not pretend I enjoy what seems to me the banality of later translations, but nor will I condemn them out of hand. It is better to bring the word of God and the hope of Christianity to people in simple language than not to bring it at all. Similarly, great religious music brings me enormous joy, but that does not mean I believe that popular music must be banned from the house of God.'

He tickled Plutarch behind an ear. Her amplified purr echoed around the cathedral and raised a general smile.

'My friends, today we pray for the soul of Canon Jeremy Flubert and for those of his colleagues who may be worried and distressed. I ask of you further that when you read of silliness and sin among the priests of your church, when you want to condemn them as old fogies or deride them as trendies, try to remember that they are just people. All a clerical collar says about anyone is that its wearer wanted to dedicate his fallible self to the service of his God.

'I leave you with a question from the Old Testament, from the book of Micah, who lived in the eighth century BC. Micah is known as a minor prophet, but I think him major, for he summed up in one simple question what to me is the essence of our religion – an essence which I believe is at the core of the Church of England. "What doth the Lord require of thee, but to do justly, and to love mercy, and to walk humbly with thy God?"'

'Not a dry eye in the house,' reported Amiss to the baroness. 'I don't think anything will make me believe in God, but as a result of that sermon I will pay my dues to the Church of England in future. David may be a rotten bishop when it comes to management or politics, but he's the sort of man who gets Christianity a good name.'

'H'm! That sermon sounds dangerously radical to me.'

'I have never known anyone as reactionary as you. You're regressing so fast you'll be back up Eve's fanny before you've finished.'

'And what's so bad about that? I'd rather be in Eve's fanny than in the European Union any day of the week. Now what else is happening?'

'The hospital won't let the cops talk to Cecil or the dean until late afternoon, so Ellis doesn't expect to be back before seven. David's stuck at a lunch with local dignitaries followed by tea with the bishop-next-door, so I'm going to chat up Trustrum and Fedden-Jones, console Alice and cook for tonight.'

'Include me in for dinner.'

'What about duty?'

'I'll have done what I have to. What'll we be having to eat?'

'Spam fritters, unless I can persuade Plutarch to catch us a toothsome rat.'

Fedden-Jones's answering machine explained that he was spending the day with friends in the country but would return on Sunday evening. Trustrum was so rattled that he invited Amiss to call on him at 12.30 for a glass of sherry. As he poured it, he said in a doom-laden voice, 'We've never had a burglary before.'

'Unless you count what happened in the sixteenth and seventeenth centuries? Let's look on the bright side. Things are better this time.'

'I'm not so sure about that. One concussed dean, one injured treasurer, one dead precentor and the loss of our valuable artefacts would have been a good haul even for the Lord Protector himself.'

Wintry wit gave way to gloom. 'The stolen goods might be retrieved, I suppose, but the chandelier is gone forever.'

'Presumably a craftsman can be found to duplicate it.'

'But it won't be the same. Don't you understand? It'll be a reproduction.'

'I daresay people won't notice.'

'I will notice. I will notice and I will mind. More sherry? I don't usually have a second glass – even on Sunday – but I will make an exception in this case.'

'Yes, please,' said Amiss, for whom the hair of the dog was proving very effective.

Trustrum resumed his seat. 'Mind you, I have got one piece of amusement out of all this tragedy. Just as I thought, all those fancy burglar alarms were a waste of money. I said we should keep our security men and was told I was out of date. Machines, apparently, were much more effective than people: electronics would do the job.'

'Is it a very sophisticated system?'

'It is certainly expensive and elaborate and no doubt difficult for an ordinary burglar to deal with, but anyone reasonably skilled in his profession who had access to the keys would, I imagine, have little trouble. In any case, Cecil must have turned the main system off when he went in to do whatever he went in to do. Perhaps the burglars forced him to switch off the treasury system as well. Who knows?'

He took a sip and sat up straight. 'But let us not mourn or speculate further on these distressing events. I have to say that I drew comfort from our bishop. I had not expected such a performance from him. I wonder if such a sermon might have caused the dean to have had a change of heart. Perhaps his accident will have the same effect; such happenings concentrate the mind.'

'Just before I go, Sebastian – curious about one thing. Why are you backing the dean over making the Rev. Bev a canon?'

Trustrum looked at his clock. 'Good heavens, I see it's just coming up to one. I'm so sorry, Robert, but you must forgive me. It is time to attend to my lunch and listen to *The World this Weekend*.'

Lunch was at Alice's house, where Amiss had never been before. She was hospitable and the place was cosy but it had an air of transience.

'I've never had my own home,' she explained. 'I've moved about too much since I left my parents. It would have been inappropriate to have anything nice in the place where I worked as a team vicar, and when I got here and realized what I was in for, I didn't have the heart to put much effort into making it my own, so most of my possessions are still at my old home.'

'I don't have any possessions at my parents' house, but I seem to have acquired singularly few.'

Alice smiled. 'But I do have some decent cooking equipment, there's a cheese soufflé in the oven and the salad is ready. Now would you like some white wine?'

'At what stage in your life did you become such a marvellous cook? That posset you made yesterday was wonderful.'

'This is not something I normally tell people, but I spent six months at a cookery school. It was the price I paid for being financed at university.'

'So far it's one I'm glad you paid. Think of it. It might have been flower arranging.'

'Don't mention that, please. I had a compulsory month of that in the summer after my O levels, when my parents were hoping I'd come to my senses and go to finishing school instead of staying on to do A levels. I hated every moment of it. I don't like torturing flowers.'

'Talk about poor little rich girl.'

She laughed. 'I shouldn't whinge. My parents are kind to me. They're just dull and unimaginative in a county kind of way.'

'Shades of what the bishop was talking about this morning.'

'Absolutely. He got the virtues and vices of where I come from just right. It was a wonderful sermon. Now sit down at the table and I'll fetch lunch.'

Agreeing that there was little point in speculating on the disasters of the night, they spent most of their time during the excellent lunch chewing over the dean and his wife.

'I don't like her one bit,' said Alice. 'She was just trying to make the dean jealous last night. Poor man, he's in a funny state. Do you think he's a manic-depressive?'

'I haven't seen enough of the dean to get any kind of grip on his personality, but I have to say his ups and downs seem pretty helter-skelterish. Tilly at least is usually predictable: cloying, boring and ultimately, I think, poisonous. I wonder what the dean was like before he met her.'

'Nice,' said Alice, unexpectedly. 'That was one of the reasons why I had some optimism about coming here. Didn't I tell you? A friend of mine worked with him in Grimsby and said he was kind and hard-working. Puritanical and rather easily shocked, yes, but conservative, not fundamentalist. Being born-again seems to have done all the damage.'

'And being married again. I suppose the two are connected.'

'Oh, I think they must be. Sally liked his first wife. She said she was sensible, jolly and more broad-minded than he was. I don't know if he was converted by this awful Tilly or by his curate.'

'My impression is that both of them were bowled over by the Rev. Bev. Understandably, I suppose. When I saw him in action he was ghastly, but impressively ghastly. And the poor old dean seems to be susceptible and guilt-ridden and precisely the kind of person who falls for that kind of bullshit.'

He accepted some more wine gratefully. 'It must have been a nasty shock for you to discover what he'd turned into.'

'It was. Everything made me miserable here. But I have to admit that despite all the terrible things that have happened, I'm much happier at the moment than I've ever been in Westonbury – mainly thanks to you. And now I've had those awful confrontations with the dean, I don't feel afraid any more.'

They chatted companionably about both their options for the future until, seeing him wilting slightly, she told him he should go home and have a nap. It was at that moment, seeing her pretty face full of motherly concern, that Amiss was attacked by one of his matchmaking impulses. This nice woman should be happy with a suitable man, he thought. What a shame she was stuck in Westonbury. And then inspiration struck. Of course, Alice and Ellis. What a marvellous pair they would make.

'Come to dinner tonight, Alice. It'll just be David, Ellis and Jack and very informal. I know they'd all be delighted to have you.'

She looked hesitant. 'Surely I'd be intruding. I can't come to dinner twice in one weekend.'

'This is hardly a typical weekend. Come on, say yes.'

'It's very kind of you. Yes, I'd be grateful for company. It's been a pretty harrowing week. What time?'

'I don't know yet. It may be latish. I'll ring when we're ready for you.'

As he kissed her goodbye he thought how nice she smelled and how soft her skin was. For a moment, he envied Pooley.

18

The palace residents were sitting round the kitchen having an apéritif.

'I'm starving.'

'Sorry, Jack. We can't start until Alice arrives and I won't ring her until we've debriefed Ellis.'

'OK, then, Ellis. What gives?'

Pooley shook his head energetically. 'God, I'm tired.'

'That's reassuring,' said Amiss. 'I hate being surrounded by superpersons.'

The bishop smiled. 'Then you'll be pleased to hear that I'm exhausted. Sorry, Ellis. Don't let me interrupt you.'

'I'll give you the bare bones of what I've found out. According to Tilly Cooper, the dean went home angry, she was tired and went to bed and left him brooding in the drawing room. She didn't notice he was gone until she woke up this morning just before five and found his side of the bed empty. She looked for him around the house and then raised the alarm.'

'So she'd passed out from the effects of Jack's punch,' suggested Amiss.

Pooley nodded. 'She was too genteel to say so, but I suspect it may be the case.'

The baroness snorted. 'Must be. You'd have to be unconscious not to notice if somebody the dean's size was or wasn't in bed with you.'

'The dean couldn't remember anything that had happened to him since the end of dinner last night. I probed delicately and ascertained that he had no memory even of his attack on Alice. He was completely bewildered and very worried about this until I put him out of his misery by telling him that the person who made the punch hadn't realized it was for teetotallers. He was too dazed to question that.'

'Hope he stays that way for your sake, Jack. We wouldn't want him to denounce you from the altar.'

'I'd quite enjoy that!'

'It looks as though having decided to take a Cromwellian approach to the Roper memorial, the dean fetched an axe from the shed, charged down the garden, wrenched off the tarpaulin and set about the edifice randomly. He managed to behead one of the winged youths, knock Roper's nose off and do serious damage to St Sebastian before raising the axe too high and hitting himself with it on the back of the head.'

The baroness jumped up, clasped her hands together as if grasping an axe and made sweeping movements up and down. 'It's possible, I suppose, but quite difficult. Though I admit I can't imagine how one wields an axe when plastered.' She sat down. 'You're sure nobody hit him from behind?'

'It's not impossible, of course. But there's hair and blood on the back of the axe.'

'Does it correspond with the size of the wound?' asked Amiss.

'We don't know. It's not like when you've got a corpse and can have a postmortem. He'd been patched up in the hospital and the wound cleaned and trimmed and sewn up by the time Godson and I came along. The plain-clothes police had no reasons to think there were any suspicious circumstances, so they didn't take the precaution of photographing the wound.'

Amiss shrugged. 'It does seem improbable that a would-be murderer was hanging around the garden on the off chance that the dean might be dancing around Roper at two o'clock in the morning and too drunk to hear anyone creeping up on him.'

'Unless the would-be murderer is Tilly.'

'I doubt if Tilly could have raised another glass last night,' said Amiss, 'let alone an object large enough to inflict damage on her husband. Considering she's not used to drink, it's a miracle she's alive herself.'

'Barely,' said Pooley. 'She's been in bed most of the day. Only emerged to visit her Norm and pray for him.'

'He will be all right, won't he?' enquired the bishop anxiously. 'I should hate to think that any permanent damage has been done to the poor fellow.'

'Don't worry, David. He has almost recovered. He must have a remarkable constitution: lying in the open air on a chilly night for four or five hours, dead drunk, with concussion and an open wound might have killed a lesser man.'

'Pity it didn't,' said Amiss.

'You don't really mean that, Robert.'

'I suppose I don't. He's not such a bad old thing really, just in the wrong place at the wrong time in the wrong century. What's the prognosis?'

'They're keeping him in overnight as a precaution, but they'll send him home tomorrow and say he'll be absolutely fine.'

'Now for poor Cecil,' said the bishop.

Pooley grinned. 'I know I shouldn't find this funny, but I fear what happened to Canon Davage cannot be viewed except as black comedy.

'It seems he decided to hang himself from a chandelier.'

'Why?'

'Because he felt responsible for the burglary, he said. We didn't press him. That can wait. The priority was to find out if anyone else was involved and no one was.

'Apparently Davage intended to make a grand gesture by lighting all three hundred and sixty-five candles on his chosen chandelier, but he got stuck on the practicalities. Each chandelier, you see, hangs from a beam on a rope-and-pulley arrangement. Davage planned to lower one, attach himself to it by a noose, light the candles, stand on top of an adjacent pew, raise the chandelier again, fasten it and then jump off the pew.'

The baroness had been following him closely. 'Sweet Jesus, that sounds like a tall order for someone stone-cold sober, let alone sauced up. How far did he get?'

'Not much further than first base. It seems his first move was to unwind the surplus rope from its cleat.'

'What's a cleat?' asked Amiss and the bishop together.

'A cleat is one of those pieces of iron that stick out from the wall and have ropes fastened to them. Haven't you noticed them?'

'Now that you mention it,' said the bishop, 'I think there are several.'

'There are indeed. Two per chandelier, in fact. One for the holding rope and the other to store the surplus. So Davage unwound the surplus rope, made a noose and put it round his neck. This is where he made his first mistake. He tied the wrong knot, so at no stage in the proceedings did this noose actually tighten round his neck.'

'Aha,' said the baroness. 'Little Davage was never a boy scout, obviously. Didn't do a slipknot, I presume.'

'Very good, Jack. No, unlike us, he was obviously never in the boy scouts. He did a bowline.'

She tut-tutted. 'Dear, dear. What a silly-billy.'

'So there he was with a noose round his neck that wouldn't tighten and therefore was irrelevant to what happened next.'

'Purely decorative,' proffered the baroness.

'As one might expect of Davage,' added Amiss.

'Next he released the rope from the holding cleat and this is where he made his second mistake. For one person to raise or lower a three-hundred-weight chandelier slowly requires them to do some clever things with leverage, but he didn't think of that. He unwound the rope rapidly, not realizing that his weight was insufficient to stop the chandelier just crashing to the ground.

'His third mistake was to fail to let go. He must have been about ten feet in the air when the chandelier hit the ground and shattered into pieces, causing Davage to descend rapidly onto the debris, break his left arm and concuss himself into the bargain.'

'Oh dear, oh dear, oh dear,' said the bishop. 'He must feel very humiliated.'

'He does. And he's distraught about the chandelier. When Godson told him about it – rather brutally – he fell silent for a moment and then looked up with wet eyes and said, "Each man kills the thing he loves." I felt really sorry for him.

Unlike Godson, who was furious at losing his Sunday.'

'Poor little wretch,' said Amiss. 'What an overreaction to a burglary.'

The baroness looked at him disbelievingly. 'What's happened to your wits? It was far more to do with the fact that he's being blackmailed by the dean.'

'What do you mean, "blackmailed"?'

'It was perfectly obvious from the conversation last night that the only explanation for Davage having ratted is that the dean has a hold on him. On Trustrum, too.'

Amiss smote his brow. 'You're quite right, of course. I just haven't been thinking properly. There's no other explanation. No wonder Trustrum is avoiding talking about it.'

The bishop came in hesitantly. 'I understand why you might think that, but I cannot think the dean would be so depraved as to blackmail anyone.'

'Ends and means, David. Ends and means. If you want to save souls, what's a little blackmail between clergymen? Well, now, Ellis. What's his guilty secret? Has your gardening superintendent had any work done on the backgrounds of the canons just in case any of them have been up to something shady?'

Pooley smirked. 'He hasn't, of course. But I ordered checks on everyone yesterday morning. There won't be any joy until tomorrow afternoon at the earliest. I just didn't have the authority to get to the head of the queue.'

'Good lad.' She smacked her right fist into her left hand. 'I'll give any of you two to one that Davage and Trustrum have form.'

'I'm not taking the bet,' said Amiss. 'I'll go further and predict that cottaging comes into it somewhere.'

The bishop wailed: 'This is all very distressing.'

The baroness leaned over and patted him on the back. 'So it is, David. We'll stop talking about it now. Robert, summon that nice child and let's have dinner.'

'I'm worried about that girl. I want you to look after her.'

Amiss whimpered, picked up his watch, saw it was just before 7.00 and whimpered again.

'I can't hear you.'

'Never mind. I can certainly hear you.'

'I thought she was looking peaky.'

'I'm doing my best for her. I've decided to marry her to Ellis.'

'That would certainly be good for her health. How does he feel about it?'

'I haven't told him and I don't really know how he feels. You know what he's like. It's not easy to know what goes on under that controlled surface. He hasn't mentioned women to me since that Asian policewoman broke his heart.'

'He's more repressed than controlled, if you ask me. Right, it's up to you then. Keep asking Alice to the palace.' She paused. 'Alice and the palace. What was that about?'

'You're thinking of A. A. Milne. '"They're changing the guard at Buckingham Palace . . ."'

'"Christopher Robin went down with Alice . . ."'

'"Alice is marrying one of the guard . . ."'

'"A soldier's life is terrible hard . . ."'

'"Says Alice,"' they cried in unison.

'Where were we?' asked Amiss.

'I was telling you to keep asking Alice to the palace for mating-with-Ellis purposes.'

'I wish you'd stop telling me to do things I'm already doing.'

'Got to make sure you're doing them.'

'In any event, I think David may be our unwitting accomplice. Last night he was trying to find some way of following my instructions about being kind to her –'

'You see, I'm not the only bossy one.'

'– when he remembered she played tennis and shyly asked her if she would do him the honour of having a game with him. It's been fixed up for five o'clock this afternoon.'

'Excellent, excellent. That'll be a good excuse for you to ask her to call in afterwards for a drink. Don't tell David you're trying to fix her up with Ellis, though. I know him. It would only make him muck everything up through self-consciousness.'

'May I go back to sleep now, please?'

'No. Wait.' There was a sound of a revving engine and a muttered oath. 'Sorry about that. I was overtaking some Frog lorry. Who do they think they are colonizing our roads? I shouted, "Waterloo" at him as I cruised by, but I fear he didn't hear.'

'Can't think why you didn't go into the Foreign Office instead of the Home Civil Service, Jack. You would have been a natch. What are my other duties?'

'Just remember that you'll get more out of little Davage than the fuzz ever would. Don't forget to visit him and seduce him into blabbing.'

'And the dean?'

'I have a feeling the dean will have enough on his hands with Tilly the Temptress. Stick to Davage. And tell Ellis that he should have a couple of cops patrolling the cathedral over the next few days. I have a feeling in my bones that things are going to get worse.'

'Don't quite see how they can. Neither the dean nor Davage is likely to get plastered a second time, so I don't foresee another round of accidents and suicides.'

'I don't know. I don't know. "By the pricking of my thumbs, Something evil this way comes," is what I feel. But I admit I may just be being melodramatic. Troutbecks have always had a bit of a taste for drama. But try to persuade him. Tell him he ignores my intuition at his peril.'

'He hasn't any power, Jack. And besides . . .'

He realized the phone was dead.

19

Amiss spent most of his day trying to keep his mind off pointless speculation by attacking paperwork with ferocity. He had just waved the bishop off to pick up Alice, with an injunction to ask her back for a drink, when Pooley arrived with a face like thunder.

'Finished for the day, are we?'

'We'd be officially finished forever, if it wasn't that Godson decided he can spend tomorrow on what he calls the paper-work – half-an-hour's work he can spin out for a whole day. As far as he's concerned, it's all over.'

'Conclusions?'

'Flubert committed suicide, the dean hit himself accidentally on the head and Davage tried to kill himself because he was drunk and therefore disproportionately upset by the burglary. Oh, yes. And the burglars were probably the shamans come back to exact revenge. Apparently Boyd had heard some gossip about them and put them forward as likely suspects. Godson's sent out a call to have them pulled in and sees no point in looking elsewhere.'

Amiss threw his hands wide. 'Well, maybe that's all correct, Ellis.'

'Come down to the kitchen. I want a cup of tea.'

The phone rang. 'What dirt has Ellis dug up?'

'I don't know yet. He's just got back and hasn't had a chance to tell me.'

'Well, get on, get on. I'll ring back in ten.'

Pooley was assembling the necessary components for what he considered proper tea, which involved a teapot, loose tea leaves, a tea cosy, jugs for milk and for hot water, and cups, saucers and spoons. Amiss waited until he had finished, the teapot had been warmed, the tea leaves added and the hot water poured on.

'That was Jack. She wants to know what the researchers turned up.'

'Everyone's clear except Davage and Flubert.'

'Oh God, no. What was there on Jeremy?'

'One conviction twenty years ago for gross indecency with a male on Hampstead Heath. He was let off with a fine.'

'Poor fastidious Jeremy. It must have been a frightful humiliation. And Davage?'

'Also humiliating. Indecent exposure at the Albert Memorial. He also got off with a fine.'

'He certainly chose his location well. You couldn't get a more kitschy piece of Victoriana than that. What possessed him?'

'He was drunk at the time, but anyway, it's always hard to understand other people's compulsions.'

'True enough. I, for instance, find it hard to grasp why you don't just sling a couple of tea bags into two mugs and put the carton of milk on the table. However, yours is a harmless compulsion. These presumably had huge blackmail potential.'

'Precisely. And yes, we raised the matter with the dean. Decently enough, Godson didn't mention anything about Davage: he just focused on Flubert. The dean swore blind he knew nothing about Flubert's past and denied vociferously that he would ever consider blackmailing anyone for whatever ends. When Godson pressed him, he became quite lively and started shouting about having his loins girt about with truth and not being prepared to have it questioned by unbelievers.'

'Oh, good. Sounds as if he's quite back to his old self. Do you believe him?'

'Yes. So does Godson.'

Pooley removed the tea cosy, and began to pour the tea. 'Strong enough?'

Amiss didn't look. 'Yes, yes. Fine. What about Davage?'

'He admitted the offence, declared it irrelevant and denied

that the dean was blackmailing him. He said the reason he was falling in with his plans was that he no longer had the stomach for battle: he just wanted to get on with his broadcasting career. As far as he was concerned, he said, Westonbury could rot.'

Amiss stirred some milk into his tea and took a sip. 'It's too strong.'

Pooley patiently passed him the hot water.

'What about Trustrum?'

'He said he was no politician, that all he wanted was a quiet life and that he wouldn't fight Davage and the dean.'

'Ellis, frankly I find it hard to see how Godson can do anything but close the case.'

'Yes, but –' The phone rang. Amiss passed it over. 'You talk to her.'

Pooley paced up and down the kitchen and told his story crisply. 'Yes, I thought of that . . . I was going to suggest it . . . Yes, I will . . . No, Godson wouldn't wear it . . . Said the budget didn't allow for night-time patrols just because a junior officer from another force had a hunch . . . I hope you're wrong . . .' He took the phone from his ear and looked at it. 'You remember all those detective stories in which the phone suddenly goes dead and you realize the person at the other end has been kidnapped or murdered. If that ever happens to Jack, we won't know the difference. And serve her right.'

He sat down. 'She thinks Tilly's the blackmailer. So do I.'

Amiss smote his brow. 'Of course, of course. That explains everything. Well, nearly everything. She's been blackmailing for Jesus. God, I must be slowing up.'

'No, you're not. I had a while to come to that conclusion. You've had only half a minute.'

'And Jack had only ten seconds.'

'Look, we know she's faster than either of us, but don't start developing an inferiority complex. Think about all the things you can do that she can't. Like what we want you to do now.'

'If you mean trying to worm secrets out of Davage, I'm already under orders, but I expect little to emerge. I can't tell him I know about his past. It would hardly be good news for your career if it emerged that you tell me your professional secrets.'

'I have every confidence in you, Robert. I'm sure you'll find a way.'

'I've brought you some flowers. Shall I find a vase?'

'How kind. How pretty. I love freesias. Now let me think. Oh, yes. Put them in the small funnel-shaped cut-glass vase you'll find beside the kitchen sink: it's just the perfect shape to show them off.'

'And I've brought you a bottle of champagne too.'

'My dear boy, is that wise? Look what it made me do last night.'

'Just one little glass for medicinal purposes. Then I'll stop it up and put it in the fridge.'

When the flowers had been arranged to Davage's satisfaction and placed exactly in the right position, just under the pope, Amiss saluted Davage with his glass. 'Let's drink to survival, Cecil.'

Davage smiled ruefully. 'To survival, though I have to say I can't say I'm much enjoying it at the moment.'

'Are you in pain?'

'Not physically. Not much, anyway. But mentally, yes. It's all very humiliating and the future looks pretty bleak.'

'Forgive me, I don't want to be nosy, but . . .'

'Why did I do it? A mixture of drink and shame. What am I if not the treasurer of Westonbury? When I found that because of my carelessness, those possessions for which I would happily have given my life had been stolen, why, then it seemed a good idea to give my life anyway, in what I fondly imagined to be a stylish manner.'

He moved in his armchair and winced slightly as his plaster cast knocked against the revolving bookcase next to it. 'And what happened? I succeeded in making myself an object of ridicule and wrecking another work of art for which I cared deeply.'

'We all make fools of ourselves at times, Cecil. And remember what we're talking about are only objects. You are a human being.'

'I see. You then would be of the school of thought that thinks you save the baby from the burning house rather than the *Mona Lisa*?'

'Every time.'

'I understand your point of view. Perhaps if it were my baby I might even hesitate a little. But I feel sure the *Mona Lisa* would win every time. There's only one of it and there are a lot of babies.' He gave a little titter. 'At least I'm consistent. I truly believe the Great St Dumbert's Staff is more important than me. I can hardly bear to contemplate its loss.'

'I ran into Ellis Pooley on my way here and he told me the police are pretty confident that the staff will be recovered. I can't think that any sensible fence is likely to welcome a seven-foot-long staff of unique design which is featured in countless books on medieval art.'

'That's not what I worry about. I could bear it going to some horrid foreign collector who gloated over it in private. What terrifies me is the fear that they'll take out the precious stones and melt down the staff.'

'Don't dwell on it now. Let's think about something else. Have you heard any news of the dean?'

'Oddly enough, I have. Less than an hour ago, I received a phone call in which he gruffly said that he hoped I was making good progress as was he, and added that he was praying for me.'

'Good heavens.'

'I reciprocated, of course. And we rang off blessing each other.'

'Has he mellowed?'

'Perhaps. It may be that what he always needed was a good bash on the back of the head. Silly old Nora.'

'It's good news, though, isn't it? Surely there's now a

chance you can work out some kind of compromise together.'

'I dare say we will.'

Amiss looked him straight in the eyes. 'I don't mean a capitulation of the kind you appeared to be mooting on Saturday night. I mean a compromise that will save the important cathedral traditions, and won't cause Trustrum to hang himself off one of the remaining chandeliers.'

Davage tittered again. 'At least he has a sort of precedent. Perhaps he could use red tape rather than rope.'

'Seriously, Cecil.'

'What can I say? I'm not sanguine. If the Rev. Myrtle joins the chapter, we are undone.'

'But you still could block him.'

'Please, Robert. I have reasons I can't tell you about. Now can we please change the subject. How's Gladys taking all this?'

'She's . . . he's not been seen since Saturday night. He rang Trustrum, said he'd been held up and left a phone number. I don't even know if he knows about you two. Listen, Cecil, I won't be made to change the subject yet. I think I know why you won't fight the dean. I think Jeremy was being blackmailed by Tilly Cooper. My guess is that she's been doing the same to you.'

'Guess away. I'm not going to help.'

'You're not going to deny?'

'I'm not going to help.'

Amiss reasoned, cajoled and finally gave up and allowed Davage to chatter to him about his plans for the next series of *Forgotten Treasures*. He had found in one of the most run-down boroughs in London a tiny Victorian graveyard crammed with elaborate crypts and vaults and cherub-laden headstones. Not only was *Forgotten Treasures* to do a programme on it, but there was an application going to the National Lottery for funds to restore it.

Davage leaned forward in excitement. 'And I'm hoping it'll start a trend, you see. There are all these wonderful places tucked away in the most . . . Excuse me, I'll just get the phone . . . Speaking . . . Yes . . . Yes . . . An unfortunate accident ... Certainly not ... I see ... There's not much point in denying it, is there? ... You feel, do you, that in doing this to me you are providing a public service? ... I see ... No ... I fear I cannot oblige you ... No ... No comment.' He put down the phone. 'Would you be kind enough, Robert, to give me a second glass of champagne?'

20

'What took you so long?'

'It was rather an eventful visit *chez* Davage.'

'We held dinner for you. Come on downstairs and tell us about it.'

'Where's Alice?'

'She came in for a drink after the match,' said the bishop, 'but then insisted on going home.'

'Who won?'

He beamed. 'I did. But she hadn't played for a long time. I think after a dozen or so matches I might be in trouble.'

As Pooley ladled out the casserole and the bishop poured out the claret, Amiss said, 'I'm warming to little Davage. He's got more guts than I'd thought.'

Pooley sat down. 'So tell us all.'

'It's not easy to put this in order, since he denied everything in the beginning and came up with the goods rather emotionally after a bombshell from outside.'

He took up a forkful of the casserole and chewed for a moment.

'Do get on,' urged Pooley.

'In a nutshell, he claims that when the dean outlined his plans for closing the choir school and turning the cathedral into a wholly evangelical centre, he told him to stuff it. He was, he said, prepared to consider reasonable compromises, but not to contemplate any erosion of the strengths of Westonbury. Then Tilly came to see him and explained that if he didn't play ball, she'd tell the tabloids about his conviction. At a stroke, she explained sweetly, that would finish his broadcasting career and make him an object of ridicule in Westonbury. He succumbed.'

'Oh, poor, poor Cecil. Which of us wouldn't? What a dreadful woman.' An awful thought struck the bishop. 'The dean didn't know about this, did he?'

'There's no reason to suppose so.'

'Why didn't Davage tell the dean that his wife was blackmailing him?' asked Pooley.

'She said that if he did, the dean would take her word against his, and she would leak the story and have him ruined anyway.'

'Does he think she blackmailed Flubert as well?'

'He knows she did, because Jeremy rang him the evening he died to tell him about a) his conversation with the dean and b) his conversation with Tilly. Apparently she caught him in the front hall of the deanery and told him she would be calling on him in fifteen minutes. Hence the phone call to me, moving me to the Dog and Duck.'

'So it looks as if it definitely was suicide,' said Pooley.

Amiss, who was picking at his food, put down his fork.

'Unless he threatened to blow the gaffe on Tilly, which he might have done. He was strong enough to contemplate ruining himself for a principle.'

'You mean she might have hanged him?'

'Possibly, if she had a gun.'

'Or perhaps with the dean's help,' said Pooley. 'He's besotted enough.'

'It seems rather unlikely that he'd be murdering Jeremy to stop the poor man telling him about his wife.'

'Sorry, Robert. My brains are becoming addled.'

'Yet there's still the stumbling block of the lack of a suicide note.'

'You're addled too, Robert. If he left a note, it would have blamed Tilly. She could have made off with it.'

The bishop had given up eating. He sat with his head in his hands listening miserably. Amiss leaned over and spoke to him gently. 'David, you'd better brace yourself. You're really going to hate this.'

The bishop sat up and looked at him in dread.

'The reason Cecil told me all this is because during my visit there was a phone call from the *Daily Filth*, asking him to comment on the revelation that he had a conviction for indecent exposure. They're going to run with it tomorrow. TV'S DIRTY OLD VICAR is apparently the working headline.'

'He's not a vicar,' said the bishop feebly.

'The *Daily Filth* doesn't worry unduly about nomenclature.'

The bishop retreated back into his hands.

'How is Davage taking it?' asked Pooley.

'This is the good news, David. By the time we got to the end of the champagne I'd brought, he said he hadn't felt so happy for weeks. "It's true, you know," he said. "Roosevelt was right: 'The only thing we have to fear is fear itself.'" He'd be free now to join forces with Fedden-Jones and fight, and was confident of getting Alice on board and perhaps finding out what Tilly had on Trustrum and stiffening his resolve. "If my series is cancelled, my series is cancelled," he said. "But maybe it won't be. After all, aren't minor offences supposed to be spent after seven years? Why should the BBC be harsher than the state?"

'Incidentally, Ellis. Why were Jeremy's and Cecil's offences still on the record?'

'They just are. They're spent in the sense that you don't have to own up to them, and they won't be taken into account if you're being sentenced for anything, but we don't banish them completely from our records.'

'And how did the tabloids get onto it?'

'If I ever find the policeman responsible for that,' said Pooley. 'I think I'll horsewhip him.'

'To within an inch of his life on the steps of your club, no doubt?'

'If I get half a chance.'

'To continue. Cecil's happiness was made complete by your call announcing the recovery of the croziers and the Dumbert Staff from the river. He said he can handle the loss of everything else. Congratulations. How did you manage that?'

'It seemed obvious to me that whether on foot or in a car, the thief would have found great difficulty in inconspicuously removing assorted croziers and a seven-foot-long gold staff from the environs of the cathedral. Even if covered, such long objects on a roof rack or poking through a window or out the back of an estate car would be highly likely to attract unwelcome attention in the early hours of the morning.'

'He might have had a van.'

'He might. But that would have been conspicuous parked near the cathedral at night. As would have been one of the shamans' trailers.

'My guess was the thief would chuck them somewhere from where they might be recovered at leisure: the river seemed the only likely place. So I went behind Godson's back and had it dredged, and bingo! we found the staff and croziers. Godson dragged himself away from his garden long enough to congratulate me and tell me we would claim it was our joint idea.'

'So are the shamans still being hotly pursued?'

'Yes, although I'm sure it's a waste of time.'

By now the bishop had had enough good news to resume tucking into his casserole. 'What is to be done about that frightful woman? Who will talk to the dean? Must I?'

'I suppose mercy requires you to wait until he's better. Why don't you confer with Cecil tomorrow about when he should be told? The poor bastard will need all his strength when he discovers that he's married to a whited sepulchre – how does it go, David?'

'"Ye are like unto whited sepulchres, which indeed appear beautiful outward, but are within full of dead men's bones, and of all uncleanness."'

'Jolly good, the Bible, isn't it? I couldn't have described Tilly Cooper more neatly myself. The dean's going to make a heroic choice between good and evil this time. My guess is that Tilly the Tart is unlikely to come out on top – if you'll forgive the expression. Now if you'll excuse me, I'll just go and ring Jack.'

The bishop shook Amiss awake. 'I'm sorry to wake you up so early, my dear boy, but I'm very worried. I can't find Plutarch anywhere.'

'What time is it?'

'Just after six.'

'Hell! So now she's been gone for about twelve hours. That's not like her at all.'

'No, it isn't. She's never stayed out all night before, has she?'

Amiss sat up and shook himself fully awake. 'There was that night she went out after supper and didn't get back till about two.'

'Yes, but if you remember, she had no difficulty in waking us up to get us to let her in.'

'She certainly didn't. I was only surprised she didn't wake up the whole city of Westonbury.'

'This is different. She didn't even come home to supper. I've looked all round the close and I can't see her anywhere. I'm terrified she's been run over.'

Amiss jumped out of bed. 'I'll come out with you.' He pulled on his clothes and they ran downstairs. As they were going out the front door, Amiss stopped. 'We should have thought of it last night when we were calling her. Maybe she's locked in the cathedral.'

'But she's usually left it long before the verger locks up.'

'I'd forgotten. Didn't Ellis say something about the cathedral being closed after six p.m.? I think they were still fingerprinting in the treasury, so they wanted it securely sealed off while the coppers were off duty.'

The bishop rushed inside and found his keys. 'Oh, the poor little thing. Let's pray that's the answer. Oh, dear. She'll be so hungry and thirsty . . .'

'And cross.'

As the bishop opened the side door into the west wall, he sniffed. 'There's a strange smell in here. It's acrid.'

Amiss sniffed. 'Nasty. Very nasty.'

'It's like the aftermath of a fire, isn't it?'

They looked at each other with dread. Amiss tried to expunge from his mind an image of Plutarch caught in a fire. They walked nervously into the body of the cathedral.

Amiss pointed to the far western corner. 'The smell's coming from that direction.'

Slowly and tentatively they walked towards the smell, which became stronger and more unpleasant at every step. Amiss put his hand on the bishop's arm. 'There's definitely been a fire, David. And I've a horrible feeling that what we're smelling is, among other things, flesh. It could perhaps have been an accident with a candle or something, and it could be that Plutarch died in the subsequent fire. It's out now, so it can be safely left. I'm not up to looking and I'm damn sure you're not. Let's go and wake Ellis. He's tougher than us. And he's seen a lot of nasty sights in his time.'

They huddled together like children while Pooley confronted the horror. After a couple of minutes he emerged, bleak of face but even of speech. He leaned against the wall for a moment. 'The good news is that I'm pretty sure Plutarch has not been a victim of that fire. The bad news is that a human being has.

'I suggest you go back to the house and have some coffee while I call for reinforcements and go on looking for Plutarch in the cathedral. If I don't find her, you can go on a more extensive hunt afterwards.'

The bishop straightened his shoulders. 'I'll go home soon, but first I must say a prayer over the remains of whoever has died. I am, after all, supposed to be a minister.'

The three of them went back into the cathedral, the bishop walking firmly ahead with Pooley. When they reached St Dumbert's Chapel, he gazed inside and made the sign of the cross. After a moment he said without a quaver in his voice: '"Naked came I out of my mother's womb, and naked shall I return thither: the Lord gave, and the Lord hath taken away; blessed be the Name of the Lord."'

He made another sign of the cross. '*Requiescat in pace.* Amen.'

'Amen,' said Amiss and Pooley.

The bishop turned around, Amiss took his arm and together they walked out of the cathedral. As they reached the open air, all colour left the bishop's face and he broke out in a sweat. Amiss propped him against the wall and held him up, for his knees were giving way. He found a handkerchief in the bishop's pocket and mopped his brow with it. 'Come on,' he said, as he saw the colour come back into Elworthy's cheeks. 'I'll take you back to the house. You've been very brave. I'm damn sure I couldn't have done what you just did.'

'No, no, I wasn't, Robert. I'm horrified by what I saw there. I wasn't brave to look. You didn't have to. I did.'

By the time Pooley arrived back at the palace, Amiss and the bishop had showered, dressed and were sitting at the kitchen table trying to talk of inconsequentialities. Pooley came and sat down and poured himself a cup of coffee. 'It's grim news, I'm afraid. Only one tiny bit of silver lining.'

The bishop looked at him dolefully. 'Do you think we could have that first?'

'Plutarch has a chance, just a small chance. She was strangled, but she's not dead.'

To his mingled incredulity and dismay, Amiss found himself possessed by emotions of rage, desolation and hope. The bishop was looking completely stricken. 'Where is she? Can we go to her?'

'She's unconscious, David. As soon as I found her – just inside the door of the north tower – I put out a call for a vet. He's with her now and he's taking her back to his surgery.' Amiss and the bishop began to speak at once. 'Yes, yes. I told him to spare no expense and gave him the number of Robert's mobile to report progress.'

Amiss leaned over and patted the bishop's hand. 'If it's any consolation, she survived being strangled once before. She's the toughest cat in the west.'

'There's no silver lining to the next piece of bad news. I'm sorry to have to tell you that it is almost beyond question that the body is that of Cecil Davage. He is not at home, his bed hasn't been slept in and a signet ring with the initials C.J.D. that looks like the one he was wearing yesterday is among the embers.

'It looks as if he committed suicide.'

Amiss's voice shook. 'He can't have committed suicide. How can he? He was fine last night when I left him. Even happy. I told you.'

'Maybe in the darkest hour of night he felt less happy. Look, I can't stay. Godson's arriving any moment.'

As Pooley left, the bishop leaned back in his chair and closed his eyes.

'David, you've got to cancel your engagements today. You're in bits.'

'I can't, I can't. Don't you remember? I'm visiting three schools and having lunch with the mayor. You can't cancel engagements like that – they'll have been making plans for weeks and it would be months before I could ever give them another date. Oh, how I hate this treadmill.' He sat up. 'Sorry, Robert. I'm being weak. I'll be fine once I'm at work. What will you do with yourself? Do you want to come with me?'

'Thanks, but no. I'll hang about, throw myself on Alice's mercy, talk to Jack, try to talk to Rachel and wait for crumbs of news.'

'Will you let me know about . . . ?'

'I promise you that wherever you are today I will get to you news of Plutarch. Tell me, do bishops say prayers for cats?'

The bishop gave a watery smile. 'This one does.'

'When I find out who did this to Plutarch I will personally tear him limb from limb.'

'Maybe it was Davage.'

'Don't be ridiculous, Robert. Davage couldn't strangle a mouse. Anyway he had a broken arm. Whoever did this must be built on the lines of a prize fighter and must also, I might add, be covered with scratches. He should be easy to find.'

'We can hardly expect Ellis to set the police force scouring the countryside for a large, strong, scratched person alleged to have tried to murder a cat.'

'Why not?'

'Be reasonable, Jack. They're busy with Davage. In their scheme of things, a cat is not important.'

'In my scheme of things, she is. Plutarch is a member of my family and therefore under my protection. Her enemy is my enemy. If the police won't do anything you'd better.'

'What? You want me to wander around Westonbury in the hope of finding somebody with a scratched face?'

'Don't be so pathetic. Start with the usual suspects. Especially the dean. He's got the physique. Keep in touch.'

Feeling like a fool, but glad of something to do, Amiss decided to call on the prime suspect. He was walking across Bishops' Green when his phone rang. 'It's Ellis. The dean's body has been found at the bottom of the north tower. He seems to have fallen from the top.'

'Is he scratched?'

'Scratched. Of course he's scratched. And bruised and bloody and battered, poor wretch.'

'I mean Plutarch-scratched.'

'Ah, yes. I'm with you now. I don't know, but I'll tell the pathologist to look out for cat scratches. I suppose it would relieve your mind to know who the perpetrator was.'

'It would also stop Jack proceeding on her mission of vengeance. She's in a very eye-for-an-eye mood.'

His mind in a spin, Amiss walked up and down Bishop's Green half a dozen times to gather his wits, until the phone rang once again. 'Ellis. We've found Davage's suicide note.'

'And?'

'It says he was going to commit suicide because he was afraid of exposure and because of his shame at his failure as treasurer, and that he decided to take the dean with him so as to save the cathedral.'

'Is that all?'

'Except for a couple of personal goodbyes to friends.'

'Ellis, this is mad. It doesn't fit in at all with what he said last night. Cecil was a softy. And a softy with a broken arm, at that. How could he have killed the dean?'

'Anyone could have pushed the dean over the tower at the corner where the masonry is missing.'

'But what about strangling Plutarch?'

'Maybe the dean did that. We don't know. Anyway I can't talk any longer. Godson wants me – probably to talk over his problems with his sweet peas.'

Amiss pressed a button. 'Get me the mistress,' he said

with an abruptness and abandonment of manners that would have done justice to the lady herself.

'I hope this is the end,' said the baroness. 'Call me a wimp, but this commuting is beginning to wear me out.'

'It's certainly the end as far as Godson is concerned,' said Pooley. 'He's already put in his report. Burglary by shamans who are still being pursued, the dean murdered by Davage and Davage immolated by himself.'

'Did you talk to him about Plutarch?'

'Godson said it didn't matter. He admitted Davage couldn't have strangled her, so said it was probably the dean.'

'But you said the pathologist saw no scratches of the kind administered by a cat.'

'Godson pooh-poohed that. His view was that there was absolutely no reason why there should be any scratches at all.'

'He doesn't know Plutarch,' said the bishop, baroness and Amiss in unison.

'I tried to explain that to him, but he was not interested.'

'Back to basics,' said the baroness. 'It's the only thing to do at these times. Either Godson is right or we're looking for another perpetrator, someone who murdered the dean, strangled Plutarch, did or didn't hang Flubert and burnt little Davage to death having forced him to write a suicide note and then presumably coshed him to make him quiet.'

'It's not like that. I can't see there being any doubt about Davage having committed suicide. He was sitting on a chair, with an empty petrol can beside him. It looks as if he lit a match, doused himself with petrol and just went up in flames.'

'Why would he choose to go in such a horrible way?'

'Most ways are horrible. This one is at least fast, if you use enough petrol. And he was a melodramatic little fellow. Also, it enabled him to die in the cathedral itself to maximum effect; he got the drama of the fire without doing damage to the cathedral. Dumbert's Chapel, being spartan and Norman, was virtually undamaged, apart from some blackening.'

'I don't like it,' said Amiss.

'Maybe not, but I fear you have to lump it. We could speculate over this forever.'

The bishop came in hesitantly. 'I'm probably being very silly, but I have to say that often when in doubt I go back to the primary source. I am, as you know, also keen on exegesis. Could you remind me once again exactly what poor Cecil said in his note?'

'I have a photocopy here.' Pooley reached for his briefcase and tossed a piece of paper to the bishop. He read it closely. 'That seems very straightforward, don't you think so, Jack?'

She perused it swiftly, nodded and passed the paper to Amiss, who read it and shouted, 'Eureka!'

He gazed uncomprehendingly around the group. 'What's the matter with you? Haven't you understood the last paragraph? The gutsy little bugger found a way to tell us someone else murdered the dean and who it was.'

'What? How?'

'It reads, "Please tell Elinor I was sorry to hear about Nora and ask her to take care of Myrtle."'

'Do you know who these people are?' asked Pooley. 'We assume they must be family but we haven't yet located them.'

'Family? You're missing the whole point! Don't you remember that Cecil in true camp style referred to those in his immediate vicinity by girls' names?'

'Not to me, he didn't,' said Pooley.

'Nor to me,' agreed the bishop and the baroness.

'Well, he always did to me.'

'So who is Elinor?'

'You, Ellis. He called you after Elinor Glyn because of your red-gold hair and his fantasies about seeing you on a tiger-skin rug.'

'What are you talking about?'

The bishop came in helpfully. 'She was a fashionable novelist and a lady of fast reputation, Ellis, about whom a well-known verse was written – I think in the 1930s. It was popular among some of my fellow ordinands for some reason I never understood, but perhaps now am beginning to. Do you remember it, Jack? "Would you like to sin . . ."'

'With Elinor Glyn
On a tiger skin?
Or would you prefer
to err
with her
On some other fur?'

'I suppose I should feel flattered. Who is Nora?'

'The dean. Cecil thought it funny to give him what he said was an Irish maidservant's name.'

Pooley's whole body went taut. 'Now for the sixty-four-thousand-dollar question. Who is Myrtle?'

'The Rev. Bev.'

'But he hardly knew him.'

'He hated him on sight when they met at David's consecration. And Cecil was a good hater.'

'Oh, my God. We never gave the Rev. Bev any thought. Why should we? The dean was his benefactor.' He punched some numbers into his mobile phone.

'We must pray,' said the bishop, 'that all will become clear in the fullness of time.'

'It's all right for you,' said Pooley, as he waited for an answer, 'you don't have to confide to a senior officer that a dead, gay canon wanted to sin with you on a tiger-skin rug.'

21

Amiss entered the kitchen to find the baroness and the bishop lying on the floor tending to Plutarch, who was lying on a bed of cushions. They were taking it in turns to finger-feed her with jellied beef consommé while crooning at her encouragingly.

'I swear I heard one of you say "Coochy, coochy, coo".'

'So what?' said the baroness stoutly. 'If you were recovering from being strangled, you might want to be coochy-coochy-cooed.'

'One of Plutarch's few virtues in the days before she became the Pamela Anderson of the feline world was that she rarely attracted outpourings of sentimental drivel.'

'Bugger off. She's a brave girl, and a clever girl, and we don't care who hears us say it, do we, David?'

'Certainly not. Without her, it would have been impossible to prove that that awful man was in the cathedral that morning.'

'I admit I would hate to have been the copper trying to construct a case based purely around the Myrtle business.' Amiss inspected Plutarch and patted her gingerly. 'How's she looking?'

'Definite improvement.' The baroness emitted an agonized yowl that caused the bishop and Amiss to jump and even Plutarch to quiver and held out her index finger for inspection. 'Look at this. She bit me. Isn't that encouraging?'

'Biting the hand that feeds her? That's my girl. Definitely the old Plutarch.'

'What do you think, David?' asked the baroness. 'Is she on course to try mashed-up salmon this evening?'

'We can try her with a little. We've got more consommé in reserve.'

'Fine,' said Amiss. 'I'll buy a tin later on.'

The baroness exuded outrage. 'A tin? A tin? I'm not having that heroine fed with tinned salmon. It must be not just fresh, but wild.'

'As you wish. As long as you buy and cook it. Now, I've got good news. Ellis has just reported that Bev has ratted on Tilly so they're off to clap her in irons. He expects to be able to tell us all at dinner.'

The baroness scrambled to her feet. 'Excellent. We'll have a proper celebration. You can make it, can't you, David?'

The bishop looked depressed. 'I can't. When I get home from the Intra-Church Symposium, I'll only have time to change and go straight out to the Lord Lieutenant's banquet.'

'Sod the Lord Lieutenant. Robert, ring him up and say David has urgent family business tonight.'

Amiss looked enquiringly at the bishop. 'Oh dear, oh dear. I don't know what to do.'

Amiss stood up. 'Then do what Jack tells you. I'll go and ring the old boy's secretary now.'

'I love this,' said Pooley unexpectedly, as he sat back in his armchair and accepted a glass of champagne. 'All my childhood I fantasized about being the Great Detective explaining to his awe-struck admirers how he had solved the case.'

'But you didn't,' pointed out the baroness. 'Robert did.'

'Oh, come on, Jack,' expostulated Amiss. 'It was a team effort. Even you made a contribution – although I still haven't worked out if it was negative or positive.'

'And there was Plutarch. And poor Cecil,' proffered the bishop.

'A fine team,' said Pooley. He put the tips of his fingers together. 'I wonder, Watson, if you have ever observed that –'

'Ellis, stop farting about and get on and tell us what happened today.'

Reluctantly, Pooley reverted to his everyday efficient persona. 'Beverley Johns and Tilly Cooper have been charged with the murders of Norman Cooper and Cecil Davage.'

'Not Jeremy?'

'No. I'm afraid he committed suicide, Robert. Tilly had the note all right; she'd kept it in case she was ever under suspicion for murdering him.'

'How did she get it, for heaven's sake?'

'She visited Trustrum after talking to Flubert and took a short cut through the cathedral when she left him. Flubert was already dead, so she looked for a note and found it on the organ.'

'Took some nerve.'

'Clearly she's got plenty of that.'

'What did Jeremy say?'

'That he hoped that by killing himself so dramatically, he would wreck the dean's plans to destroy a great musical tradition and expose his wife's ruthlessness and immorality in trying to win consent through blackmailing him with a twenty-year-old conviction.

'He saw no point in staying alive when his choice was either to watch the ruin of everything he had spent his life building up, or to be humiliated by the press for yielding many years previously to an overwhelming temptation.'

Amiss gazed miserably at the carpet.

'There was a message for you, Robert. After sending his thanks and blessings to his colleagues and friends, he asked that his new and valued friend, Robert Amiss, should be given as a memento the armchair which he liked so much and in which he had sat so companionably.'

Amiss looked up. 'That makes me feel both better and worse. Press on, and take my mind off Jeremy.'

'The Rev. Bev and Tilly each accuse the other of being the prime mover. What seems beyond dispute is there was terrific sexual chemistry between them. Tilly was a bank clerk when she met Cooper. She says she married him on the rebound and regretted it shortly afterwards, especially when she realized he was a manic-depressive – though according to Johns she was to turn that to her advantage by controlling Cooper's drug intake: when it suited her, she replaced with placebos the lithium that kept him relatively stable.'

The baroness snorted. 'I bet it's balls about marrying him on the rebound. A bit of clerical rough would have been right up that little tart's street. And she'd have enjoyed making him a slave. Tough on him that the attraction wore off.'

'Johns arrived at their church as curate within a couple of months of the wedding. He's half American and had spent some months in the Deep South with an evangelical church picking up ideas which Tilly found intoxicating. Their affair began almost immediately. He says that, like Cooper, he was sexually in thrall to Tilly.'

'Hah,' interjected the baroness, 'I told you so.'

'She seems to have led them both by the nose . . .'

'Surely you're getting your organs mixed up?'

'Shut up, Jack. She persuaded Cooper to swallow the whole born-again agenda and let Johns do what he liked. So Cooper's church, which had been doing well because of his genuine and effective evangelical efforts, turned into a wildly successful rave centre and more and more Cooper confined himself to pastoral work and presiding over low-profile services.'

The bishop looked confused. 'Was this woman a genuine believer or a hypocrite?'

'Both. She wouldn't be the first moral inadequate who confused the razzmatazz of born-againery with the substance – for a time, anyway. However, if the Rev. Bev is to be believed, Jesus didn't have a look-in once she decided she wanted to marry Bev and get rich by setting up their own church in the Bible Belt. This made it necessary to get rid of Cooper: born-agains don't like divorced preachers.'

The bishop looked anguished. 'Surely Johns resisted this?'

'He claims he did at first. He went on about Eve giving Adam the fruit of the forbidden tree.'

The bishop shook his head. 'The oldest excuse of men: "The woman whom thou gavest to be with me, she gave me of the tree, and I did eat." I fear I have little sympathy with that line of defence.'

'Money was the problem. Tilly took out as much life insurance on Cooper as she dared – about a hundred and fifty thousand pounds – and while she was looking out for possibilities of getting more, there was a stay of execution on her husband. When he was offered the deanery she encouraged him to take it in the hope there would be rich pickings. Specifically, she was hoping there would be some way of getting her hands on some of Reggie Roper's legacy. She was very peeved when she realized that was not going to be possible. According to Bev, through sheer temper, she then made an attempt to kill the dean.'

'The highly polished pulpit steps?'

'Precisely, Jack. Well spotted.'

'She and Bev then reverted to plan A, which was to stir up the canons to such an extent that one of them would either murder the dean or be given the blame when the lovers did the deed. According to Johns, Tilly had donned a disguise and paid a private eye to dig up whatever dirt there was on the chapter.

'They also turned their attention to the treasury and decided to rob it at a propitious moment. Meantime, the Coopers went off on their long-awaited visit to Born-Again Land and Tilly came back mad with lust for the power and money acquired by successful preachers. She decided to bring forward the murders of the dean and Davage, who had been selected as the most obvious fall guy.

'Last Saturday, Tilly tipped off Johns that the coast would be clear. He broke into Davage's house and took his huge bunch of keys, which are numbered by case and which included a key clearly marked "alarm". The police would have known that simply by hanging around the cathedral for a few days any professional burglar could have cased the joint, spotted Davage with the keys and even seen him disable the alarm, so no suspicion could legitimately fall on any insider.'

Amiss looked sadly around his friends. 'I'm afraid Cecil was right when he said he was careless.'

'Maybe "innocent" is a better word,' said the bishop. 'One cannot always be on the watchout for venality amongst one's fellows. One question, if I may, Ellis. Did the wretched man attack the dean that night?'

'He says no and Tilly says yes, which leads me to suppose that she did.'

'But she was as pissed as a newt.'

'Not really, Robert. I'm sure that performance with me had as much to do with her strategy of keeping the dean jealous as to alcohol-related indiscretion.'

The baroness snorted. 'I was watching. Your trouble, Ellis, is that you're too modest.'

'At all events, she wasn't as pissed as the dean. Remember, he was a genuine teetotaller, while she was a fake. Johns says she drank plenty on the quiet – and had developed a taste for cocaine. My guess is that she wound up the dean to go and attack the memorial in the hope that he would injure himself and bleed to death, that when he didn't return she investigated and found him passed out from his exertions and that she hit him on the back of the head with the axe and left him there for a few hours hoping he'd die. Acting the concerned wife, she raised the alarm early in the morning. But that's academic, since she arranged for Johns to kill him a couple of days later.'

'How did they get the dean to go up the north tower at night?'

'Not difficult if a friend who has come to visit you, and whom you're trying to persuade to become a member of your chapter, expresses a desire to see Westonbury in the moonlight from the top of the tower. Up went Cooper and Johns, over the edge went Cooper and down came Johns. Unfortunately for him, when he was almost at the bottom of the stairs, Plutarch came bounding up.'

Amiss laughed. 'Sorry, but it is grimly comic if you consider the state of mind of the two as they collided. In one corner we have an unusually hungry Plutarch, who had just spotted that the door separating her from the kestrel's store of goodies was open, salivating at the thought of what might await her at the top of the stairs. In the other we have a murderer hastening to kill a second brother in Christ and get the hell out of Westonbury. I'm surprised they both came out alive.'

'Johns's face and hands are in a very, very nasty mess and

two of his earrings had been pulled out, leaving nasty wounds. Plutarch is unquestionably not a cat one would wish to meet on a narrow, dark staircase.'

The baroness wrinkled her forehead. 'Why didn't the idiot throw her in the river to hide the evidence?'

'I suspect he wasn't thinking very clearly by then. Must have been close to blind panic. And in great pain. Remember he was an amateur at burglary and murder and probably lacked your criminal instincts.

'He fetched the equipment he needed from his car and stashed it in St Dumbert's Chapel, went to Davage's house, made him write his suicide note – presumably by threatening to hurt him – and took him over to the cathedral where he fed him whisky laced heavily with sleeping tablets. He insists Davage became unconscious as soon as he got to the chapel. Johns tied him to a chair with several rounds of cotton thread, which is as effective as string or rope but can be guaranteed not to survive a fire, put Davage's fingerprints on the petrol can, doused him with its contents, set fire to him and ran for home.'

'Was Tilly not involved?'

'Apparently not. She persuaded him it would be too risky for her to leave the deanery, since she was so instantly recognizable.'

'I suppose it was quite clever of them to work out such a foolproof method,' said the baroness grudgingly.

Pooley shook his head. 'Not foolproof at all. I won't go into details or I'll put David and Robert off dinner, but even when a body is incinerated to the extent that Davage's was, the contents of the stomach are preserved. A bit like a potato that you cook in a fire. That's how we knew he was much too heavily drugged to have been able to do the deed himself.'

'That's quite enough, Ellis. We take your word for it.'

'So the pathologist reported that he must have been unconscious when the fire started.'

Very hesitantly, the bishop leaned towards Pooley. 'I don't want to be materialistic, Ellis, but is there any trace of those of our treasures that are still missing?'

'I think we've recovered the lot. Johns was so badly

marked he didn't want to go out, and he had not had a chance before then to find a hiding place or a reliable fence. The top of his wardrobe is crammed full of rings, reliquaries and other odds and ends.'

'Thank God.'

'Happy ending, then,' said the baroness, standing up.

'Except for Jeremy, the dean, Cecil, Tilly and the Rev. Bev,' said Amiss.

'And nearly Plutarch,' added the bishop.

'Stop being so pedantic. You know what I mean. Come on, then. It's almost eight and I'm starving.' As she reached the door she turned and observed carelessly. 'I think I bought too much food. Shall I ask that child Alice to join us for dinner?'

'Why not?' said Pooley.

EPILOGUE

Amiss looked about him nervously. 'I don't like the look of this place. Why have you taken us to a back street in Southall to what looks like a fifth-rate Indian restaurant. It's got to be that they serve something really, really horrible that cannot be found in salubrious establishments in the West End.'

'Well, I suppose it's not for the squeamish.'

'Curse you, Jack, I am squeamish.'

'It's time you learned to be less so. I'm giving you two a treat. There is nowhere, but nowhere, in the United Kingdom to touch this place for fish-head curry.'

Amiss and Pooley looked at each other.

'Red-hot fish-head curry, of course.'

'What else have they got?' asked Amiss faintly.

'You're not going to be feeble, are you? What's the point of coming here if you're not going to eat their speciality?'

'I don't even want to look at their speciality. Christ, I can't even eat whitebait, because their little eyes put me off. And they're disguised in batter.'

'Ellis, are you a pathetic wimp like your friend?'

Pooley stiffened his shoulders. 'Certainly not. Do your worst.'

'There you are, Robert. Ellis is an embodiment of the courage and determination acquired on the playing fields of Eton.'

'Pshaw!' said Amiss. 'More an embodiment of the misplaced macho bravado acquired in the police canteen, if you ask me. Me, I value moral courage, so I don't mind telling you I want a meal that consists of ingredients I won't feel ill contemplating, cooked in a sauce which won't take the roof off my mouth and give me the runs for a fortnight. Is that too much to ask?'

She clicked her tongue disapprovingly. 'Sometimes I don't know why I hang about with you. I might be better off with a real man like Ellis.'

'Thank you for the compliment, Jack, but I think you would probably find me falling short in some other respects. I lack Robert's essential . . . flexibility.'

She nodded. 'H'mm! You have a point, I suppose. He's probably easier to push around.' She clicked her fingers and a waiter materialized. 'My friend and I will have the fish-head curry. Give him' – she pointed disparagingly at Amiss – 'something suitable for cowards.'

'No fish heads,' said Amiss firmly. 'Nothing hot.'

'Mutton?' asked the waiter.

'That'll be fine.'

'Madras?'

'Too hot.'

'Korma it must be then, I suppose.' The waiter shook his head. 'You can get that anywhere. Why do you come here and not have the fish-head vindaloo?'

Amiss maintained a frosty silence.

'Bring us plenty of beer,' said the baroness.

The waiter, who seemed to know her well, returned within two minutes carrying three jugs, which a couple of minutes later were augmented by a vast tureen which he placed in the centre of the table. A large bowl of rice followed, along with three plates, two of which were lined with leaves. Finally, with a contemptuous gesture, the waiter placed a nondescript container of something brown and harmless-looking beside Amiss.

The baroness tossed her leaves aside. 'In Kuala Lumpur this is served on a bed of banana leaves: regrettably in this joint they use plastic. Now, Ellis, pay attention. You will find that when the eyes are white and popping out, the fish heads are perfectly cooked. Dive in.'

The next fifteen minutes consisted mostly of the sound of teeth cracking on fish craniums, loud excavations within the tureen and intermittent cries of joy as the baroness found particularly succulent morsels, which, she insisted on explaining to Amiss, were usually to be found around the eyes, cheeks and gills.

Amiss did his utmost to block out either the sight of his companions' dinner or the information he preferred to be without. He took great pleasure from seeing Pooley having frequently to mop sweat from his face.

When at last the baroness finished, she wiped her mouth, emitted a large belch and threw down her napkin. 'So how was yours?'

'All right, thank you. Nothing special.'

'That's because they have contempt for those who come along and demand sheep's balls rather than fish heads.'

'Jack, I wasn't eating sheep's balls, was I?'

'Quite possibly. How would I know? Mutton covers a multitude.'

Pooley began to choke. 'Drink some more beer,' instructed the baroness. He took a vast gulp, stopped choking and burped.

'That's more like it.'

'Pleasant, Ellis?' asked Amiss.

'It tastes very good indeed once you get over the initial shock. Thank you, Jack. This has indeed been an experience which I will not easily forget.'

She beamed. 'I like people to eat properly. There is more to life than cucumber sandwiches and China tea.' She waved a hand at the nearest waiter and shouted, 'Beer.'

'Speaking of cucumber sandwiches takes me back to Middle England. What news from the close, Robert?'

'Trustrum finally came clean with me yesterday over an unprecedented third glass of sherry. Apparently Tilly just turned up at his house the evening Jeremy died, explained that she wanted him to do what she told him and said if he didn't she'd accuse him of attempted rape. He panicked and capitulated immediately. He's followed too many stories of men being dragged through the courts on unsubstantiated charges of sexual harassment to doubt that his life could become a misery.'

'Blimey!' exclaimed the baroness. 'You've got to hand it

to her. I don't know that I'd have thought of such a simple method of getting my own way.'

'I doubt if you'd be able to carry it off quite as convincingly as Tilly,' said Amiss. 'Otherwise, David labours on conscientiously doing things he hates, and Fedden-Jones, Trustrum and Alice try to keep the cathedral running while waiting for a new dean.'

'I thought Alice was looking much happier when I was down last weekend,' said Pooley.

'She's in good form, but she's not cut out to be an administrator.'

'Well, she's not going to be one for much longer,' said the baroness. 'I sorted her out this morning. She's going to become chaplain to St Martha's, with a part-time curacy in the seediest part of Cambridge. That should keep her busy and happy.'

'Congratulations, Jack.'

'And David's going to resign and take up a St Martha's Fellowship in Philosophy.'

'Good God!' said Pooley. 'Isn't that an abrogation of responsibility?'

'Balls, Ellis. He's giving up what he's bad at and going back to what he's good at.'

'Can he live on that?'

'Cornelia had made several clever investments that can be converted into an adequate pension. Besides which, he'll be able to live on his wife's money. She's got oodles.'

Amiss and Pooley exclaimed so loudly that three waiters came rushing over; the baroness waved them away.

'He's going to marry Alice. I've told them to get on with it. The girl's in her mid-thirties and wants to breed. David had some scruples because it isn't even a year since Cornelia died, but I told him she would have agreed with me. And she would.'

'But . . . but . . . but . . . Alice marrying David! Dammit, he's more than twenty years older than her.'

'She'll love that. She'll be able to look after him. Yes, I know you wanted her to marry Ellis, but that would never have done.'

Pooley directed a startled look at Amiss. 'You wanted her to marry me?'

'Well, I thought it might be a good idea. Didn't you like her?'

'I liked her. But I was never attracted by her.'

'Nor her by Ellis, Robert. I'm surprised you couldn't see that. It was David she looked at meltingly. Besides, Ellis and she would have been ill-matched. She needs someone inadequate. His self-sufficiency would have broken her heart.'

Amiss shook his head in bewilderment. 'How did I miss what was going on between her and David?'

'Because you were fixated on Alice and Ellis. I've been plotting this from the very beginning. The breakthrough came this morning, apparently, when she beat him at tennis for the first time and he was unable to restrain himself from kissing her. One thing led to another and you not being there to tell, they rang me up. He was babbling Betjeman at me: "Love-thirty, love-forty, oh! weakness of joy,/The speed of a swallow, the grace of a boy."'

'I suppose I'm delighted, really,' said Amiss. 'I didn't know how he was going to get on without me. I'll have to leave in a couple of weeks.'

'What'll you do?'

'Apart from moving in with Rachel, I've actually got a good chance of a job I like the sound of. Don't ask me about it: I'm superstitious.'

The baroness took a mighty gulp of beer. 'Now there's just one more matter to dispose of. Ellis, why are you avoiding Mary Lou?'

Pooley looked horrified. 'What do you mean?'

'You know very well what I mean.'

'Mary Lou kindly invited me to dinner when she was in London last month. It was very pleasant.'

'Balls. She said the sexual electricity was flashing between you, but you suddenly made an excuse about having an early start the next morning and rushed away. Since then you keep being too busy to see her.'

'Really, Jack, this is an unwarrantable intrusion into my private affairs.'

'Bollocks. This is all because you're being high-minded because she's had affairs with Robert and with me, isn't it? You don't want to upset either of us.'

Pooley sat up straight like a little boy who has decided to own up. 'Very well, then. There is quite a lot in what you say. I suppose I could have sorted things out with Robert, but frankly, I draw the line at sharing a lover with you.'

'If you'd given her the opportunity, she'd have told you that's all been over for ages. It's just that I enjoy teasing Robert about it. Mary Lou and I had a fling, but we both thought it a bit much for the mistress and the bursar to be having it off. Noblesse oblige and all that.

'We're just allies and comrades now – and whatever my faults, I'm not a dog in the manger. Mary Lou is essentially hetero. What she needs is a good man.'

Amiss was looking dazed. 'I know I'm self-evidently bad at this, but Ellis and Mary Lou wouldn't have occurred to me as a likely pair.'

'For God's sake, Robert, contemplate your friend. What took him out of the background from which he comes?'

'His romanticism, I suppose.'

'And what does he need above all else in a woman?'

Amiss thought for a moment. 'Someone who will make him lose control.'

'Don't you think the bold and gorgeous Mary Lou fits the bill rather more than that nice Wasp, Alice Wolpurtstone?'

Amiss took the mobile out of his pocket. 'I brought this with me to return to you, Jack.' He handed it across the table to Pooley. 'Take it outside,' he said, 'press three and ask for Dr Denslow.'

Scarlet-faced, Pooley hurried out of the restaurant.